OPPOSITE ATTRACT

JACQUELINE LEE

CHAPTER 1

MEGAN

APARTMENT HUNTING IS HIDEOUS. I'm talking about plucking-out-your-eyeballs-and-stomping-on-them hideous. Especially when your budget is, to put it politely, on the deprived side of average. Which in New York means you can give up dreaming about a cozy little studio apartment for one and instead start contemplating whether a roommate with eight cats is better or worse than a roommate who dabbles in satanic rituals.

I have a good feeling about the apartment I'm heading to now though. My potential roommate is a twenty-three-year-old vegetarian non-smoker who works in the STEM field. If I were writing a list describing my perfect roommate, it would read close to this guy.

Also, I like the area. It's a short commute to work for me, which on a bleak January day like today is a massive plus. The apartment building itself turns out to be a squat, square-shouldered thing that has probably developed a complex from being compared with the taller, sleeker buildings surrounding it. But it has an elevator, which is a bonus, even if the metallic groaning and moaning does have me scanning the walls to locate the emergency phone.

I make it to the fourth floor. Someone has painted the door of 4B a cherry red. My favorite color. I'm hoping it's a good sign as I take a deep breath and knock.

While I wait, I plaster my best apartment-hunting expression on my face. It's my I-don't-leave-my-dishes-in-the-sink-and-I-always-hang-up-the-bathmat look. It requires a lot of cheek muscles.

A guy opens the door.

"Hi, I'm Megan. I messaged about viewing the apartment?" I squeak this out because, holy shit, I've just clocked how good-looking this guy is.

"Sure, come in. I'm Josh, by the way."

He's wearing square-cut glasses that highlight his deep-brown eyes. With his tousled blond hair, Kings of Leon T-shirt, jeans, and bare feet, he gives off an aura of geeky-cool.

My heart sinks as I follow him in and take off my coat. This guy is way too handsome. He won't want to room with a girl because he'll be worried about having to constantly fend me and my friends off.

My mind runs rapidly through my potential sales pitch. *I think you're cute, but don't worry, I have good self-control. I promise I won't walk around the apartment in my underwear trying to tempt you.*

Actually, since my underwear tends toward saggy full briefs and sports bras, the washing machine is the only thing that ever gets up close and personal with them. In the few short relationships I've had, any time a guy and I head to the bedroom I make sure my underwear disappears faster than Houdini. It's a neat trick of mine. And probably the only trick I can boast about in the bedroom.

Josh shows me around the apartment. It's been done up

nicely, even if the kitchen cabinets are a bright turquoise that will probably haunt my vision when I close my eyes tonight. I try not to gush too much but come on! He has *Ctrl, Alt, Del* cushions and a periodic-table shower curtain.

Unfortunately, I'm pretty sure I'm giving off the same needy vibe as a puppy at the animal shelter. *Please let me live with you.*

We come back into the living room, where he gestures for me to have a seat. The couch is sink-into-it comfortable, and I can too easily imagine myself cuddled up here watching the giant television on the opposite wall. I don't snuggle now though. Instead I sit on the edge, tucking an errant curl behind my ear, feeling like I'm about to sit my driver's exam.

"So, Megan, tell me about yourself." As Josh smiles I notice he has a small gap between his front teeth.

Swallowing my nerves, I outline the bare facts. I'm from Oklahoma originally but came to New York for college and completed a master's in science communication. I now work at *The Science Journal*, trying to turn complex scientific papers into something more easily digestible.

"Cool, I love *The Science Journal*. You guys did a great article on epigenetics recently."

Oh, God. This guy couldn't be more perfect if he had a hot tub. Not only has he heard of the publication I write for, he remembers the lead article from the last issue!

"I did some of the interviews for that," I say, and his grin spreads even wider.

"Really? That's so awesome. I did a few biochem classes at college—almost chose it as my major but decided to go down the tech route instead. I'd love to code for a biotech company sometime."

My shoulders relax as Josh and I chat about college

majors and first jobs. We're both two years out of college, just starting out in the industries we want to work in. It would be so amazing to be able to talk the same language as my roommate. My current roommate, Celeste, is a beauty therapist. Since I don't speak makeup or fashion and she doesn't speak geek, in-depth conversation between us is quite limited. I was still gutted, though, when our landlord announced our eviction so he could move his mother into our apartment, and Celeste decided to move in with her boyfriend, leaving me homeless.

"So, are you into celebrities? Like, do you watch any of those celebrity reality TV shows or *E! News*?" he asks.

It's a bit of a random question, given we were just talking about the genetic code. I try to keep the frown from my face as I answer.

"Um...no?" I'm not sure if this is a positive or negative but being upfront and honest has got to be the best policy. I hope so, anyway. "I don't watch much TV, but when I do, I tend to watch Discovery Channel. Or sometimes I have a Netflix binge if I find something I really like."

Josh's expression gives nothing away about whether my answer was right or wrong. "What about sports? Do you follow any?"

"I don't follow anything, but I'm okay with watching them. Except football." Oh, God, why did I blurt that out?

Sure enough, Josh raises an eyebrow. "What's wrong with football?"

"I just don't like it. I come from a state that's obsessed with football and football players at the expense of every-thing else. It's a philosophical stand of mine."

He doesn't need to know the real reason I don't like football. It's not something I share with anyone. Ever.

He tilts his head to the side, like I'm some newly discovered species. "But you wouldn't mind if I watched some games?"

"No, as long as you wouldn't expect me to watch. Or talk about it afterwards."

Josh breaks out into a giant grin. "I can definitely keep my end of that deal. So, when can you move in?"

I blink. "Really?"

"Sure, the room is yours if you want it."

Hope surges in my chest, but I dampen it down. "Don't you have other people to interview?"

Josh shrugs. "A few. I'll just message them and tell them the room is taken."

"Oh...okay. Do you want to check out my references?" What am I doing? It's like I'm trying to talk him into being diligent when he's just offered me the room. Nice one, Megan.

"I count myself as a good judge of character." Josh continues to smile. "You're exactly the type of roommate I've been looking for."

I can't help but smile back.

❧

"When are you moving in with the hot guy?"

I'd made the mistake of showing Josh's profile picture to my friend Ashley at work. She's been salivating worse than Pavlov's dogs ever since.

"Tomorrow." I tear my eyes away from my laptop and lean back in my chair, looking up at Ashley who is hovering by my cubicle. Our office is open plan, and it's obvious Brett at the next desk over is listening closely to our conversation. Although that might just be because Ashley has long blonde hair and a figure that attracts male stares the way a magnet captures iron filings. She's kind of my polar opposite in appearance, as I'm only 5'5" with dark hair and the type of figure that makes me feel like a fraud when I go bra shopping. Despite our external differences, it can be scary how closely we think alike sometimes.

"Do you want me to help you move?" she offers.

"Thanks, but it's fine. I've got a van coming in the morning. Besides, I don't have much stuff."

Ashley reaches over to fiddle with the pendulum on my desk, pulling out one ball so it ricochets into the next and starts all the balls moving. "So, do you know if your new roommate has a girlfriend?"

"I've got no idea." I shrug, pretending I haven't given much thought to Josh's relationship status. Which is a total lie. I've been contemplating it then scolding myself for thinking about it. Because having a crush on my roommate is up there with my sole attempt at pole dancing—generally a bad idea all round. A few friends have raised concerns about me rooming with a strange guy, but I've done the prerequisite online stalking, and Josh seems to be the upfront, nice guy he came across as. Well, he hasn't appeared on any Reddit forums discussing how to lure unsuspecting girls to room with him and then chop their bodies up to feed to his pet eels. Not under his real name anyway.

"Do you know that forty-eight percent of single roommates end up hooking up within the first year?" Ashley says.

"Really?" I eye her suspiciously. "What study does that statistic come from?"

She doesn't lift her gaze from the pendulum. "I can't remember where I read it."

Ashley is queen of making up random statistics to back

up her arguments. Conveniently, she can never remember the source. Which is actually an incredibly bad trait for a scientific journalist.

"I have no plans to hook up with my new roommate," I declare primly.

"You need to do something to spice up your love life," Ashley says.

"Maybe I should just sprinkle myself in paprika?" I suggest.

She grins. "If not him, he might have a cute friend."

When I arrive at the apartment on Saturday morning Josh is as charming as he was at our first meeting. The moving van turns up, and he helps ferry my stuff into my room and sticks around to assist me in putting together my bookshelf.

I don't know why, but the bookshelf takes forever to reconstruct. Josh and I both have master's degrees, so it's a bit embarrassing we can't master Ikea instructions.

"I don't think that's coming down anytime soon." He gives the shelf a gentle tug when we finally finish. "I'll leave you to unpack."

I diligently fold and put away my clothes into my drawers. I'm hanging stuff in the wardrobe when Josh comes back into my room, frowning. He runs his hands through his hair so it's tufted up at the back, which is adorkable.

"Sorry, I don't want to ditch you on your first night here, but something's come up and I need to go out of town."

What kind of mysterious thing comes up at the last minute that involves leaving town? Is my new roommate a secret spy? Melodrama, meet Megan.

"Yeah, sure, I'll be fine." I give him a bright smile. The

last thing I want is for Josh to think he needs to babysit me. And while I was looking forward to having a roommate bonding session, there's lots of time for that.

"Message if there's anything you need to know."

"Cool, thanks."

After he leaves, I spend an enjoyable Saturday night finishing my unpacking and taking boxes to the recycle chute.

I go to bed around ten, and lie there listening to the unfamiliar sounds of the apartment. My room borders the kitchen, and the fridge gurgles weirdly through the wall.

I hear a door slam, and footsteps out in the hallway. Soundproofing was obviously not a priority when they built this place. I know the front door is locked. I've double-checked it. Yet I still find myself listening for the door handle turning. Having a vivid imagination is great most of the time, but I wish I could dial back the dreaming-up-axe-murderers part.

Eventually I drift off to sleep, only to get abruptly pulled out of my dreams a few hours later.

My door is ajar, a triangle of light from the hallway now spilling onto my carpet.

My blurry eyes and sleepy brain try to make sense of this.

I'm positive I shut my door before I went to bed. My heartbeat pounds in my ears, generating a soundtrack to accompany my rapidly drying mouth and the surge of fear flowing through my body.

Over the noise of my blood pumping I hear another sound. A rustling noise at the bottom of my bed.

A scream attempts to claw out of my throat but gets stuck halfway.

Someone is in my room.

CHAPTER 2

BRANDON

I AM the king of bad decisions. On my first night back in the city, instead of having a quiet night, I agree to go to a club opening with Mike and the guys.

The instant I walk in, I know it's a mistake. This place is all leather walls and shining poles, and waiters and waitresses dressed as dominatrices. Maybe the name The Sin Club should have been my first clue? Hey, I've never claimed to be the smartest guy in the room.

So, instead of getting to shoot the breeze and play some pool with the guys, I'm fending off scantily clad chicks dressed as all kinds of sin. Which, okay, might sound like I've walked into a wet dream fantasy of most guys. Four years ago, when I was first drafted, I would have agreed, but partying up hard is definitely not what the doctor ordered. Especially tonight.

However, it's impossible to turn away people who approach you for selfies, unless you want to star on all the *Celebrities Who Are Assholes* blogs out there.

On my way back from the bar with the next round I

find myself sandwiched between two blondes, one dressed as gluttony and one dressed as lust. I'm pretty sure my smile is more of a wince.

"WTF Brandon, you're trending on Twitter," Mike exclaims when I finally make it back to the table. He's staring down at his phone.

I groan and grab his phone, scrolling through the pictures of me with various sin girls being tweeted and retweeted. Awesome.

My team just got knocked out during the first round of the playoffs in a game we shouldn't have lost. Against a team we shouldn't have lost to. News reports of me partying it up are definitely not going to impress team management. And with free agency looming over me like a 200-pound linebacker, impressing team management is pretty fucking important.

Unfortunately, a week before our first playoff match, photos of some of the guys letting loose at a nightclub after a team function made us look like a bunch of boozy idiots who only think with their dicks. I didn't even participate in the game of drinking shots off the stripper's body. But I was there, so I got slammed regardless.

The New York press are like rabid dogs, and I'm one of their favorite toys. Occasionally they play nice. But most of the time they're not afraid to use their sharp teeth.

I stand. "I'm bailing."

Mike's eyebrows shoot up. "Seriously?"

"Seriously."

The damage is already done, but at least I can stop any more images of me making their way onto the internet.

Disappointment runs rampant across Mike's face.

I try to tell myself it's because he enjoys my company.

The cynical part of me can't help wondering if it's because he's concerned that the amount of female attention he and his friends receive will go down once I leave.

"Okay, man. Catch up again soon." Mike holds his hand out for a fist bump.

I bump it back. Mike was one of my good friends at college, but we've been drifting apart for a while now. Mainly because he can still go out and enjoy himself without worrying about what stories the tabloids are going to invent.

Yeah, I know. Poor little football star. It's a wonder a miniature orchestra doesn't follow me around playing sad violin music.

Outside in the freezing night, I step around a guy vomiting in the gutter and the thought of going home to an empty apartment is less appealing than eating the contents of the gutter.

I want some company. And there is only one person who likes me enough that they won't mind me unloading on them at two a.m. on a Sunday morning. I head to my little brother's place.

I'm hoping it's one of those nights when Josh is up coding at all hours, but when I unlock his apartment door with my spare key the place is dark. No signs of life in his room. Damn. Although I want to talk to him, I'm not enough of a selfish bastard to wake him just so I can share the details of my pitiful night.

I'll crash in his spare room and talk to him in the morning.

Which is a nice idea in theory—until I discover the room is already occupied.

I'm fumbling around, trying to remember where the

damn light switch is, when I'm suddenly aware there are noises coming from the bed. My breathing hitches, and my pulse starts to gallop. Adrenalin charges through my body on a takeover mission.

I'm pretty much the definition of freaking the hell out.

I've always been a big horror movie fan. And the first thing you learn from watching lots of horror is that noises in the dark are never a good thing.

Thank fuck my fingers find the switch then, and the room floods with light. Right in time to see a projectile heading straight for me.

Luckily I manage to dodge the missile, and a book falls harmlessly to the floor by my feet.

A girl is scrambling halfway out of the bed, staring at me as if I'm the zombie apocalypse. She grabs a cellphone from the bedside table.

"Who the hell are you?" The words fly out of my mouth.

"Who am I? Who are *you*? What are you doing in my apartment?" She continues to grapple with her phone, her chest rising and falling rapidly.

"*Your* apartment? This is my brother Josh's apartment."

She stops suddenly and stares at me. "You're Josh's brother?"

"Yes, I'm Josh's brother. Who are you?"

"I'm his roommate."

"Josh got a roommate?" Shit. Thanks for the heads-up, little bro.

"Um...yeah..." She rummages around on the end of her bed, grabbing a blue cardigan to pull over her pajama top.

"Sorry. I didn't realize Josh was getting a roommate. You can put the phone down," I say, when I see her fingers are back to hovering over the screen.

She narrows her eyes at me. "How do I know you're not a serial killer?"

"If I was a serial killer, don't you think you'd already be dead?"

"Maybe you're one of those predators who likes to play with their prey first."

"What kind of playing are you talking about?" I ask. I can't help myself. It's a natural reaction to a cute girl.

She gives me a scathing look. "Seriously? You've just crashed into my room in the middle of the night, and now you're hitting on me?"

That sobers me up. I get a flash of my agent's face and think about how this might play across the front page of a tabloid. Fuck.

I hold my hands up. "Sorry. Sorry. Listen, we'll wake Josh up, and he'll tell you I'm his brother."

"Josh isn't here."

I frown. "Where is he?"

"He had to go out of town at the last minute. I don't know where he went."

My shoulders drop. I know exactly where Josh is. No matter how many times I tell my kid brother that he shouldn't be at Mason's beck and call, he ignores me.

Josh definitely got the smarts in the family, there's no denying that. However, when it comes to Mason, his brain seems to go into deep freeze. "Okay," I say. "I'll crash in Josh's room then."

"You're going to stay?" She follows me out through the kitchen into the living room.

"Yeah. Why?"

She comes to a stop by the couch and crosses her arms. "I'm not comfortable having a strange guy sleep in the apartment."

Hmm. She hasn't recognized me yet. Interesting.

"I'm not a strange guy. I'm Josh's brother."

"Well, you're strange to me."

It's weird. It's been a long time since I've met someone and been challenged to prove that I'm a good guy. Most of the time people are falling over themselves to impress me.

I blow out a breath. "Fine. Ask me five questions, any questions, and I'll answer honestly."

"What?"

"Ask me any five questions you like, and I'll answer them. Then I won't be a strange guy anymore. I'll be a guy you know five random things about."

She lifts her chin and stares down her nose. This girl has a killer glare. I'm surprised the government hasn't harnessed it as a weapon—I can feel my balls shrinking.

But something about the idea of asking me five questions seems to appeal to her. I can see it on her face. She bites her bottom lip, which draws my attention to her mouth. She has sexy, full lips.

"What's the thing that scares you the most?" the lips ask.

"Heights," I say automatically. I'm lying, of course. While heights do scare the crap out of me, I fear other things more.

"What's the most embarrassing thing that's ever happened to you?"

"Easy. Sixth grade. Falling off the stage in the school play."

I'm lying again. It's a good thing I'm not Pinocchio right now, or there would be some incredible nose growth going on.

"If you had a superpower, what would you wish for?"

"To fly."

She doesn't realize that I've been answering versions of these questions for years. Reporters love asking cutesy questions like this, as if football fans really care about whether I eat my broccoli stalks or not. I'm pretty sure most football fans just care how far I can throw the ball.

She tilts her head. "How does wanting to fly go with your fear of heights?"

"I plan to fly very close to the ground."

"How close are you and Josh?"

"I'd give us about an eight and a half on the brother-closeness scale."

I watch for her reaction. I don't even get a twitch of her lips. To be fair, it wasn't that funny. But women usually fall over themselves laughing when I'm mildly amusing.

"If you're so close, how come he didn't tell you he was getting a roommate?"

"I've been out of town. I guess it slipped his mind."

Actually, I'm betting Josh deliberately decided not to mention it to me, considering the last roommate debacle ended up with me needing to get a restraining order. I've been covering the lost rent for him for the last six months, but I know part of the reason he wanted a roommate was for the company. During the season I'm not around much, although in the off-season we usually hang out all the time. And no one, especially not the pundits, could've predicted my off-season would start so early this year.

I say to the new roommate, "Okay, I think that's your five questions used up."

She blinks. "What? I haven't asked you five questions yet."

I tick them off on my fingers. "What scares me, most embarrassing thing, superpower, how close Josh and I are, and why he didn't tell me he was getting a roommate."

"That last one didn't count as a question. It was a follow-up," she protests.

"Fine. Ask me another one then."

She pauses. "If you could construct a house out of any food, what would you choose?"

My eyebrows fly up. I've never heard that question before. "I guess...cheese."

"Cheese?"

"Yeah, I love cheese. Plus it lasts a long time, and there are different softness levels to construct different parts of the house."

She seems to agree with my logic because she nods. "Good answer."

"So, can I stay? You can call Josh if you want. He'll vouch for me."

"I'm not going to call him at this time of night."

I glance around the living room and spot a family photo on a bookshelf. It was taken outside our house and shows Mom, Dad, Josh and me. We look like a cookie-cutter version of an all-American perfect family. Of course, at six three I dwarf the rest of my family but she can't fail to see how Josh and I are a blend of our parents, with blond hair like Mom and dark eyes like our dad.

I grab it off the shelf and thrust it at her. "Look, here you are. Proof I'm Josh's brother."

She takes it from me and examines it. "Nice haircut," she finally comments.

"Thanks. I was going for a cross between Justin Bieber and a shaggy golden retriever. It was the fashion at the time."

This time I'm rewarded by a tilt of her lips, which I match with my own grin. Until her next words. "Where's your Stanford T-shirt?"

That's right, this photo was taken right before Josh left for his first year of college. He's wearing his maroon T-shirt and Mom and Dad dug up their faded Stanford sweatshirts. I'm dressed in plain blue.

"I didn't go to Stanford," I mutter. "I went to Penn State."

Something flashes across her face. "All my family apart from me went to Oklahoma State," she says. "Three generations, both sides."

"Where did you go?"

"Columbia."

She says the name with a tinge of pride, but I don't miss the flash of loneliness in her expression. I get it. It's not easy being the odd one out in a family.

The fact that she returns to gazing at the photo now with sympathy on her face causes a weird spike in my stomach. I need to reset this scrimmage, fast.

"Columbia, eh? So, you're smart *and* beautiful," I say.

She looks at me, startled, and I realize she's not just cute —she is actually beautiful in an understated, stern-librarian way, dark hair curling as it makes its way to her shoulders. Her blue eyes catch mine, and whatever she sees in my gaze causes her pupils to dilate.

My body decides to get into the action, and my heart rate increases while I hold my breath. I'm sure I'm not imagining the heat that sizzles in the air between us.

She breaks eye contact, pulling her cardigan closer. "Seriously? You need to do some major work on your pickup lines."

Despite her words, a faint flush tracks its way up her cheekbones.

I swallow a smile. "Maybe you can help me out with

them sometime." I wink. Because this is back in my comfort territory. Flirting with a girl.

She rolls her eyes. "I'm going back to bed."

I bite back my offer to join her, instead watching as she goes and double-checks the lock on the front door then heads to her room.

"See you in the morning," I call cheerfully after her.

CHAPTER 3

MEGAN

WHEN I COME into the kitchen the next morning, it takes a few moments for my eyes to focus. The turquoise cabinets are definitely a shade too bright for this time of the morning. Or any time of day, really. After my vision finally settles, I realize Josh's brother is standing at the breakfast bar, helping himself to breakfast.

"Good morning," he says.

"Good morning." My reply is as friendly as the iceberg that sank the Titanic. Seeing this guy casually pouring himself some of my cereal irks me. I'm even more annoyed when I remember my response to his compliment last night. The moment of mutual gazing.

I'll admit, he's a good-looking guy. Okay, okay, he's freaking gorgeous. He's got the same brown eyes and blond hair as Josh, but where Josh's features are soft around the edges, this guy is all about the chisel. Chiseled nose, chiseled cheekbones, chiseled chin.

He's a lot bigger than Josh too, and he moves with a fluid gracefulness that makes you think he could pull off a pirouette in mid-stride.

I honestly thought I was a deeper person who responds to someone due to their personality, rather than based on what they look like. Apparently not.

As I grab a plate out of the pantry I notice Josh has a row of carnivorous plants on the windowsill. I have to bite down my grin, because carnivorous plants are so cool. I had a Venus fly trap named Wanda growing up.

"I didn't introduce myself properly last night. My name's Brandon. Brandon Seaton." Brandon's deep, smooth voice interrupts my admiring of the plants. He emphasizes his last name like it contains some special magic.

I turn back to face him. "Yeah, I figured that if you're Josh's brother you'd have the same last name as him. I have incredible deductive powers."

A quirk appears at the corner of his mouth. "You didn't tell me your name?"

"It's Megan."

"Great to meet you, Meg."

I freeze. Okay, I get that Meg is not a highly original nickname for someone called Megan, but somehow, hearing him say that in his deep jock voice, causes something inside me to stir. And not in a good way. For a moment, I'm taken back to similar voices calling me Meg in some of the worst moments of my life.

I blink, and the past retreats. Although it leaves me with a weird impulse to test what size prey the carnivorous plants can consume.

"It's Megan," I repeat. "Not Meg. And did you just use the last of the milk?"

"Oh shit, my bad."

"And that's my cereal you're eating."

"I thought Josh's taste had improved." He continues to chew unapologetically.

I study him out of the corner of my eye as I put bread in the toaster.

I should be playing nice with Brandon. After all, he's Josh's brother. If Josh ever asks him, "What do you think about Megan?" a positive answer is in my best interests.

But something about this guy rubs me the wrong way. No, scrap the something. *Everything* about him rubs me the wrong way. Because I've seen more than my fair share of Brandon's type. He's a stock-standard pattern they must make at the arrogant jock factory. Someone who is used to flirting with anything that has a pulse, charming his way through life.

And there's the fact that I know he lied to me last night. I wrote an article last year about body language and how to tell if someone is lying, and Brandon was definitely not telling the truth on some of those questions.

So, I can add pathological liar to the list of his qualities.

The toaster is slightly too enthusiastic in doing its job, and the aroma of charred bread fills the room just as my toast pops.

"Sorry, I should have warned you. Josh's toaster tends to misbehave," Brandon says as I scrape off the top layer of black and start spreading peanut butter.

"It's okay." Though it's a concerning sign about how much Brandon hangs out here, the fact he's so intimately acquainted with Josh's appliances. I thought I was getting the perfect fellow nerd as my roommate; I had no idea a cocky jock came built-in as a compulsory extra in the deal.

I'm about to take my toast and retreat to my room when the sound of the front door opening stops me.

Josh is whistling as he comes in but pulls up short when he sees Brandon and me. "Hey, Megan," he says before shifting his gaze to Brandon. "Didn't expect to see you here." The casualness in his voice is forced.

"I thought you were out of town." Brandon raises his eyebrows.

They have a weird standoff for a few seconds, until Josh breaks eye contact and moves past Brandon to open the fridge.

"I decided to come home early." He pours himself a glass of orange juice. "What are you doing here?"

Brandon lounges back against the counter. "I dropped by last night. Crashed in your room. Now Meg and I are just getting to know each other."

"Call me Meg again, and I'll castrate you," I say in my sweetest voice.

Josh chokes on the glass of orange juice.

"Castrate me? With what?" Brandon looks amused.

"With the grater. I'm sure whatever you've got down there can be easily grated off."

Brandon's mouth drops open while Josh starts to laugh. He gives me a quick wink.

Poor Josh. I don't need to use my imagination to know what it was like growing up with a jock brother who hogged the glory spotlight. I've lived that reality. Twice over, actually, since both of my brothers were addicted to football, just like my dad. Football is a second religion in Oklahoma, and I'm a notable atheist.

After I finish my toast, I stack my plate into the dishwasher.

"Megan was telling me the other day she can't stand football," Josh says conversationally.

Brandon stares at me. "Is that right?"

"Yep, I'm pathologically allergic to it," I reply. "I never watch or read anything about football."

"How do you avoid watching anything to do with football?" Brandon bends down to put his bowl in the dishwasher.

"It takes considerable practice. And good reflexes to turn off the TV the moment anything football-related is on."

"You'd never go out with a football player?" Josh's eyes sparkle.

I'm obviously helping him in some kind of point-scoring game against his brother and I have no problem playing along. I give an exaggerated shudder. "I'd prefer to gnaw off my own arm."

Brandon studies me with a peculiar look on his face. "You know what they say—opposites attract."

"That theory works for magnetism, but not for relationships," I reply.

Josh's grin grows wider. "She's got you there."

Brandon continues to study me, his weird expression not wavering.

"She sure does," he finally agrees.

CHAPTER 4

BRANDON

I END up hanging out at Josh's apartment quite a bit over the following weeks.

I could claim I'm keeping my head down because all those tabloid headlines saying things like *Brandon Seaton Embraces his Sinful Side* didn't exactly make it into my mom's scrapbook of clippings. Or my agent's.

As expected, I got the hard word from Frank that with my free agency pending and having just had an awful last playoff game, I don't need to give teams reasons not to offer me a big contract. He reminded me that staying out of trouble should be my top priority. And surely nothing meets the definition of keeping out of trouble more than watching Discovery Channel documentaries with my brother and his new roommate.

But there's something else that keeps attracting me back, and it's not just that I'm eager to expand my knowledge about the mating habits of the African dung beetle.

It's Megan.

Not that I'm thinking about her in that way—because, let's face it, she couldn't be further from my type. There's just something refreshing about hanging out with someone who has no idea who I am. Someone who doesn't want to talk about the playoffs and why we lost that last game and what's happening with my free agency decision. Someone who's not impressed by how far I can throw a football.

In fact, Megan doesn't appear to be particularly impressed with me at all.

I turn up one Tuesday night, and I see the twist of her scowl before she buries it.

She's on the couch, holding Josh's geeky *Ctrl* cushion on her lap while Josh is in his usual chair closest to the TV.

"Hey, we were just about to watch a documentary on the Hubble telescope," Josh says.

"Okay. Count me in." I plop down on the other end of the couch from Megan. I've got to say this for my little brother, he knows how to choose a couch. I mocked him when we went couch shopping together because he turned it into a scientific test and insisted on rating every model on various criteria. But the end result is a navy-blue couch that's softer than the NFL commissioner's stance on rogue umpires.

As Josh sets up the show, he and Megan trade astronomy puns, and I realize something.

She likes him. As in *likes* him.

Which means my little brother hasn't been completely upfront and honest with his new roommate.

My stomach hollows. This is like watching a train wreck in slow motion yet I can't tear my eyes away.

She's flirting with him but doing it subtly. Obviously science nerds have this whole other mating strategy that's not used by the average Joe. The girls who hit on me are normally pretty obvious. Hair flicks interchanged with some eyelash batting and *accidentally* brushing against me.

Meanwhile, Megan is going for the whole turn-him-on-with-my-brain thing. After they finish up with the bad astronomy jokes, Megan starts talking about how the Hubble telescope was named after the person who provided evidence for the big bang. Her eyes are bright, and she tucks a strand of hair behind her ear as she talks, looking cute and vulnerable.

"I thought *The Big Bang Theory* was a TV show," I interrupt.

Megan presses her lips together. "It's a theory about the origin of the universe. I'm pretty sure the TV show was named after it, not the other way around."

Right. Shit. Way to show my ignorance.

I settle back. "Sounds like it could be the name for a Swedish documentary about orgies."

Megan's eyes widen. "Seriously?"

"Don't mind Brandon, he's missing a filter or two," Josh says.

I shrug, pretending not to care. "Just saying."

"On that note, it's probably time to start watching." Josh reaches for the remote, and the TV springs to life.

I catch Megan sending sneaky glances at Josh as we watch, and something stirs deep in my gut. Maybe it's my competitive side waking up. I've never had a girl ignore me to flirt with my brother before. Or maybe it's my insecure side. Because if I had to rely on seducing someone only by brainpower I'd be screwed. And not in the fun way.

Just as the documentary finishes, Josh's phone starts to chime. He retreats to his room to answer it, and I resist the urge to roll my eyes. My brother's very-in-the-closet boyfriend has forced Josh to get back in the closet too. Not that he'd ever fully emerged, but he did come out to our parents in his senior year of high school. He was about to come out at school too, which was incredibly brave of him in a small town. I was crushing college football at the time, and I arranged to run some coaching clinics at my old high school. The idea was that I would be hanging around, reminding any homophobic jerks who needed a memory refresher that if they messed with my little brother they were messing with me too.

But the day before he came out at school Josh decided to trial coming out to the boy next door, and in response, Mason kissed him.

Unfortunately, Mason belongs to the type of religious family where biblical teachings on tolerance and loving thy neighbor don't apply if the neighbor is also a boy. And since Mason needs to hide the amount of time they spend together under the guise of friendship, Josh has never been able to be openly gay. They've done the long-distance thing —with Mason back in Maryland and Josh in New York—for the two years since they finished college. To me, that's a hell of a long time to spend pretending to be something you are not.

But hey, maybe I can't exactly hand out lectures about denying your identity, because the other day when Megan asked me what I did as a career, I told her I was in sports management. Which is kind of true. I do have to manage myself.

"What do you want to watch now?" Megan glances at me.

The promo for the next show is already playing. It's called *Naked and Afraid*, and apparently, it chronicles the lives of a male and female survivalist who meet for the first time and have to try to survive in the wilderness naked for 21 days. Which pretty much sounds like the most awesome premise for a reality TV show ever.

"This looks good." I nod at the screen.

"A reality show?" Her words contain scorn.

"Hey, you shouldn't judge something before you've experienced it."

I stand up and go into the kitchen, grabbing a Coke for myself and a Dr Pepper for Megan, because I've already worked out she has an addiction.

She accepts the can with a brief thanks, already leaning toward the TV as the two contestants are introduced.

"I bet he used to play football," she says.

"How do you know?"

"He just has that look."

"What look do football players have?" I ask.

"Generally they have a bigger head than the general population." She smirks at me.

I layer my voice with innuendo. "Which head are you talking about?"

Megan splutters on a mouthful of her drink. "You did not just say that!"

Fuck. What's with me tonight? It appears all I can do is say crass stuff. I decide the best course of action is to keep my mouth shut. We watch as the contestants strip naked to meet each other. They blur out the good bits, sadly.

"This is the worst show in the world," Megan says finally.

"And yet you're still watching it."

"Sometimes things are so bad they're almost good."

"Ten bucks says she's going to be the first to crack under pressure," I say.

Megan narrows her eyes. "Twenty says it's the guy."

Of course it's the guy. She has to deal with his break-down while trying to cook them dinner and deal with a horde of monkeys trying to steal their hunting equipment. She handles the entire situation impeccably.

Megan turns to me with a grin, her eyes sparkling. I grab twenty bucks from my wallet. Our fingers touch as I go to hand it over, and I feel a jolt of...something.

I drop the note, and it slips through Megan's fingers. We both lean down to grab it, and I'm close enough to smell the coconut and vanilla of her shampoo. My arm brushes against her arm and goose bumps spring up instantly. The jolt intensifies until my whole body hums like a fucking harmonica.

Okay. So it appears I'm not completely immune to Science Barbie's charms after all.

However, Megan doesn't appear affected at all by our encounter. She straightens up, grasping the twenty-dollar note, and smiles triumphantly. "I think I might frame this."

CHAPTER 5

MEGAN

LIVING with Josh is as great as I expected. We move from roommates to friends seamlessly over the next fortnight, and inside me there's a little spark of hope that the next progression might happen just as naturally.

Unfortunately Josh shows no sign of being interested in me romantically. And trust me, I've been searching for signs more actively than UFO enthusiasts search the night sky. Because there is no way I'm going to put myself out there and risk all the potential awkwardness unless I'm absolutely certain my feelings are reciprocated.

One Saturday night we're heading out the door together when Brandon arrives. I swear Brandon spends more time at our apartment than he does at his own. Josh seems to enjoy his company, so I've bitten back my complaints.

"We were just going to grab some frozen yogurt. You want to come?" Josh asks him.

Brandon flinches. "Probably not a good idea."

I let out a breath I didn't even realize I was holding. It's not just that I want to spend time alone with Josh. Somehow, when Brandon's around there's always this weird tension buzzing between him and me, and not just when we're trading insults. It's like antimatter—one of those phenomena science can't find an explanation for.

Josh ducks back into his room and emerges holding a red baseball cap and dark sunglasses. "Here." He thrusts them at Brandon, who puts them on.

I raise an eyebrow. "Is there a reason why you're dressing Brandon up like that even though it's mid-January, forty degrees, and dark outside?"

"We've got to cover up Brandon's beauty or the girls start mobbing him," Josh says.

I roll my eyes. I have to concede, Brandon is male-model gorgeous. However it's egotistical of him to assume that females can't control themselves around him.

"Yeah, I understand. I struggle with the urge to mob Brandon daily." My words are deep-fried in sarcasm.

"And yet you find the strength to resist," Brandon says.

"It's my superpower," I reply.

We head into the elevator, also known as taking your life into your own hands. I swear the metallic groaning and creaking gets worse every time.

Brandon stands next to the door, and as I lean past to press the button I catch a hint of his cologne. He smells like a fresh mix of lemon and cedarwood, two of my favorite scents. I have to restrain myself from shuffling closer to him. After just mocking the idea of mobbing him, planting my nose on his skin might be slightly hypocritical.

We make it to Frozen Palace and I volunteer to queue up while Brandon finds a booth near the back and Josh heads to the bathroom.

I'm studying Frozen Palace's poster that's inviting me to

suggest my own new flavor of yogurt, when a guy sidles up behind me.

"Excuse me, is that Brandon Seaton you just came in with?"

I turn to look at the guy. He's the pure definition of a jock, in letterman jacket and jeans. His two friends standing beside him are dressed identically.

"Um...yeah." My shoulders have hunched up automatically. I force myself to unclench.

"Oh, my God, I thought so."

"Do you know him from somewhere?" I ask.

He gives me a weird look. "Yeah, I know him from football."

"Oh, do you guys play on the same team?"

The guy's look morphs into astonishment, and he starts to chuckle. "Yeah, sure we play on the same team. I'm the starting receiver, didn't you know?"

He and his friends crack up laughing. Heat tracks up my cheeks. *Jocks.* I frigging hate them. Especially when I'm the butt of a joke I don't understand.

And I really don't understand what's going on now, because as I collect our orders and weave my way back to the table it's like I've stumbled into one of the sixth dimension's alternative universes. I can hear Brandon's name echoing around, like the walls are whispering it. I put the tray on the table with a thump.

Brandon looks at my face and frowns. He's taken off his sunglasses but his cap remains in place. "What's up?"

I don't want to admit I'm hallucinating his name. I'm about to tell him I ran into his friend, when suddenly the friend turns up at our table.

"Sorry to disturb, but can I grab an autograph?" He thrusts a pen and napkin at Brandon.

My forehead wrinkles in confusion as Brandon puts on a smile. I know Brandon well enough to know it's a fake smile. But he obediently picks up the pen and signs the napkin.

"Your friend wanted to know if we play on the same team," the guy chortles.

Brandon glances at me. I give him a flat glare back.

"Yeah, she's not really into football," he says.

Sidling back in my seat while he talks to the idiot guy, I shield my phone from scrutiny while I google Brandon. What I read makes me swallow hard. Twice.

Right, so apparently there are some negatives about determinedly remaining ignorant about everything in the football universe.

Like not knowing your roommate's brother is the *Freaking Starting Quarterback for the New York Goliaths.*

Trying to keep what I know has to be a freaked-out look off my face and cultivate a nonchalant air, I put my phone back on the table and slide it away from me. I pick up my lemon frozen yogurt and dig out a spoonful. The bitterness bites my tongue.

Brandon finishes up signing the autograph, and the idiot jocks retreat. He glances at me, his eyebrows shooting up at whatever he sees on my face.

Maybe I haven't got my nonchalant look quite perfected yet.

"So, you've discovered my little secret," he says. He's trying for a mocking tone but there's a whiff of something else underneath. Disappointment?

I swallow. "Yeah, Google informed me that rich people pay you an obscene amount of money to throw a piece of dead cow around in a paddock. The knowledge is life changing."

Brandon's lips quirk up in a grin and Josh, arriving back from the bathroom in time to hear my snide remark, has an equally amused expression.

"I take it you've been outed?" he asks, sliding into the booth.

"Interesting choice of words." Brandon gives Josh a loaded stare I don't understand.

Josh flicks a glance at me. "You know what I mean."

"Actually, Josh, I'm kind of interested why you didn't think to give me the heads-up about who Brandon is? Like drop it casually into conversation? Oh, by the way, Brandon's a famous football star."

"It was more fun this way," Josh says.

I snort. "Yeah, it was about as fun as head lice."

Josh laughs as another group of wide-eyed autograph/selfie hunters approaches our table.

"Just don't believe everything you read on Google about me." Brandon turns his attention to them.

Which leads me to my next form of entertainment for the evening: finding all the random facts about Brandon splattered over the internet. He's everywhere. Brandon hugging Beyoncé. Brandon meeting the vice president. Apparently there used to be a giant ad of him advertising underwear on display in Times Square, until it caused too many accidents and they had to take it down.

The fact that I never recognized him really doesn't say great things about my knowledge of popular culture.

"Did he really date Kendall Jenner?" I ask Josh quietly as Brandon signs his umpteenth autograph.

Our joke earlier about Brandon being mobbed suddenly feels prophetic. Although it's not just girls swarming around him like electrons swarm around the nucleus—Brandon's being equal-opportunity mobbed.

Josh shakes his head. "No, he's never dated Kendall. He worked on a charity thing with her, and then the press jumped to all kinds of assumptions."

"And this thing about him eating a 12-ounce steak every morning for breakfast?"

"He did that for a few months when he was trying to bulk up."

I continue my googling. "There's all these articles speculating about his free agency. It's insane."

"Yeah, it's pretty intense," Josh agrees.

I try to focus my search on the non-football-related stuff. Just because I've inadvertently been spending time with a professional football player doesn't mean I'm changing my stance on the game. "Did he really have to go to court to get a restraining order against two women on the same day?" I ask with an eyebrow raised.

"Yeah, that one's actually true."

"Seriously?"

"Yeah. He's had a few stalkers."

"Okay." Skepticism is threaded through my voice. To me, Brandon is like a lingering smell you can't get rid of. The idea that you would actively seek out that odor is a strange concept.

Josh pushes the glasses back up his nose, looking uneasy. "One of them was my old roommate, actually."

I almost drop my spoon. "What?"

"She was a big football fan, and she kind of went off the deep end when Brandon hung out at our apartment. She stole my spare key to his place and snuck into his apartment, and he came home and discovered her naked in his bed."

"Holy shit," I squeak. I'm aware my eyes are so wide I could audition to be a Disney princess.

"Yeah, it got a bit awkward in the end."

"I can imagine."

Josh gives me a smile. "That's why I really liked the fact you don't like football. It was a total bonus you didn't actually know who he was."

Hmm. I would have preferred that Josh chose me because he sensed our potential connection, rather than for my anti-football, not-likely-to-end-up-lying-naked-in-Brandon's-bed qualities. "It still would have been nice to have had a little heads-up," I mutter. "You know, so I didn't look like a complete idiot.

Josh gives me a sheepish look. "Sorry."

I can't help throwing him a small grin. Josh has probably had to put up with a lot of people liking him under false pretenses because of Brandon—copping the negatives of Brandon's celebrity without any of the bonuses.

The Brandon groupies retreat—happy smiles on their faces just because they got to interact with Brandon for a few minutes. It reinforces what I've always suspected about most football fans' IQs.

"What secrets are you telling?" Brandon's eyes dart between us, a frown on his face.

"Oh, it's all about you," I say.

He leans back and shakes out his arm, the frown on his face not wavering.

"You guys want to get out of here?" he asks.

"Sure," Josh says.

Brandon scoops up his frozen yogurt, which he hasn't even had a chance to eat. It's melted into a puddle of strawberry goo that would probably be easier to drink now. He chucks it into the trash as we leave.

We get stopped once on the way home by some rabid fan who recognizes Brandon despite his large coat, hat and glasses. Brandon obligingly grins as the guy smushes up against him for a selfie. Personally I don't think I could handle having my personal space invaded all the time, but Brandon seems fine with it.

"And that's what a public excursion with Brandon is like," Josh says after the rabid fan retreats.

"I kind of understand why you prefer to hibernate in our apartment," I say.

Josh sneaks a glance at Brandon. "Actually, that's been more of a recent development." His eyes twinkle with some mischief I don't understand.

Brandon narrows his eyes at Josh. "Yeah, after we lost in the first round of the playoffs and I had a whole lot of random strangers hissing death threats at me."

"See, that is exactly why I hate sports," I say as we step into the elevator.

Brandon seizes up like I've just announced a plan to kill the queen. "What do you mean?"

"Well, you have all these people angry and upset at you —and for what? Because there was one game where things didn't go your way?" The elevator gives a shudder and I put out a hand to brace myself.

Brandon's so involved in the conversation he seems able to ignore the fact that we're perilously close to plummeting to our doom. He turns to face me, arms crossed. "Actually, it was more of a ten-minute period where our defense completely lost focus and the other team scored two touch-downs, and then our offense couldn't generate anything in return."

His words help distract me from the fact that the shuddering has turned into a kind of strange vibrating. We're still moving upwards. However it feels like the elevator is a tad unsure about this decision.

"That's even worse," I say. "Ten minutes defines your life when there's just so much luck involved."

"Ten minutes didn't define my entire life. Just this season."

Josh points out, "Technically, depending on what happens in free agency, those ten minutes could determine the course of your career."

Brandon whips his head around to glare at his brother. "Whose side are you on?"

Josh raises his hands in an innocent gesture. "Neither side. I'm not brave enough to put myself in the middle of you two."

The door opens on the fourth floor, which is a major win, since this elevator sometimes spits you out on random floors just to mix it up.

I step out, take a moment to appreciate what a brilliant invention solid flooring is, then continue to argue with Brandon. "All sport has that kind of randomness, right? Like Olympians—they all train for years and years, and it's often just one performance, sometimes a split second, that determines if they are winners or losers."

"That's life in general," Brandon says.

I shake my head. "In arts or science you're normally judged on years of your work. It's not defined by such a small time period, so chance plays less of a factor."

Brandon narrowed his eyes. "Yeah, but you get that sometimes in science too, right? Like how the microwave was developed by that guy studying radars after he realized the chocolate bar in his pocket had melted."

My surprise is echoed on Josh's face.

"What? I have actually been watching all those documentaries too, you know," Brandon says.

Unlocking the door to apartment 4B gives me a thrill.

It's so perfect for me and it's starting to feel like home. With Josh's encouragement, I've hung my famous-scientist framed prints. So Marie Curie, Einstein and Charles Darwin all frown down from behind the couch as we head into the living room. They look as unimpressed with Brandon's arguments as I am. Einstein is even poking out his tongue in disgust.

"Just because serendipitous moments occur in science doesn't invalidate my point," I say.

"What moments?" Brandon flops down on the couch.

"Serendipitous. It means, something that happens by chance."

I sit down on my end of the couch and turn toward him, while Josh takes his normal chair. Somehow these have become our usual positions. The middle cushion of the couch lies between Brandon and me like no-man's-land.

"Oh, right, but what I'm saying is chance plays a part in arts and science too," Brandon says.

Hmm. I revise my earlier thought. The apartment is *almost* perfect. If only it didn't come infested with an argumentative football player.

"Not nearly as much as in sport," I counter.

Brandon and I continue to argue back and forth about the relative merits of sport versus other professions. Brandon maintains that the randomness is what makes sport more exciting than other professions. I contend that it means success in sport is far less valid than success in other endeavors.

Josh gives a large yawn. "Right, I'm going to bed. Don't stay up too late arguing, you two. And I don't want any blood on the furniture."

"Night, Josh." I give him a nice smile, which fades as

soon as I look back at Brandon. He's watching me with dark eyes.

There's no way I'm conceding any ground to Brandon on this one, and from the determined jut of his chin he's not giving up soon either.

It might be a long night.

CHAPTER 6

BRANDON

SO, if I was hoping that finding out I'm a famous football star would change the way Megan treated me, her attitude in the next week would have left me sadly disappointed.

I know she doesn't like football, so I wasn't expecting adoration or anything like that. However, I'd have taken a little bit of grudging respect. I mean, not to be egotistical, but I am good at what I do.

If anything, her disdain is even more pronounced, because now she's got my career to mock too. It's like an extension of our argument the other night, where despite the hours spent arguing, nothing can dislodge her contempt for sport.

"Hey, Brandon, what did the football coach say to the broken vending machine?" Megan asks on Thursday night when we're on the couch.

I squint suspiciously at her. "What?"

"Give me my quarterback." Megan scrunches up her nose as she grins in triumph. She's got her glasses on, which I know she only wears when her eyes are tired. It must have been a full-on day in Nerd Magazine land.

"That is the lamest joke ever," I reply.

"Yeah, well, football fans aren't known for their advanced senses of humor."

"How can you judge football fans when you avoid everything football related?"

I'm rewarded by an epic eye roll. Seriously, if eye-rolling became an Olympic event Megan would be a guaranteed podium finisher.

"I grew up with a football-mad family in Oklahoma. I might not follow football now, but trust me, I learned a lot by osmosis growing up."

"What's osmosis? Some kind of weird Oklahoma thing?" I ask.

She splutters. "Ah, no, osmosis is not a 'weird Oklahoma thing'. Did you not pay any attention in high-school biology?"

Shit. Looks like I've just exposed my ignorance. Again. When in doubt, cover up with something funny.

"I spent a lot of time trying to convince my lab partner, Anita Jackman, to let me explore her biology. Does that count?"

I'm rewarded by eye roll type seven. It's when she's secretly amused by me. I can tell by the crinkles around the corners of her eyes.

I wait for a few seconds, counting in my head. *One. Two. Three...*

"Osmosis is the movement of water from an area of high concentration to low concentration through a semi-permeable membrane. It's generally how water gets into cells."

Ha. I knew it. Megan can't bear to leave me uneducated. It's kind of like hanging out with a talking version of Wikipedia. "Thanks for the lesson," I say.

Her attention has been diverted away from me. "Shush, it's back on."

We're watching *Naked and Afraid* again. It's kind of become a weekly thing to watch the new episodes, and we've spent a lot of time in between catching up on the first few series. Megan, despite her initial protests, is now as hooked as me. I think for her it's mainly because the women always seem to outshine the guys. They usually pair up macho hunters with these hippy, Earth-mother-type women. And maybe it's because the guy's mindset is to conquer the wilderness while the woman tries to work with it, but generally it's the men who can't hack it.

Need to step it up, men. You're not exactly doing wonders for our gender.

I sneak a glance at Megan. There's something about the way she leans forward slightly while her shoulders remain rigid, like her whole body is concentrating on what's going on. It's...cute. Although using the word cute to describe Megan feels on par to describing a grizzly bear as cute. Sure, grizzly bears might look like something you could snuggle with, but they also have the potential to maul you.

Megan must feel my gaze on her because she shoots me a puzzled look.

Oh, yeah, that's right. There's a naked chick on screen swimming through crystal clear tropical water to reach another island. I really should be concentrating on that.

I tell my teammate Connor about *Naked and Afraid* the next day when we're out shopping together after a hard morning in the gym. We're heading up an escalator, and other shoppers are giving their neck muscles good workouts as they do double takes. Even if they don't recognize us, Connor is six four and built like the linebacker he is. When us footballers are together, we tend to stand out in a crowd.

"Like, seriously, you've got to check it out. They're trying to survive in the wilderness, and they're naked. It's epic," I explain as we step off the escalator. The toy store is set over multiple levels. A toy store plus escalators would pretty much have been my definition of heaven when I was a kid.

Connor nails me with a skeptical look. "This is why you bailed on the trip to Puerto Rico? So you could spend your time watching reality TV?"

"Nah, I'm still bummed about getting knocked out. Didn't feel like partying at the beach."

"You're not distancing yourself from us because you're planning on bailing in free agency, are you?"

My stomach clenches, as it always does when I see or hear something about my free agency. Which is basically any time I go on social media or look at any sporting news website. "Nah, man, I'm a Goliath for life. As long as they want me," I manage.

I know Frank has been in intense discussions with Goliaths' management. I'm trying to stay away from all the drama and hype about whether they'll offer me a good contract or look for another quarterback. Although I might be stalking Adam Schefter's Twitter feed the same way I would've stalked a free buffet in college.

"Of course they want you. Coach loves you," Connor assures me.

"Jason Smith and Harris Adams are free agents this summer," I remind him. "And after what happened in the playoffs, the owners might decide they want to mix things up."

Connor scoffs. "Jason Smith's got an arm like an eighty-year-old woman. You're safe, man. You should be asking for as close to the max as you can get."

I shrug. "I leave that shit to Frank. That's what he gets his cut for."

Frank knows my preference is to stay in New York, but I'm willing to hear what other teams will offer. I'd be stupid not to. Seeing other guys in the league being forced to retire early has made me realize I've got limited years playing football, so I need to maximize my earnings while I can. Because although I hate to admit it, Megan was right when she said that random chance *is* a big factor in sport. One bad hit and your career could be over.

"Next season is our year," Connor declares. "I heard rumors they're thinking of signing Max Endecott. We're going to have the team to go all the way."

"I hope so."

"Anyways, you missed an awesome time at the beach," Connor says as we reach our destination. "A real friend would have turned up and drunk piña coladas regardless."

"Dude, I'm walking down the Barbie aisle with you. If that's not friendship, I don't know what is."

We're shopping for Connor's five-year-old daughter Annaliese, who is the result of a random one-night stand when he was in college. I'm pretty sure Connor wasn't prepared to be a dad at twenty-one, but from what I can see he's managed to make it to the pros while still being a hands-on dad to his kid. And for that I've got to give him big ups.

"Nothing says friendship like Barbie shopping," Connor agrees. He stops and picks a box off the shelf. It's pink. Like nearly everything else in this aisle. You'd think product marketers could get a bit more creative. "What do you think about this one?"

The Barbie staring back at me through the plastic has a more than passing resemblance to a stripper. In fact, I'm pretty sure that's a pole painted in the background of the packaging.

"Am I rating the Barbie for her hotness, or for her suitability for what you want your daughter to grow up to be?" I ask.

He sticks it back on the shelf. "That's a good point. I should get her a Doctor Barbie or something."

I'm halfheartedly helping Connor scan the shelves when I spot it. Science Barbie. All dressed up in a lab coat with a tiny pair of goggles and holding a microscope.

I grab it, the stiff plastic wrapping crunching under my fingers. "I've got to buy this."

Connor snorts. "Are you getting lonely at night?"

"Shut up. It's for Josh's roommate. She's a science geek."

From his expression, I can see Connor doesn't get it. "You're buying a doll for your brother's roommate?"

"Yup." Giving Megan the Barbie will antagonize her. But deep down she'll find it funny. I can already envision her smirk that she'll work hard to bury as she conjures up ways to insult me. She'll probably call me a Ken doll and make some comparisons to my genitalia being equally non-existent. And I'll reply asking how her vital measurements stack up against Barbie, and I'm sure she'll start lecturing me about feminism and what Barbie's impossible standards have done to little girls. Which all amounts to fun times in apartment 4B.

"Are you okay?" Connor's giving me a weird look now as he chooses a firefighter Barbie off the shelf.

"Yeah, why?"

"You're kind of grinning to yourself."

I realize I've just been having a mental conversation with Megan.

Shit, that girl is taking up far too much real estate in my brain.

CHAPTER 7

MEGAN

"SO, how are things going with your roommate?" Ashley asks me as we take a seat at the bar. It's Friday night, so it's busy, but Ashley has come prepared, dressed in a low-cut sweater. Combined with her killer smile, it means as soon as she removes her coat we get served. Which makes me bristle, and the bartender retreats with a confused look after I reward him for handing me a wine with a scowl for his blatant appearance-based favoritism.

"Josh and I are getting along fine," I answer. I shift my stool a little closer to hers because it's noisy in here, with a game blaring on the screens above the bar, along with the usual noises of clinking glasses and people chatting.

Ashley raises an eyebrow. "So, no progression from fine to *fine?*" She says the last word with a lewd wink that left subtle behind several levels ago.

I sip my wine, and the tartness explodes on my tongue. I'm not usually a big drinker, but after the full-on week I've had at work some chemical help to relax is exactly what I need. "No, absolutely no progression."

"Why not?" Ashley asks.

"Because hooking up with your roommate is a worse idea than hydrogen airships." I'm reminding myself as much as I'm telling Ashley.

"Oh, come on, you talk about the guy all the time. And you know, proximity is such an important part of attraction." She leans forward, her eyes glinting. "Tell me honestly—is there a spark there?"

I pause to consider. Is there any spark between Josh and me? I feel like I'm rubbing and rubbing pieces of wood together, and it's barely smoldering.

Brilliant. A fire-making metaphor. I really have been watching too much *Naked and Afraid*.

"I'm not sure," I say truthfully.

Ashley gives me an evaluating glance that causes fear to stir in my stomach. Ashley's thinking face is never a good thing.

"Maybe you should stir things up," she suggests, spearing an olive from the plate the bartender just delivered.

"How would I do that?"

"Take home another guy. See how he reacts." Ashley nods at a group of guys playing pool nearby. "Lots of candidates here tonight."

"Um...no. I'm not picking up anyone at this bar."

"Why not?"

"Well, firstly, you chose a sports bar. And I made a pact with myself when I was seventeen that I would never date a jock." I leave off the important word—I vowed that I would never date a jock *again*.

"You realize that sports bars provide the best ratio of men to women of any bar, right? I was simply increasing our odds. I didn't realize you'd taken a vow of celibacy for athletes."

She scans the bar. "What about him? I guarantee he's not a jock." She points to a guy who couldn't be more the definition of laidback hipster if his low-slung jeans started quoting Bob Dylan.

He looks almost as out of place here as I do. Unlike Ashley, I didn't bother to take a change of clothes to work, so I'm still wearing my professional turtleneck sweater and tidy slacks. If I'd been the one buying the drinks we'd still be waiting.

"No," I reply flatly.

"Why not?" Her forehead screws up like she's trying to understand the mathematical basis for string theory.

It's hard to explain to Ashley how I feel. If she sees someone she likes, she goes for it without pausing to think. But I'm not confident about pursuing guys. I don't need to use my college psychology classes to work out where it comes from. Traumatic event in my formative years? *Tick.* I could be a case study, I'm so textbook. But knowing the origin of my neurosis doesn't mean it's easy to change.

I fiddle with my wine glass as I debate confiding the truth. I've never told anyone before. Of course, it's not exactly private—half the people in my hometown know, because my humiliation was a very, very public thing—but I've never volunteered the information up myself.

Maybe talking about it will reduce the power it has over me? Maybe I could turn it into a self-deprecating joke? Like, hey Ash, you'll never believe the crazy thing that happened to me in my high school senior year?

But my heart skitters at the thought of talking about it, even though it was six years ago now. It's especially not something I want to discuss when I'm surrounded by loud jocks and TV screens blaring sport.

I fall back into a convenient default. "I don't do the casual thing." I sit up straight. "Anyway, I think it's time we instituted our own version of the Bechdel test for our conversations."

Ashley grins.

The Bechdel test measures whether a film features at least two women who talk to each other about something other than a man. It's a sad indictment on our society that about half of the movies produced fail this test. It's even sadder that my night with Ashley so far has also failed this test.

"Fine, fine, have it your way. What do you want to talk about? Hey, did you see that recent meta-analysis that links gut microflora to treating anxiety?"

"Really?" I make a mental note to get some probiotic yogurt next time I'm grocery shopping.

"Yeah, the brain-gut connection is fascinating. There's so much emerging research that shows how the balance of bacteria in your intestine affects your mental health. I'm thinking of pitching the idea to Tony—see if I can turn it into a cover story."

"That would be incredible."

Ashley and I are both still chasing our first cover story. But that's okay—some people have been at *The Science Journal* for over ten years without ever getting on the cover.

"What about you? Did you get that article on solar cells finished?" Ashley asks.

"Yeah, I finally finished it this afternoon. I'm researching an article on DNA scissors and also..." I hesitate before plunging on. "I'm trying to line up an interview with Dianne Marshall."

Ashley's eyes widen. "Really? I thought she didn't give interviews."

"I know. But she was the lead researcher on that recent neuroscience article in *Nature*. And she's kind of been my hero for a while now. So I thought it was worth a shot."

"Good luck with that." Ashley nicely leaves off the '*You'll need it.*'

I'm a realist—I already know I'll need the luck of a four-leaf clover combined with a lucky rabbit foot multiplied by the number seven to secure an interview with Dianne Marshall.

We chat a bit more about potential stories for work. This is why Ashley's so great. She'd only been there a year when I first started, but she immediately took me under her wing, like a blonde mother hen with great bangs. She's been both a valuable sounding board and a vocal cheerleader at work for me ever since.

As Ashley and I stand up to leave, a familiar face pops up on one of the large television screens.

It's Brandon, in all his football gear. He doesn't look happy. I'm guessing this is a replay of the playoff match where the Goliaths lost.

I've never seen Brandon fully dressed to play before. It's weird to see a face I know so well in such a different context, with the green field and bright lights and a stadium full of people behind him.

On screen, he's taken off his helmet, and a bit of his hair is plastered on his forehead. The shoulder pads make his wide shoulders look even broader than usual. The sound is turned down on this TV, so I can't hear what he's saying.

"Since when are you interested in football?" Ashley asks when she notices I've paused halfway across the bar to watch.

"I'm not. That's just Josh's brother."

Ashley whips her head around. "Where?"

I nod to the screen, where Brandon is still talking to the reporter. His eyebrows are drawn together in the same frown he used the other day when I suggested the national chess championship deserved to get more coverage than football.

"Josh's brother is an ESPN interviewer?" Ashley's eyes widen.

"No, he's the player being interviewed."

Ashley studies the screen. "That's Brandon Seaton," she says finally.

"Yeah, I know."

"You're telling me that your roommate's brother is Brandon Seaton?"

"Yeah. He's an arrogant jackass though. And he's forever hassling me. Like, the other day he bought a Science Barbie. Just to mock me."

"Brandon Seaton bought you a Barbie?" Ashley's voice rises an octave in the space of the sentence.

"Yeah. It's okay though. I've just ordered a Ken doll that's dressed as a footballer in revenge."

And I've got some evil plans for the doll once it arrives. Brandon will rue the day he dared to enter the world of Barbie.

Ashley just blinks at me. "You have in-jokes with Brandon Seaton? How am I just hearing about this now?"

"It's no big deal."

She's shaking her head as we continue walking. I shrug into my coat and wrap my scarf around my neck, but the cold New York February night still greets me like a blow when we push open the door. Our breath immediately starts to make our own personal clouds in the air.

"What other things are you hiding?" Ashley turns to me when we reach the pavement. "Are you best friends with one of the Kennedys? Going on vacation with the Dalai Lama?"

CHAPTER 8

BRANDON

"BRANDON, GREAT TO SEE YOU." Frank meets me at his office door with a strong handshake.

I follow him over to the leather couches, and we sit.

Frank is the last person you'd expect to be a sports agent. He's about five foot five and skinny, with a shock of almost-white-blond hair. When he's surrounded by the professional athletes he represents, he looks like a child who's been brought to work by his father on Take Your Kid to Work Day.

But he's one of the most hard-assed agents out there.

Frank narrows his eyes at me contemplatively. "I gotta say, since you and I last talked you've done a great job of keeping your nose clean."

"I always obey you, Frank. You're like my Jedi master."

Frank smirks. "I only wish some of my other clients would listen as well. You know that technically we're not allowed to be talking yet, but I gotta say, all the stuff I'm hearing out of the Goliaths' camp is positive."

I feel my shoulders relax. "That's good to hear."

"Yeah. I wasn't sure, given the playoff debacle, but I'm

getting a good vibe off of them. Our plans are still the same though: I go out to other teams when the negotiating period begins, see what else is out there. You want to stay big market though, right?"

"Yeah, definitely."

"Some of the West Coast teams could bite. I hear there are a few locker room problems with the Bighorns. They might be looking to shift Clifton Wells on. You interested in LA?"

"I'd prefer to stay in New York, obviously, but I could handle living in LA," I say. "It's worth a conversation."

"Yeah, and we want Goliaths' management to know we're prepared to look around. They're going to have cap space issues if they're not careful, and we don't want them stiffing you just because they think you're desperate to stay here."

"I trust you on this one, Frank. Bring me the best deals, and I'll decide once I know what's on the table."

"That's my job."

The sooner free agency is behind me, the better. I know that whatever contract I sign is going to be dissected like a frog in biology class. It's one of the awesome parts of professional sport—everyone gets to have an opinion about how much I'm worth.

"I've got another thing to talk to you about. This ad campaign you're doing with Kleinfielders—they just sent me the brief," Frank says.

"Yeah?"

"So, they want you dressed up in their suit next to a seal."

"What?"

"I actually went back to clarify it wasn't a typo, but no, that's the plan, apparently."

With all the questions rolling around in my brain, I decide to go for the logistical one. "Where are they going to find a seal in New York?"

"At the new aquarium, apparently. That's where they want you to do the shoot."

"Aren't those things vicious?"

"I'm assuming they're going to pair you with a friendly one."

I raise my eyebrows. "You're assuming?"

"Pretty sure the brand doesn't want the publicity of you being attacked by a sea creature."

"How has a seal got anything to do with high-end clothing?" I'm no expert in branding, but I can't see any obvious link.

"No idea. Those ad executives must be smoking a whole lot of weird shit." Frank stares at me. "You okay with it? Because I can argue it if you want."

I shrug. "Yeah, it'll be fine. I've done crazier stuff."

"I don't want to know about it. As long as it doesn't make the tabloids."

I roll my eyes. "I mean I've done crazier things for advertising. Remember the time I had to roll around in the hay for that Addison shoes ad?"

"Oh, that's right."

Frank and I hash out some other endorsement deals and promotional stuff. Football is a weird career, in that people mistakenly think you work less than six months of the year. The off season is definitely less intense, but there's still work to be done.

I do a good two-hour session in the gym every morning and evening, because I take keeping my body in condition very seriously. It's always tempting to slack off for a few weeks after the season's over, but I know from experience it'll make climbing the hill back to full fitness a whole lot more painful.

As I leave Frank's office my mind drifts back to free agency. Fuck, I just want the whole thing to be over. The endless speculation and uncertainty.

I want to get a good deal from the Goliaths and stay put, with the coaching staff I know and my teammates that I like. But nothing is guaranteed in this business.

To distract myself from thinking about the alternatives, I grab my phone out of my pocket and quickly tap out a message to Josh.

Me: *What are you doing on Saturday?*

Josh: *No plans, why?*

Me: *Want to come watch me film an ad with a seal at the new aquarium?*

Josh: *That sounds like a once-in-a-lifetime opportunity for mockery. I'm definitely there.*

Me: *Awesome.*

Josh: *You coming over tonight?*

Me: *Nah, can't. I've got a charity thing for Active Coaches.*

Josh: *Pity. I think you really want to see what's happened to Ken now.*

Fuck. That's been the theme of the last week—me turning up to Josh's apartment to discover what nasty surprise the Ken doll has had inflicted on him.

Megan, of course, has taken the Barbie and Ken thing to another level. She didn't just buy a football Ken—she continues to find new and innovative ways to torment him. At first it was all about physical torment, like hanging him by his neck from the light fittings. But now she's really going all out.

The other day I arrived in their apartment to find a

whole setup on the counter, with Ken wearing an apron and some kind of black spandex outfit, taking muffins out of an oven in a Barbie kitchen. Even my comment about how Megan was just acting out one of her fantasies couldn't budge the smirk from her face.

When I reach the lobby I realize I'm doing it again. I spend a lot of time scripting conversations in my head with Megan where I manage to one-up her. My success rate in real life isn't as high.

Maybe I need to consult an exorcist who specializes in removing Science Barbies from people's brains.

Saturday finds me dressed to kill in a thousand-dollar charcoal suit with a faint check pattern, a crisp white shirt, and burgundy tie. I'm looking extremely sharp for someone about to get up close and personal with a marine mammal.

I'm trying to tap down my nerves, because sweat and expensive suits don't exactly go together, but my eyes keep darting to the gates of the enclosure, wishing I was on the other side of them. They've set up the photo shoot inside the pool area where the animals usually come to perform, although thankfully the stands are empty of spectators right now. I'm currently trapped between a concrete wall and the pool. My opportunities to run are limited.

"Ollie is a mature male California sea lion. He weighs over 800 pounds," Emily, the sea lion trainer, tells me as I try not to let my anxiety show on my face.

Apparently my costar on the shoot is going to be a sea lion rather than a seal. I'm not sure of the difference but don't know if it's another instance of where I didn't listen well enough in biology, so I don't want to look dumb and ask.

"Sea lions actually do really well in captivity, and they can live up to thirty-five years compared to twenty-five to thirty years for animals in the wild," Emily continues, and I try to focus on her words rather than wondering if sea lions can smell fear.

I don't know what I expected from a sea lion trainer, but probably not a five-foot nothing, barely hundred-pound girl who looks like she's not long out of her teenage years.

"Just think of them like defensive linemen," Emily says. She has these dark eyes that match her dark curls. She's cute, but my priority right now is staying alive rather than hitting on a sea lion trainer. Besides, I already have one science-geek Barbie in my life. I don't think I could handle another.

I seize on something familiar. "You a Goliaths fan?"

"Yeah, I've been known to watch a game now and then," she says with a smile.

Emily and I start to chat about football and I find myself relaxing. She asks me lots of questions about other members of the Goliaths, and randomly her queries keep on circling back to Connor. Sounds like she's a bit of a fan of the big man. I make a mental note to tell him. Maybe he could bring Annaliese for a behind-the-scenes encounter sometime.

Monique, the director of the shoot, is tapping a foot impatiently as she talks to the photographer, Chris. It's ironic, because Chris has dreadlocks and neck tattoos and looks so far from the target consumers for pricy suits. But hey, I'm just hired to stand here and look good, so what do I know?

"Um...Emily, can we get the sea lion out here and start taking some shots?" Monique asks.

"Hang on a sec." Kimberly, the makeup person, runs in to do a swipe of my face with a brush. I try not to sneeze as it tickles my nose.

Emily turns to me, going into business mode. "The most important thing with sea lions is to remember that they're not as friendly as they look. Ollie is well trained, but he's still a wild animal with sharp teeth. So just listen to me and follow my instructions, okay?"

I suck in a sharp breath. "Okay."

While Emily goes to get Ollie, I look up and see Josh has arrived in the enclosure.

He's not alone.

Megan gives me the biggest grin I've ever seen. The Godzilla of grins. One laced with anticipation.

Fuck, Josh brought Megan? The opportunity for ridicule in this situation is immense. It's like I'm handing it to her gift-wrapped in gold on a platinum platter.

I watch Megan as she follows Josh around the edge of the pool to where a cluster of ad executives are watching the proceedings from a safe distance. She's got her hair tied back in a ponytail, but a few strands have escaped. Dressed in an oversized red sweater, she looks cute and cuddly as she settles into a green plastic chair. It's like with sea lions—appearances can be deceiving.

At least Megan's arrival has distracted me from the impending arrival of my costar.

That all changes when Emily walks into the pool area, followed by the sea lion. He comes up to about her waist and lumbers after her, staring at her with the same devotedness you'd expect from a dog. It might be because Emily has a plastic container strapped to her waist that's full of fish.

I wrinkle my nose as they approach. There's a faint aroma around Ollie that reminds me of old fish combined with the uncleaned bathrooms of a seedy nightclub.

"Okay." Emily gives Ollie a signal, and he jumps up so his hind flippers are resting on the ground but his front legs are on this platform set up three feet away from me.

On the platform, Ollie is nearly the same height as me. I give him a closed lip smile. I have no idea if sea lions are actually like dogs, but I don't want to bare my teeth in case it's interpreted as a challenge.

Chris is clicking away madly while I try to maintain the usual expression I use for modelling. Josh calls it my manly pout. Apparently, it involves looking slightly bored but with a flicker of secret amusement. When I did my first photo shoot, I practiced it in front of the mirror for days. Now it comes as naturally to me as lifting my leg before the snap.

Finally, Chris drops his camera on his chest. "Can you interact with it more, Brandon?"

"His name is Ollie," Emily says with a glare at Chris.

I'm pretty sure that's an important life rule—don't piss off the person who's controlling the sea lion.

"Place your hand on its shoulder," Chris suggests, raising his camera again to get ready to take the photo.

I throw a nervous glance at Emily. Yeah, like I'm doing anything to the sea lion without her permission. I don't have a death wish.

"What's going on?" Monique, the director, trots over toward us.

"I want to try for something more edgy," he says.

Monique purses her lips. "Why don't you just stick to the brief?"

"It's a crappy brief." Chris tosses a stray dreadlock over his shoulders. "We could get something really special here."

Monique and Chris start to argue in low tones while I sneak a peek at Ollie. He looks as skeptical as I do about the whole proceedings.

Kimberly comes to take the shine off my forehead. Apparently being in close proximity to Ollie is giving my sweat glands a serious workout.

"Is that your brother over there? He looks like you," she says redundantly.

"Yeah, that's him."

"He and his girlfriend are so cute."

I whip my head around to stare at Josh and Megan. They've shifted their chairs closer together. Megan leans across and whispers something in his ear, and he turns to give her a wide smile.

A shard of something hard splinters through my stomach. What kind of game does Josh think he's playing? A stabbing pain in my jaw alerts me to the fact I'm clenching my teeth so hard it's like I'm trying to crush rocks with my molars.

When I glance at Kimberly one side of her mouth quirks in a knowing smile.

"Brandon." Monique comes over to me, and I'm glad to shift my attention to her. "Are you comfortable interacting more with the sea lion?"

I turn to Emily. "Um...yeah. As long as Ollie is comfortable interacting more with me."

"He should be fine. He'll follow my instructions, and he's used to being with people. Just don't make any sudden moves," she says.

No sudden moves. Okay. I can do that.

"Let's see what you can do," Chris says.

I shuffle reluctantly closer to Ollie, and Emily gives Ollie a signal. He lifts a flipper and puts it on my shoulder. I keep as still as I can, like I'm a kid playing freeze tag, while Chris starts snapping away happily.

"That's great," he says. "Angle your shoulder in, Brandon, more toward the front. That's it. And look at seal."

"Sea lion," Emily and I both correct at the same time.

I follow his instructions, and Ollie and I are now gazing meaningfully into each other's eyes. His are pools of liquid brown. He also has long whiskers that look sharp enough to poke my eye out.

"What else can he do?" Chris asks.

"I can get him clapping for you," Emily offers.

"That would be fabulous."

It happens in an instant. One moment Ollie is next to me clapping his fins together, the next moment his breath is in my face and I have the mouth of a sea lion pressed against my lips. I stagger back, wondering that the hell just happened.

Only the laughter rollicking around the set lets me know that I didn't just imagine making out with a sea lion.

"Oh, I'm so sorry," Emily exclaims. "It's just that in his routine, normally after he claps his flippers he kisses the trainer. The crowd loves it."

"Did you get a picture of that?" I ask Chris.

"Sure did."

I flick a glance to where Josh and Megan are sitting. Maybe there's a chance they were both taking an extra-long blink and missed the whole thing?

Megan's pursed her lips and is trying to conceal her amusement, but she can't hide how hard her eyes laugh at me. Josh isn't so restrained. He's laughing out loud. Seeing their mutual amusement doesn't improve my feelings about the whole situation.

"Don't worry. I'm pretty sure cross-species love isn't

quite the angle the brand wants to take. It won't make it off the editing floor," Chris says.

"Good to know," I mutter.

Kimberly dashes forward to fix my makeup again. I'm not sure she can do anything to tame my red cheeks though.

After a few more shots Chris declares he's finished. Nearly everyone on set is still smirking to themselves as Ollie faithfully follows Emily away.

I will have to check with Frank how much they're paying me for this ad campaign, but I'm pretty sure I just earned every cent.

I wash all the makeup off my face (taking extra time to scrub my lips) and change back into my jeans and shirt, jamming a baseball cap on my head. It's in the mid-fifties today, which makes it a balmy day for New York in February, and the sunshine means wearing a hat and sunglasses won't look weird for once.

I emerge to find Josh by himself. He cracks up laughing the moment he sees me.

"Do you mind?" I ask.

"Dude, you just made out with a seal."

"It's not a seal. It's a sea lion."

"Sorry. I probably should learn the name of my brother's intimate partners. Or at least the correct species classification."

"Where's Megan?" I have a twinge of hope that she's been called away to some scientific journalism emergency. I know I'm just delaying the inevitable, but I'll take it at the moment.

Josh indicates his head. "Talking to the trainer."

I look over and, sure enough, Megan is deep in conversation with Emily. They're laughing, and because there's also nothing delicate about Megan's laugh, I can hear it from here.

There's something about Megan when she's laughing. Maybe it's because her whole body commits to it. I swear even her little toes must shake.

It amuses me to watch her laughing, even though there's a high chance they're laughing at me.

I guess the whole thing would be funny—if it had happened to someone else.

Megan comes back over to us, traces of a grin still evident on her face.

"Go on. Hit me with it," I say.

"What?" She widens her eyes innocently. "All I was going to say is, it turns out even a sea lion can't resist the charms of Brandon Seaton."

"I'll give you five thousand dollars if you never mention this again," I offer.

Megan screws up her nose as she pretends to think. "Nah, not worth it."

"What were you talking to Emily about?" I ask in an attempt to swerve the subject in another direction.

"I had an idea for an article for *The Science Journal*. I thought it would be interesting to talk to animal trainers about how behavioral studies influence their work."

"That's a great idea," Josh says.

"You think?" Megan smiles shyly at him. "It's a bit different to what we normally do. I'm not sure whether my editor will go for it."

"You could bring in all the neuroscience of behavioral training, the history of all that Pavlovian stuff," Josh says.

Megan's eyes brighten. "Yeah, that could work really well."

"You guys want to go see some sharks?" I interrupt.

"Sure."

Megan and Josh continue to discuss her work as we amble toward the shark exhibit.

"I'm trying at the moment to line up an interview with Dianne Marshall," Megan tells Josh. "You know, the researcher from Princeton who's doing all that work on the structure of neurons."

"Oh, wow, that's amazing," Josh says. "So much of our understanding of neural networks is underpinned by brain science."

It's like they're talking some cryptic language I don't understand.

Stepping inside the shark exhibit is like stepping into another world. The light is different in here, with a blueish tinge over everything.

Sharks loom over the top of us, emerging from the dim and then disappearing as quickly as they came.

Megan stops to read one of the signs of the exhibit. She turns to me with mischief in her eyes. "Killing machine, primitive brain, follows it's primal urges. I could really just be reading your Tinder profile, Brandon."

"I don't have a Tinder profile. I don't need one. I have fifty girls a day telling me on Twitter they want to have my babies." I throw her a wink.

She rolls her eyes. But quickly she resumes her conversation with Josh.

I stare overhead at the sharks. For some reason the feeling sweeping over me makes me think of a kid who is the last one picked for a team. Which is stupid, because I was always a good athlete. I was one of the first ones picked for every team.

I turn my attention to reading the exhibits. Who knew there were so many different types of sharks?

"Hey, did you know that shark embryos attack each other?" I say.

I've got Megan's attention now. "Really?"

I point out the information on the display.

"That puts a new spin on sibling rivalry," she says after she reads it.

Sibling rivalry. The words spin in my head as I watch Megan and Josh resume their conversation.

Josh and I have always had a pretty peaceful brotherly relationship. He was the weedy kid with the glasses who wanted to rescue ants rather than fry them with his magnifying glass. Being the big brother, I've always looked out for him. But right now I have an irrational urge to give him a wedgy or something.

After we finish looking at the sharks we head to the cafeteria.

"I can't believe they have fish on the menu here," I say as we sit down. "It just seems a bit weird. Like having Hannibal-Lector-themed restaurants or something."

Megan tips back her head and laughs her full-body laugh. I find myself grinning at her, and for a second a light feeling inflates my chest.

But then she turns back to Josh.

Again.

I eat my fish and chips slowly and observe the spectacle unfolding in front of me. Because the flirtation has really stepped up another notch. Megan's eyes sparkle as she toys with her salad, and she has this smile dancing across her face.

I was the first person Josh ever came out to. I still remember him turning up in my room one night. He'd hovered in the doorway, looking like he was about to bolt.

"Can I ask you something?" Josh was fourteen at the

time. His voice had broken, but it had an unfortunate habit of going higher when he was nervous. It went through about three octave changes in the space of that sentence.

"Sure, what's up?" I'd been sitting at my desk, pretending to do homework in case parental units stuck their heads in, but really I was just surfing the net.

"Do you...like...ever think about other guys...like, in that way?" Josh had directed most of his question to the carpet but snapped his eyes up to me at the end.

Even though I was a self-absorbed seventeen-year-old I instantly knew my reaction mattered. That what I said could affect how Josh saw himself for the rest of his life.

"Nah, I don't think about guys like that," I said carefully. "But there's nothing wrong if you do. Just go with whatever feels right for you."

Josh flushed a deep red. "Yeah, okay."

After that it just became one of those accepted things between us.

It's not my place to say anything now. I would never, ever out Josh against his will.

But I'm getting more and more pissed off as I sit there watching Megan direct all her attention toward him.

When she goes to the bathroom I lean toward Josh and drop my voice. "You need to tell Megan you're gay."

Josh looks up from the remains of his tuna melt, startled. "What? Why?"

"She likes you." For some reason, the words hang heavy in the air.

Josh's expression falters. "She doesn't like me like that."

"Trust me, she does. I'm probably a bit more qualified in the area of how to tell if a girl likes a guy—wouldn't you agree?"

"I'd say you're overqualified." Josh gives a quick grin,

but it fades. "Shit, do you really think she's interested in me like that?"

"Yes. That's why you need to mention the fact that another thing you have in common is that you both like dick."

Josh shakes his head. "You're so full of class."

"I try." I fix him with a stare. "Seriously. You need to tell her."

"I can't—" he begins, but our conversation is cut short when Megan reemerges.

I make sure my furrowing eyebrows and glare send him a clear message. *This conversation is not over.*

"Ready to go see the coral reef?" she asks.

"Sure. The symbiotic relationship between the coral and algae is fascinating," Josh says.

Megan gives Josh a glowing smile, and I shoot him a look that he misses because he's smiling back at her.

Nice one, little brother. Because mutual smiling always shuts down attraction.

As I trail after them, a question sneaks into my mind. *Why does it bother me so much?*

I'm being a good guy, looking out for Megan, making sure she doesn't get hurt. That must be why.

CHAPTER 9

MEGAN

I PITCH my idea for an animal behavior article profiling the people who train animals for a living, and my editor loves it. Which is good, because I still haven't got a reply from any of the multiple emails I've sent Dianne Marshall. I'm not sure what else I should do. There's a fine line between being persistent and stalking someone, and I'm concerned I'm flirting with it.

On Thursday night, I'm finishing up editing an article about the ozone layer when Ashley appears at my cubicle.

"Hey, d'you feel like doing something tonight?" she asks.

I can't help my immediate reaction. *But it's a work night.* I decide to ignore it. "Okay. We could go grab a drink somewhere?"

"Actually, I was just thinking that I feel like a girly night in. Maybe watch a movie?"

"Sounds good."

"We'll have to do it at your place though, because my TV isn't working at the moment."

"Sure."

"I'll need to dash home and feed Copernicus first. Meet you there?"

I get home and change into sweatpants. When Ashley arrives she's changed from work clothes too, but she's now dressed in skinny jeans and a tight top, and it appears her hair has been newly blow-dried. Ashley's effortlessly beautiful anyway, so seeing her fully made-up causes a sniffle of suspicion to begin in my mind.

As soon as I let her in she does a quick scan of the living room like she's a metal detector looking for buried treasure.

"He's not here," I say.

"Who's not here?" she asks with wide eyes.

"Josh. Or his brother. They've gone rock climbing."

"Okay." She shrugs like it's no big deal.

I suppress my smile.

We decide to watch *Hidden Figures*—because, you know, you can never get enough of girl power, social justice and NASA.

We're just at the bit where Kevin Costner's character is tearing down the bathroom signs when Josh arrives home. Brandon is with him, of course.

Ashley sits forward, raking through her hair with her fingers and adjusting her top to show off the achievements of the push-up bra inventors.

"Hi, Megan. And who's this?" Brandon asks in a flirtatious tone, giving Ashley the once-over.

"This is Ashley. She works at *The Science Journal* with me," I say reluctantly. "Ashley, this is my roommate Josh and his brother Brandon."

She gives them her bright smile, all white teeth. She'd be a good ad for toothpaste right now.

"Hi," she coos.

My eyebrows shoot up. Seriously, there are some pigeons out there who could come to her for lessons.

"Nice to meet you. Any friend of Megan's is a friend of mine," Brandon says smoothly.

"Any friend of Megan's should show better taste than to be a friend of yours," I mutter.

Brandon clutches at his chest. "Ouch. That wounds."

"Can something actually puncture that ego of yours? I thought it was like Teflon; unbreakable, and nothing actually sticks."

Josh rolls his eyes. "It's nice to meet you, Ashley. Don't bother listening to these two. The Four Horsemen of the Apocalypse could show up and it wouldn't stop them bickering."

"Right," Ashley says slowly.

Josh comes and perches on the side of the couch. "Is this *Hidden Figures*? Great. It's one of my favorite movies."

"Dude, you have to hand back your man card for admitting that," Brandon says.

I cannot leave a comment like that untouched. "Seriously, how much of a walking stereotype are you? Hand back your man card for admitting to liking a movie that includes women and social injustice? What type of movies are acceptable to you, oh staunch one?"

"That's easy—*Diehard*, *The Fast and the Furious*, *Fight Club*," Brandon says, ticking them off on his fingers. "If we're going totally old-school, I'll allow *Braveheart*."

I can see by the way the side of his mouth has tilted that he's deliberately trying to get a rise out of me, but I can't help biting. "None of those movies include women who have anything intelligent to say."

"Some of my favorite movies include women, I'll have you know."

"Like what?"

"Like *Baywatch*." Brandon smirks.

"Oh, very funny. Besides, oh macho one, I'm pretty sure I saw you shed a tear the other day when Jenny died in *Forest Gump*."

"That was totally allergies," he replies.

Ashley's head is moving back and forth between us like an overactive pendulum.

"Do you mind if I watch the movie too?" Josh moves from the side of the couch to his usual armchair. "I love this part."

"No, that's fine," Ashley says.

"I'll grab some snacks." Brandon retreats toward the kitchen.

Ashley presses play, and I settle back down, but I'm finding it hard to stay focused on the movie since I'm watching out of the corner of my eye to see when Brandon notices my next Ken doll piece of brilliance.

He's just grabbed a packet of my favorite caramel popcorn—I've trained him well—when his mouth goes into a firm line. He's trying for annoyance, but the dimple on the left side of his face betrays him.

Ken is poised in his normal position on the counter, only this time he's making out with a sea lion. I hope Brandon appreciates how much effort it took to find a sea lion figurine in the right size to realistically make out with a Ken doll. It involved a lot of googling.

He flicks a glance over at me. I scrunch up my nose into a cutesy smile, which he rewards with an eye roll. I swear, when I first met him Brandon never used to roll his eyes. He's picked up the habit from me.

~

I'm in the lunchroom the next day when Ashley plonks herself next to me.

I used to eat lunch at my desk, but then I read some research on how eating at your desk is so unhygienic it would actually be healthier to eat in a bathroom. So now I religiously make the twenty-foot trek from my desk to the employees' kitchen. The kitchen is kind of gross because no one ever cleans up after themselves properly, so honestly, it would probably be just as hygienic to stay at my desk. However I don't have the stomach to take bacterial swabs to find out. Sometimes ignorance is bliss.

"So, that was fun, hanging out at your place last night," Ashley says as she unwraps her sandwich. "Josh and Brandon are great."

"Yeah, it's a fun place to live."

I watch her closely as she takes a bite of her sandwich, trying to decide how I should broach the subject. I want an impartial observers' opinion about whether Josh might be interested in me, but given how much I've resisted her comments about hooking up with him I'm setting myself up for ridicule if I admit I'm interested.

"So, now that you've met him, do you still think I should hook up with my roommate?" I finally say with a wry eyebrow raise, like I'm point scoring with a rhetorical question rather than fishing for information.

Ashley swallows her mouthful. "Josh is a great guy, but I didn't see any spark between you two."

I try to hide my disappointment. "Oh. Okay."

Ashley levels me with a look. "Don't get me wrong—there were more sparks flying last night than in a welding factory. But not between you and Josh."

My forehead creases like a used tissue. "What sparks are you talking about?"

"Um...between you and Brandon."

"Me and Brandon?" Technically I understand the words coming from Ashley's mouth, but my brain is struggling to grasp the context she's using them in.

"Yes."

"Sparks of hatred aren't really what I'm looking for."

In a singsongy voice she says, "That's not what I saw."

I frown. "What? Brandon and I totally rub each other up the wrong way."

"It looks to me like you'd both like to rub each other the right way."

My mouth drops open. "Seriously? I'm going to need brain bleach to get that image out of my head."

"You want to remove the image of you getting up close and personal with an incredibly gorgeous celebrity football player? Is there something wrong with you?"

"It's not all about looks. Sure, he's nice to look at, but the moment he opens his mouth his attractiveness plummets into a black hole."

"He's funny and charming."

"Maybe to you."

"I think you protest too much," Ashley says.

"Seriously, your theory is wackier than the moon conspiracy theory. It's up there with the flat earth theory and the anti-vaccination brigade. Another off-the-wall theory that is backed by absolutely no evidence except what the person inventing the theory wants to see."

Ashley has a smug smile on her face. "We'll see."

I decide not to bother giving much thought to Ashley's idea. After all, perception in the animal kingdom is actually an incredibly subjective thing. Bees, for instance, can detect ultraviolet light that is invisible to us, so what they see when they look at a flower is completely different than what we see. Dogs can hear sounds we can't hear. And Ashley appears to have developed the ability to see and hear things on the crazy spectrum.

Tonight is one of those rare nights when Brandon isn't at our apartment. It's like a blood moon or an eclipse or some equally unlikely astronomical event. I should be using this as a chance to bond with Josh, to establish some sort of connection that doesn't involve his brother.

Instead: "Where's Brandon?" I ask.

Okay, so maybe not the right way to start. But his absence is such a conspicuous thing. Having a large, obnoxious quarterback on the couch is something I've gotten used to. Like an offensive piece of furniture that your eyes just stop seeing after a while and you only notice when it's gone.

"He's at some black-tie charity event," Josh says.

His hair is rumpled up at the back. Brandon's hair does that too, I've noticed. Just a little tuft that seems immune to hair products. It's weird the quirks genetics throws up.

"Do you want to watch a documentary?" I ask.

"Sure. And we can play one of my favorite games. Stalking Brandon by social media and photo bombing him," Josh says.

Yeah, not quite how I imagined my Brandon-free night going, but I'm intrigued. "What do you mean, photo bombing him?"

"I find all the coverage of Brandon on social media and send him back the images with my own commentary."

"I'm in."

Mutual mocking of his brother counts as bonding, right?

I slide a look at Josh as he thumbs through his phone.

Josh is so cute. And he's nice. We have lots in common. All really good building blocks for a relationship. I'm aware I don't get that giddy rush of desire when I see him, but I don't need the starry-eyed, plot line of a romantic movie. I thought I had something leading toward that once before, and I learned you can't trust that type of emotion.

Josh is single. I'm single. As far as I know he hasn't been out on a date since I came to live here. Is that normal for a twenty-three-year-old guy? I mean, I know he's really focused on doing well in his job and he works incredibly long hours but not even a single date? Though who am I to judge? It's not like I've been dating either. Maybe he's just selective like me. A tiny sliver of hope squirms inside me. Perhaps his lack of a dating life has something to do with the fact he's happy to hang out with me. Should I say or do something to show I'm open to the idea of being more than friends?

But the thought of making a move dries my mouth out as if I'm sucking on desiccant sachets.

"Here, someone's tagged him in their photo on Facebook." Josh flashes his phone at me.

There's a picture of Brandon wearing a tux and holding a glass of champagne, surrounded by a group of elegantly dressed men and women who are all smiling for the camera. He's wearing his fake smile—Brandon's real smile involves a whole lot more eye creasing.

I get a strange feeling in my stomach as I stare at the photo. Intellectually I know that this is a celebrity footballer's stomping ground, being at a flash party surrounded by the rich and famous. It's just that I think of Brandon's natural habitat as the couch in our apartment, lobbing out insults at me.

I realize I've been looking at the photo for too long

when I notice the weird look Josh is giving me. So I hand him back the phone.

Josh does a screen capture of the image then overlays it with the message *Latest News: Brandon Seaton adopted by wealthy patrons.* He gives me a giant grin. "And now we wait for his response."

"Oh, I'm so in on this game." I do a quick Twitter and Instagram search. Photos of Brandon are popping up all over the place. "What's his number?"

I feel a bit weird as Josh gives it to me and I add it to my contacts. I mean, I've known Brandon for a while now, but we've never exchanged messages before.

I screen-capture a picture of Brandon between two girls and flick it back to him with my own caption. *A Brandon sandwich. Who knew meat could be so thick?*

My phone quickly beeps with a reply. *Is this the number of Science Barbie?*

Me: *I plead the fifth.*

There's a brief delay before Brandon's message pings in my phone. *You're in great company. These are your fellow Fifth Amendment devotees.* And he sends me a link to all the famous people who have plead the Fifth Amendment. It's not exactly the best group of people to associate with.

Me: *Thanks. At least it's better than this list.* And I send him the 50 most infamous criminals in sports history.

Brandon: *I'd prefer to be on that list than this one.* And he sends me a list of the top mad scientists from history.

And okay, I have to concede that science definitely allows you a bigger scope to commit atrocities than sport. Nazi scientists versus Mike Tyson is not really a competition.

While I'm trying to think of a good reply, another Instagram alert comes up on my phone. Someone has snapped a photo of Brandon sitting at a corner table, with the caption *OMG Brandon Seaton is here. Go Goliaths forever.* In the photo, Brandon is looking down at his phone, his forehead creased, wearing his half-irritated, half-amused smile. It's his normal smile when he and I are engaging in one of our usual debates.

It's weird to think random people are taking photos of him while he's messaging me.

Josh is on the chair, busy on his phone, and it's chirping away.

"Is that Brandon replying to you?" I ask. If so, I'm incredibly impressed with the speed of his messaging skills. Must be all those reflexes honed from being a professional sportsperson.

"Ah, no. Sorry, I'm just messaging a friend," Josh's face flushes as he drops his phone on the coffee table. "Hey, are you doing anything the weekend after next?" He's trying to keep his voice casual, but I can see his Adam's apple bobbing as he swallows.

My heart starts to beat faster.

"I don't think so." Fingers fumbling, I quickly swipe my online calendar and check the date. "I had planned to maybe see a film festival thing with Ashley, but I can skip it." I raise my eyes to his, trying to disguise my hope.

Josh rubs the back of his neck. "It's just I need a huge favor. I'm going to a wedding of some family friends back home, and I kind of need a plus one. Just as friends, of course. I'll pay for your flight. We can stay with my parents, if that's okay with you." Josh stumbles through the words, averting his gaze.

Oh my God.

I was just thinking only a few minutes ago how great it would be if things progressed further with Josh, and now he's inviting me to a wedding! Thanks, universe. And while we're in granting-Megan-wishes mode, I also wouldn't mind a solution to global warming and a larger focus on scientific education in elementary schools.

What's even better, the wedding is in his hometown. I've never been to Maryland before, so it'll be interesting to see a new place. Plus we'll get to spend the whole weekend together, just the two of us. I mean, he's stressed it is just as a friend, but there must be something behind his nervousness in asking me, right?

A romantic setting away from our apartment might be exactly what we need to take our relationship to the next level.

I manage to plaster a neutral expression on my face. "I'd love to come."

CHAPTER 10

BRANDON

MEGAN'S FOLDING a basket of laundry on the coffee table in the living room when I arrive the next day.

"Do you actually have your own apartment?" she asks me as she folds a pair of sweatpants. "Or do you just sleep in the basement and emerge here during the day?"

"I hang from my feet in the stairwell. It's far more comfortable."

I'm rewarded with eye roll type three. Which I've determined means she considers my comment so lame it's not worth expending any more effort than eye muscles.

"Where's Josh?" I ask. I'd been planning to talk to him about free agency. Not that there's anything to talk about yet, but the constant speculation is starting to grind me down. Josh is always good at helping me keep things in perspective.

"He's playing racquetball with a friend."

"Right."

I grab my phone from my pocket and check Mason Bloomfield's status on social media. Surprise. Surprise. He's just updated his location to Central Park. What a coincidence that Josh is out and Mason happens to be in town. I try to squash my flash of annoyance that Josh is prepared to put up with the scraps of a relationship Mason is prepared to give him. He deserves so much more.

"Do you know when he'll be back?" I ask, stashing my phone away.

"No. He didn't say."

I pick up two socks and start matching them up.

Megan pauses in her folding to stare at me. "What are you doing?"

"I'm helping you fold your laundry."

"Um...thanks?"

"It's no problem. You know what a nice guy I am."

She raises one eyebrow mockingly. "Is this your way of trying to steal women's underwear?"

"You always see the best in me, Megan. Besides, I do have other options to get up close and personal with women's underwear. Although we may have to discuss these." I grab a pair of panties that look like they've come from a nun's drawer. You'd struggle to classify them in the same category of clothing as the lacy G-strings I usually see.

Megan snatches them from me, her cheeks aflame as she stuffs them back in her laundry basket. "Leave my underwear alone, okay? You can fold towels or something."

I obligingly pick up a towel and fold it. Then I pick up one of her T-shirts. The fabric is soft, and it has a picture of a cat with a plus sign near its head, and the caption *Cation* underneath. I don't get it, but I'm guessing it's one of those science in-jokes. I snort as I fold it in half. Her and Josh really do have the science geek thing nailed.

I look up to find Megan watching me with skepticism. "You're folding that in a weird way."

"This is how I always fold T-shirts."

"Well, it's weird."

"You'll have to tell that to my mom. She's the one who taught me to fold them this way."

"I'll tell her that when I meet her next weekend," she says.

I put the T-shirt down and stare at Megan as her words echo in my head. "You're meeting my mom?"

"Yeah. Josh invited me to go to a wedding in your hometown. We're staying with your parents." She's trying to play it cool but I can sense the happiness and triumph in her words.

Meanwhile, I feel like I've just been sacked by a linebacker.

No way.

No fucking way.

My little brother can't have done what I think he's done.

Megan's staring at me with a confused expression. Some of my anger must be playing a game on my face.

I have to take deep breaths through my nose to calm myself, because I haven't felt this angry since the last *Game of Thrones* episode.

"You okay?" Megan asks.

"I'm fine," I manage to grind out through clenched teeth.

After she finishes her laundry and puts it away she heads out to meet her friend Ashley. I stay put in the apartment. Josh doesn't respond to my messages, so I watch hockey on TV while I wait for him. All the smashing of people into boards fits my current mood.

I can't believe Josh is taking Megan to Mason's brother's wedding. Especially since it appears he still hasn't told her the truth. Being an asshole is not Josh's normal mode, so I'm guessing this has Mason's fingerprints all over it.

Finally, I hear the sound of his key in the lock.

He comes in, stopping when he sees me on the couch.

I stand, folding my arms across my chest. "Just the person I wanted to see."

"What's up?" Josh asks. I must be doing a shit job of hiding my mood because his whole body radiates wariness.

"Where were you?" I ask.

"Playing racquetball." He avoids my gaze.

"Is that what you kids are calling it nowadays?" Sarcasm coats my words.

"So funny. Anyway, I don't have time to talk. I'm going out for dinner, and I need to get changed." He walks away down the hallway.

I follow him to his room, looming in his door. "Oh, trust me, you've got time to talk. Because I want you to please tell me you haven't just invited Megan to be your beard at your boyfriend's brother's wedding."

Josh freezes for a moment, then goes to retrieve a shirt from his closet. "Yeah, I needed a plus one for Adam and Cassidy's wedding, so I invited Megan. It's no big deal." He's trying to keep his voice casual as he wrenches off his T-shirt, drops it into his laundry hamper, and then puts on his shirt.

I continue my big-brother stare down. I know Josh well. He breaks easily under a disapproving stare. It's something Mom and Dad used to their advantage throughout our childhood.

Josh's cheeks tinge pink, and he manages to mangle buttoning his shirt. He curses and starts again. I wait, continuing the stare down.

"All right, all right. Mason freaked out about me being at the wedding without a date so I RSVPed with a plus one. And then I kind of forgot about it, so I had to ask someone at the last minute." Josh is talking fast and over-explaining - both things he does when he knows he's been caught doing something he shouldn't have done.

"What? He thinks people will look at you going stag and immediately work out it's because you're having sex with the best man?" I load my sentence with as much derision as possible.

Josh's face gets this pinched look that reminds me of when I used to put him in a headlock when we were kids. "You don't get it."

"No, you're right—I don't."

"You don't get it because society is never going to judge you about your sexual preferences, is it? No one cares what you do in the bedroom." There's a depth of pain in his voice as he leans down to tug off his shoes.

Actually, I'm pretty sure the New York media would love to know the details of what I do in the bedroom, but I don't point that out.

We never talk about what it's like for him being closeted. It's just one of those things. And yeah, I get it. I get it must suck. But that's still no excuse for what he's doing to Megan.

I watch him as he retrieves his dress shoes from the closet and sits down on his bed to lace them up.

"Fine. Take Megan as your date. But you need to give her the heads-up before you go." My tone leaves no room for an argument.

Josh stands up and runs his hands through his hair. "I can't. I promised Mason I wouldn't tell anyone else. He's already freaked out by the number of people who know about us."

I snort. I'm fairly sure I could count the number of

people who know about Josh and Mason's relationship on one hand—me, and some of their friends from college. Josh has never even told our parents about their relationship, which speaks volumes about how infectious Mason's paranoia is and the level of control he's always had over Josh. Our parents do know Josh is gay, and I've seen how Mom is bewildered about why he's so adamant about not being openly out. If only she knew the answer lay over the neighbor's fence.

"You're taking her to the wedding under false pretenses. It's not fair on her."

"I stressed to her we'd just be going as friends."

"That doesn't mean she's not going to hope for more."

But I can see I'm not getting through to Josh. It's like Mason blots out everything else on his brain.

"I promised Mason. I'm not breaking my promise to him." Josh sets his jaw.

Unfortunately I'm all too well acquainted with how stubborn my brother can be when it comes to matters associated with Mason Bloomfield. It's a standoff; neither of us is going to relent. Shit. Josh knows I'll never out him to anyone. But I can't let him do this to Megan.

I grab my phone out of my pocket and scroll through my contacts.

"What are you doing?" Josh sounds slightly panicky.

"If you're doing this, then I'm going to be there." Ignoring his alarmed gaze, I select the right contact and press call.

I'd been invited to the wedding too, although I'd sent a polite refusal, glad I'd had an easy out because it clashed with a sponsor's event. I'm not a big fan of Mason's extremely right-wing family, and watching Mason deny his relationship with my little brother never rates highly in my things-I-enjoy-doing category.

The phone only rings twice, and then Mason's father, Max, is in my ear. His voice is too smooth, like black ice.

"Brandon Seaton, this is a surprise! How's everything going?"

"Hi, Max. Everything is going good. I just have a small favor to ask."

Max chuckles. "Ask away. Anything for you."

I happen to know Max uses me in his stump speeches all the time. Apparently, he talks about his next-door-neighbor's kid who used to practice in the backyard for hours on end kicking a football, how my perseverance and passion paid off and I made it to the NFL.

"I know it's last minute, but I've had a change of plans, and I'd like nothing more than to attend Adam's wedding if there's still room for me."

Max starts to splutter. "That would be great. I'm sure there's still room for you. I'll check with Adam and Cassidy, but I know they've had some last-minute cancellations, and they'd love you to attend."

That's one of the upsides of being a celebrity. Everyone wants to boast that you attended their event.

"Great. I look forward to seeing you then."

"How're those free agency negotiations going?" Max asks, his voice laced with anticipation.

"The official negotiating period hasn't opened yet and I'm not making any decisions until I see what's on the table." I go with my standard line, but it reminds me I've signed on to spend an evening dodging free agency speculation from Max and his cronies. Fun times.

I manage to wind up the conversation. When I lower

my phone Josh is glaring at me. I meet his gaze with a steely one of my own.

At least by being there I'll be in a position to deal with things if it all goes to shit.

CHAPTER 11

MEGAN

MY ENTHUSIASM for going to the wedding dampens slightly when I hear Brandon's coming too. Brandon's always good for amusement, but a background of mocking or arguing doesn't exactly set a romantic mood. And it appears Brandon and I can't be in the same room without the soundtrack of at least one of the two.

"Flying in economy—this must be a novel experience for you," Josh says to Brandon as we board the plane.

"I know. I'm seriously slumming it. I hope you appreciate my sacrifice," Brandon says over his shoulder as he moves down the aisle. Somehow, even in the cramped confines of a plane he still manages to move gracefully.

"Actually, having you taking up more than your fair share of the seat and wrestling with you over the armrest is one flashback to childhood I can do without," Josh comments.

"These seats weren't exactly built with six-foot-three guys in mind. It's not my fault. Megan's the smallest—she can sit in the middle."

"That's so biased against smaller people. I had to do that with my brothers growing up in the car," I grumble.

We reach our seats. Brandon has the window seat on his ticket, but he draws back before sitting down.

"You want to swap seats?" he asks Josh.

"Okay," Josh says, giving him an understanding look as he slides past us.

"I forgot about your fear of heights," I say.

"That's nice. I didn't," Brandon says.

"I thought you were okay with flying though."

"I'm not too bad as long as I'm not looking out the window and reminding myself that we're enclosed in a small metal tube sixteen thousand feet in the air."

Josh takes the window seat and I sit in the middle, with Brandon on the aisle. I'm literally sandwiched between two gorgeous Seaton men. I'm aware many women would probably trade body organs to be in my position.

Josh is hunched over, sending a message to someone on his phone. He does spend a lot of time on that thing and guards it closer than a male crab guards its mate.

After stashing my carry-on under my seat and straightening up, I glance over at Brandon. He's grabbed the emergency instruction card and is studying it like his life depends on it. Which I guess in some ways it does. Yeah, really not the thing to be thinking about just before takeoff. I don't need to add my overactive imagination into the mix.

As the plane screeches down the runway Brandon grips the armrest and does this deep breathing thing I've seen him do when he's trying to calm himself down. He's usually doing it on the back of me making some derogatory comment about football though. It appears he's overstated how fine he is with flying.

As tempting as it is to taunt him, I'm not that mean.

Instead, I put my hand on top of his. It's an instinctive reac-tion to stop someone freaking out. "So, Josh told me you mentor some kids from underprivileged neighborhoods. How did you become involved in that?"

Brandon gives me a look that tells me he knows exactly what I'm doing. But he still answers me. "My teammate Connor got involved with the Active Coaches program a few years ago and he recruited me."

"And how do they select the kids for the program?" The plane has reached its full speed, hurtling down the runway.

"Generally teachers or coaches recommend them. They're normally kids who've got family stuff going on, who need a positive role model in their life."

There's that momentary lurch as the wheels leave the ground.

To distract Brandon from the fact we are climbing rapidly into the air, I continue with my rapid-fire question-ing, asking how many kids he's mentored and what they're like.

Brandon obligingly describes some of them.

As he talks, I tilt my head back on the headrest. He does the same, facing toward me. His dark eyes scan my face, and I feel the soft puff of his breath when he laughs at some-thing I say.

It feels...intimate. Like we've just woken up in bed together.

I blink.

Where the hell did that thought come from?

The seat belt sign switches off with a *bing*. It's only when the flight attendant starts charging through the cabin with the drinks trolley that I realize my hand is still over Brandon's.

Suddenly all my awareness is focused on that one point

where our bodies intersect. The back of his hand is warm against mine, and his skin is softer than I'd expected. I have this weird urge to run my fingertips along his hand. Purely for scientific purposes, of course, to investigate whether his skin is really that soft. Luckily I manage to get hold of myself before I do anything stupid.

Have I gone completely mad? I'm trying to progress things forward with Josh, so holding hands with his brother might not be the best thing. I withdraw my hand slowly, tucking it back on my own lap where it belongs. I don't meet Brandon's gaze.

I glance at Josh, but luckily he's engrossed in the latest issue of *New Scientist*. Which is the competing magazine to mine, but still.

I lean toward him. "Anything interesting in there?"

"Yeah, there's a really interesting article about the migration of the North Pole," he says to me.

This is why Josh is so great. We're interested in the same things. "Oh, cool. What are they saying?"

"It's skittering worse than a centipede on Ritalin."

I shuffle closer to him so I can get a look at the article. Josh angles it toward me.

"Wow, that's really interesting," I say as I have a quick scan.

It's weird. You'd think the magnetic north, also known as the place where all compasses point to, should be in a fixed position, but it's actually not. In 2001 it was west of Ellesmere Island in northern Canada, but since then it has been moving toward Russia at around 35 miles per year. The article was raising an even more intriguing idea that the North and South Pole might reverse, and all compasses will suddenly point at Antarctica rather than the Arctic.

Josh and I spend the rest of the flight chatting about the

concept. I'm aware part of the reason I'm concentrating on this interesting scientific principle is to avoid dwelling on that moment with Brandon earlier. Brandon—whose every movement in his seat next to me seems to register in my consciousness, despite my best efforts.

But the magnetic north stuff is actually fascinating. It's crazy to think that something we take as a given, fundamental fact about the world - that compasses point to the north - could change in an instant.

I've never been in a relationship long enough to do the meet-the-parents thing before. Not that Josh and I are in a relationship, but if things progress in that direction, it matters what his parents think of me. So I'm slightly nervous as we disembark from the plane at the small airport of Salisbury.

I immediately recognize their father waiting at the arrivals gate. Even if there wasn't a photo of him in our living room, I think I would have picked him out as related to Josh and Brandon regardless. They both got their dark eyes from him, although instead of blond, he has brown hair that's shot with gray. He's Josh's height, which means Brandon's got at least two inches on him.

He embraces his sons, grinning the whole time.

"This is my roommate, Megan," Josh says. "Megan, meet our dad, Kevin."

"Megan. So nice to meet you." He envelops me in a bear hug too.

"Thanks for letting me stay with you," I say shyly as I pull back.

"Oh, that's no problem. We've got plenty of room. Well,

we had to put mad Uncle Jack in the backyard, but he says the dog kennel is almost as comfortable as his own bed."

What the hell? His words ricochet around my mind, and I'm not sure how to react until Kevin bellows out a large laugh.

"I'm just kidding round." He gives me a wink.

"Oh," I say.

"We don't really make him sleep in the dog kennel—we let him have the broom closet," Kevin continues and I give a tentative smile.

"Don't mind Dad. He's got an offbeat sense of humor," Josh says as he shuffles his bag onto his other shoulder and starts to head toward the luggage carousel.

"Bizarre is the word you're looking for," Brandon says.

"So there's no Uncle Jack?" I venture.

"No, he's a figment of Dad's imagination." Josh turns to look at his father. "See, this is why we don't bring people home to meet you."

"Well, one of the reasons, anyway," Brandon mutters, sliding a dark look at Josh.

Josh narrows his eyes and shoots Brandon a glare behind his father's back as my forehead creases in confusion.

Kevin continues his banter as we drive to their house in Amberly, a half-hour drive from the airport. Josh and Brandon continue to rib their father, and Kevin reacts with a booming laugh.

Josh has already told me his parents own an engineering company. Judging from the size of the house, it's a very successful business.

Josh bounds up the path ahead of the rest of us and meets his mother with a huge smile and a matching hug. Brandon hangs back, letting them do their thing.

I swallow as she pulls away from her embrace with Josh to glance at me. She's dressed elegantly in a green cashmere sweater and navy pants, her blonde hair cut into a chin-length bob.

Fathers are one thing, but mothers are a whole other proposition. Will Josh's mother look at me and instantly know I have designs on her son? Will she think I'm good enough for him?

A recent article I wrote on the maternal protective instinct in the animal kingdom gallops through my mind as I cautiously climb the steps to the porch.

"Megan, this is my mom, Lauren," Josh says, beaming. "Mom, meet Megan."

Lauren looks me up and down, and the oxygen particles in my lungs freeze. Then she flashes me a smile that's larger than the Grand Canyon and smushes me into a hug. "It's so great to meet you, Megan."

CHAPTER 12

BRANDON

USUALLY WHEN I'M here there's a honeymoon period where I'm happy to be home, before my parents start to piss me off.

Today that honeymoon period lasts about twenty minutes.

Because my mother is fawning all over Megan. There are deer farms with fewer fawns than are currently frolicking in our kitchen.

The kitchen has always been the center of our house. Although my parents have an ornate dining table in the formal dining room plus two living rooms full of comfortable couches, somehow we always seem to end up crowded around the plain wooden table in the kitchen.

After Megan has gotten herself settled into her room, she comes back down to find Mom, Josh, and me in the kitchen. Mom and Josh are sitting across from each other at the table in their normal gossip position while I'm leaning against the counter. I don't know how many times I came home from football practice to discover Mom and Josh hunched over a hot drink, laughing about something. Josh is the definition of a mama's boy. He used to tell our mother everything. I swear she had a better handle on the school gossip than the cheerleaders did. The only interesting tidbit he's ever hidden from her is the fact he's got himself a boyfriend. Which is kind of a major omission.

There's a delicious smell in the air, which I can only hope means Mom has made some of her famous cinnamon rolls.

"Have a seat, Megan." Mom gives her a bright smile.

"I love the color of the walls in here," Megan says, which makes Mom smile wider. She painted the lavender herself.

"Thanks. Lavender is supposed to be relaxing and cheerful. The boys mock me for having a purple kitchen, but I love it."

"I think it's fantastic." Megan sinks into a seat. "There're lots of studies that indicate how color can affect someone's mood."

"Do you want something to drink?" Mom offers. "Coffee, soda, juice?"

"A coffee would be great, thanks."

"I'll make it." Josh stands up. "You want another cup, Mom?"

"No, I'm fine for now. Thanks, hon."

I'm hovering by the counter as Mom starts interrogating Megan about her work. It's obvious Josh has already primed her and I should've known Mom would lap up Megan's job.

Next to me I see Josh pause, his hand hovering over the sugar. He looks like he's about to interrupt the conversation to ask Megan how she takes her coffee. How has he not noticed that she always sneaks half a teaspoon of sugar into her mug?

I nudge him and indicate half a spoon.

He raises his eyebrows but obeys. He holds up the milk, and I nod.

My brother seriously needs to pay more attention to the habits of his roommate.

Josh pours Megan her coffee. He sits back down at the table and slides the mug across to her.

"Thanks." Megan flashes him a huge smile.

"You should tell Mom how you got to interview the head of the Climate Change Commission," Josh says.

"Oh, that was so interesting. It was fascinating to learn all about the models they are basing their predictions on..."

They continue to talk about sciency stuff. Mom watches Megan and Josh interacting with a growing smile on her face. Josh is sitting next to Megan, prompting her to tell Mom things, laughing at her jokes.

They look every inch the perfect, nerdy, high-achieving couple.

I really don't want to examine closely why that bothers me so much. The skin on my hand prickles as I remember Megan's hand on mine on the plane. I know she was just trying to stop me freaking out, but the memory unsettles me.

I see through the window that Dad is mucking around out in the yard, restacking the woodpile. Given it is technically spring next week I don't think organizing the woodpile is a priority, but my father loves to be busy. I guarantee Mom would have made Dad promise not to go to work today, so instead he'll be inventing jobs to do around the house.

I slip out the back door. No one in the kitchen looks up from their conversation.

"Hey, Dad," I say when I reach him.

Dad looks up. "Oh, hey, son."

"Can I help you with that?"

"Sure. That's why I had kids—for the slave labor," he says with a grin.

I grin back and start lifting up pieces of wood and restacking them into a neater pile. I see Dad slide me an appreciative look when I lift three large logs at the same time. He doesn't try to match me though—he's never been one of those guys who tries to keep up with his sons to try to prove he's still got it.

"Does this count toward your off-season training?" Dad asks.

"Something like that," I grunt as I grab two more giant logs and put them down to form the base. We work in silence for a few moments. Soon I'm perspiring under my sweater.

"How's the free agency thing going?" Dad finally asks.

"Okay. Frank doesn't think they'll franchise tag me, but he thinks the Goliaths will make me a decent offer. They don't have much cap space though, so I guess it depends on what other teams are prepared to offer. Not having a decent playoff run might hurt me."

Dad's eyebrows knit together in thought.

Josh is undoubtedly my mother's favorite, so you'd assume I'm close to my father. But I'm pretty sure I've caused him lots of head scratching over the years as he's wondered how he managed to produce a son like me.

My father likes watching football as much as the next guy, don't get me wrong. But I'm sure he never expected to have a son who became a professional player. He's always had a hands-off approach to my football, has always trusted my coaches to guide me in the right direction. The day of the draft he sat next to me at the table, surrounded by other draft prospects and their families and wearing the world's biggest how-the-hell-did-I-end-up-here expression.

But now I suddenly want him to have an opinion. I want him to give me advice on my career, tell me what I should be doing.

"I'm sure you'll work out whatever is best," he says instead.

My shoulders slump as I lift another two giant logs. Yeah, looks like I'm not going to get any help here. I don't know why I even bothered to hope for anything different.

Mom comes out onto the back porch just as we're finishing up.

"I think I'll re-oil the door to the garage. That squeaking's been driving me crazy," Dad says.

Mom stays on the porch, one eyebrow raised skeptically as she takes in the woodpile. "Did that wood actually need to be restacked?"

"Nope."

She huffs out a laugh, and we share a smile.

"Where are Josh and Megan?"

"Josh is showing her some of his old science fair stuff."

I roll my eyes. Of course he is.

Mom's smiling to herself as she puts her arms over the railing of the porch, surveying the backyard. It's not at its best now, just coming out of winter, but come summer it's Mom's pride and joy. My parents spend lots of time out here when the weather's nice.

"So, what do you think of Megan?" I blurt out the words without even realizing what I'm doing.

"Oh, she's wonderful," Mom breathes.

Hmm, 'wonderful' wouldn't be my go-to word for Megan. I try to decide what I'd use instead if someone held a Taser to me and forced me to describe Megan in positive terms. Interesting? Challenging? Perplexing?

"She and Josh make such a lovely couple," Mom continues to gush, and I snap back to attention.

Shit. I've always suspected Mom secretly hopes Josh is actually bisexual rather than gay.

"I think there's one small problem with Megan, which is why I think you should hold off on the *His* and *Her* towels for now."

The lines on Mom's forehead deepen. "What problem is that?"

"The fact that she doesn't have a dick."

Mom purses her lips. "Don't be crude."

I fold my arms across my chest. "Okay, I won't be crude if you stop trying to pretend Josh is something he's not."

"People's sexuality can change, you know. It's very fluid."

My mom is a lovely person. But she also must have ostrich ancestry somewhere in her family tree, because she can stick her head in the sand with the best of them.

To be fair, it's not completely her fault. After all, she's never actually seen Josh with a guy. It's like he jumped out of the closet to surprise them, then jumped straight back in and slammed the door shut.

I get it. I get why Mason can't be openly out when his father has made a career of lecturing people about upholding traditional family values. I get why Mason—who's going to law school at his Dad's alma mater and plans to work as the third generation of his family's law firm—needs to be discreet. And I even kind of get why Mason doesn't want Josh to be openly out, because it might raise questions about the amount of time they spend together.

I just hate seeing the impact Mason's paranoia has on

my brother's life. And I hate the fact that Josh can't even be honest with our parents about who he loves.

Of course, I don't tell Mom any of that now.

"Mom, Josh had a poster with pictures of Adam Lambert on his wall that he kissed every night as a teenager. He's definitely gay."

"Sometimes people fall for the person, not the gender. I was watching a documentary on that just the other day. And Josh hasn't ever had a boyfriend. He might be open to other options. Sex is only one part of a relationship, you know."

Actually, Josh has a very serious boyfriend, and it's your next-door neighbors' son.

I file that in the cabinet of *Things I wish I could say to my parents*. It's quite full.

"And I think the fact that he's chosen to bring Megan home as his date speaks volumes," Mom continues.

"Yes, it speaks volumes about the way society judges people for being gay. Trust me, Mom, Josh is never going to be interested in Megan like that."

Mom gives me her secret smile. It's the one she used to give me when I asked questions about Santa Claus and the Easter Bunny. "Stranger things have happened," is all she says.

I head back inside and wander up to my room. Josh and Megan's laughter echoes from along the hallway.

I kick the door closed. Ouch. That fucking hurt.

This was my room growing up, but Mom is not one of those people who keeps rooms as a shrine to her kids. I think she was pretty happy to get rid of all the teenage boy stuff and smells and turn our rooms into elegantly decorated guest rooms.

But she has held on to some of the trophies and awards

that Josh and I got over the years, and my old room is the place where they are all displayed on shelves. My football and baseball trophies, along with Josh's science fair medals and spelling bee ribbons. If they combined us they really would have the perfect child.

There's a knock on my door.

"Come in."

Josh pokes his head around the door.

Great. Exactly who I want to see.

"Hey, how's it going?" he says, cracking open the door wider.

I don't bother with any preamble. "I told you inviting Megan to the wedding was a bad idea."

"Why?"

"I just had to remind our mother about the definition of gay. She's talking about what a lovely couple you make."

"Oh." Josh's face falls.

"Yes. 'Oh.'"

Josh shuffles from one foot to another, rubbing the back of his neck. "Um...anyway, I was wondering if you could do me a favor..."

"What kind of favor?"

"Show Megan around town this afternoon?"

"Why? What are you going to be doing?"

Josh's face flushes, and he develops an interest in studying my most-improved-player trophy from freshman year.

Irritation floods through me. "Let me guess, you're going to be doing Mason."

"Sshh." Josh's eyes dart to the door, which makes me even angrier that he has to constantly hide stuff in the house he grew up in.

"No way. You're not ditching Megan to go for a secret hook-up with your boyfriend," I say.

"*Please*. It may be my only chance to see him this weekend." Josh gives me his pleading, puppy-dog eyes.

I shake my head. Partially in disbelief at myself that I know I'm going to let him get away with this. "Fine. But you owe me. Big time."

"Hanging out with Megan isn't exactly torture," he says.

"I'm pretty sure it's somewhere on the torture spectrum for me. And you need to spend part of your time with Mason convincing him that you should tell your roommate and your parents about your relationship."

"I'll talk to him about it," Josh promises.

I snort. I don't know why I bothered to waste the words.

It turns out I'm not a natural tour guide. To be fair, I don't have quality stuff to work with—there's not that much to see in Amberly. My hometown is just your typical small Maryland town.

I show Megan the high school, the main street with the few historic buildings, and the weird-shaped igloo house that was built by some hippies back in the seventies.

We end up at McTyler's, which was the popular hangout spot when I was in high school. The shakes flavors haven't changed, and it appears neither have the teenagers.

We watch a group of guys in their varsity letterman jackets mucking around at the jukebox, pushing and shoving each other while keeping an eye on a group of girls at a booth near the entrance.

"I bet you were like that in high school." Megan narrows her eyes over her lime milkshake.

"Like what?"

"Sauntering around as if you owned the place."

I can't lie. High school was a great time. College even more so. Rolling up to classes occasionally, playing lots of ball, girls flocking everywhere I went.

All the perks of my life now, but back then I didn't have the complications of press attention and worries about the future. You think you're bullet proof when you're a teenager. You don't realize that everything has an expiration date.

"I miss high school sometimes," I admit.

"Really? I would have thought that your life now is like high school on steroids."

"Nah, in high school people liked you for you. Now everyone has their own agendas. Like, I never know if people genuinely like me or just want to hang out with a famous football player."

Megan stirs her milkshake. "Who was your girlfriend in high school?" she finally asks.

"Janna Adams."

"Let me guess, head cheerleader?"

"Yeah. How did you know?"

"Do you think Janna would have been interested in you if you'd been president of the chess club?"

Her words sink in.

"Fuck. Thank you for shattering that illusion."

"You're welcome." She grins at me over her milkshake.

I stare back at her. There's something about Megan's smile that always makes me want to lift the corners of my mouth to match it. Even when she's only smiling because she's mocking me. I don't quite get why I endorse something that's at my expense.

"Can we grab a selfie?" It's one of the teenage boys we

were watching earlier, who's been pushed forward while his mates hang back watching us. He swallows, and his Adam's apple bobs.

"Sure."

I put on my best professional smile, and suddenly their cool façade has gone and the boys are just boys. I chat with them, asking them what positions they play on the high school team and whether Coach Lennon is still making them do up-downs.

They in turn ask me questions about where I'm planning to play next season. I stick to the party line I've been trotting out. *I don't know.*

When they leave, Megan's watching me. "How many selfies do you think you've been in?"

I shrug. "Thousands, probably."

"You're really good with the fans, you know. Like it comes across genuine, not at all fake. And that means a lot to people."

All the mocking, self-deprecating things I can say boil up inside me, but die when I meet Megan's gaze. She's staring at me seriously, and I don't want to throw it back in her face. Especially as something warm is spreading through my chest at her praise.

"I just try to treat them how I'd want to be treated," I mutter. "Like, I was once a high school football player who would have been star-struck to meet a professional player."

"You must be getting sick of everyone asking you about free agency," she says.

"Yeah, I guess." I think back to my conversation with my father this afternoon. Funny how everyone is obsessed with my free agency except my own family.

"So what's the big deal about it?"

"It just means I'm not under contract anymore and I can sign with whatever team I want."

"Oh, right. So there's a chance you could be moving?"

"Yeah, but only if the Goliaths don't want me, or another team is prepared to pay a whole lot more than them. The odds are I'll be staying in New York, so don't start thinking you'll get the couch to yourself."

Megan gives a small grin. "I can't imagine ever leaving New York."

"Really?"

She fiddles with the salt and pepper shakers on the table. "Yeah, I knew within a week of moving to New York for college I'd never want to live anywhere else. New York fits me like no other place ever has."

There's something vulnerable in her expression that stirs something inside me. I'm about to ask why she feels that way, but I'm cut off by another round of selfie hunters. This time it's three women in their thirties who smush in extra close to take a group shot.

When they finally finish up and walk away Megan's shaking her head.

"I really don't understand why people get so excited about the fact you can throw a ball a long way," she says.

The sound that leaves me is halfway toward a laugh. "I know you don't."

CHAPTER 13

MEGAN

I ACTUALLY DON'T THINK Josh's parents could be more perfect for me if I'd designed them using a Megan's Incredible In-laws Kit.

The apple that is Josh didn't fall very far from Newton's science tree.

At dinner, the conversation flows as smoothly as the wine and we talk about epigenetics and the complications that arise from DNA testing. Their comments are insightful and interesting, and I relax. I'd say it feels like home, but I could never have this kind of conversation with my own family.

During dessert Lauren starts telling all these childhood stories about Josh trying to invent a new type of rocket fuel and blowing up the kitchen. And the time he decided to take the washing machine apart and put it back together but ended up with three leftover parts that he had no idea what to do with.

The tips of Josh's ears go red, and it's cuter than kittens purring out rainbows. I haven't laughed so much for ages.

My eyes slide to Brandon. His jaw is clenched, and he's

glaring at his pecan pie like its existence personally offends him.

My smile fades. What's up with him?

His dad seems to pick up on Brandon's mood and tries to include him by telling a story of taking the boys to see a baseball game for Brandon's birthday. But even then, most of the story is about Josh and how he started calculating the batting averages of all the players on the fly.

"And then there was the time we left Brandon at a rest stop when he was twelve and didn't realize for two hours that he wasn't in the car."

"Yeah right," I say. I'm finally adjusting to Kevin's sense of humor and give a small snort.

"Actually, that's true," Josh says.

Shit.

"It turns out I'm quite forgettable," Brandon says, his face strangely blank.

"Oh, it's just we were caught up in an epic game of word dominos, and you never liked to play, Brandon," Lauren says. "So we didn't notice the fact you weren't saying anything. It wasn't until we reached the camping ground that we realized you weren't in the car."

"I'd tried to call you from the payphone but you didn't pick up," Brandon says.

"I always keep my phone on silent when we're playing word dominos," Lauren tells me. "I'm quite competitive and take the whole thing a bit seriously."

"A bit seriously? That's like saying Greta Thunberg takes global warming a bit seriously," Josh comments and Lauren laughs.

I imagine twelve-year-old Brandon standing by himself at a rest stop, waiting for his family to remember him. My heart gives a weird twinge.

"Brandon was always a mature kid, even at twelve. I thought he'd be fine. But it was still a long trip back to the rest stop," Lauren says.

Brandon gives a half smile that doesn't reach his eyes. He stands up and starts clearing plates off the table.

I get up to help him.

When I arrive in the kitchen Brandon's standing at the sink, scraping the leftovers into the garbage disposal. His shoulders are hunched up, like he's a puppet and someone has pulled the strings tight.

I bring my stack of plates over and hover next to him. I want to say something that gets rid of the tense look on his face. As much as it always annoys me, I'm itching for him to switch on his smug I'm-Brandon-Seaton-you-can't-help-but-love-me grin that he's trademarked.

"Right." Lauren comes through the door with an armload of dishes. "We were thinking about playing Scrabble tonight. Do you like Scrabble, Megan?"

"I love Scrabble!" I can't hide the delight in my voice.

"Of course you do," Brandon mutters, pushing past me as he goes back out to the dining room.

"Kevin's on washing up, so why don't you come and help us set up, Megan?" Lauren says brightly.

"Okay."

It turns out the Seatons don't just have an ordinary Scrabble set. They have a mahogany one with a raised, gilded grid that holds the tiles in place.

"Wow, now that is what I call a Scrabble board," I say.

"Josh gave it to me last Christmas." Lauren gives a wide smile. "It's my favorite Christmas present ever."

"Even better than the year I made you socket earrings?" Josh's eyes sparkle.

"Oh, that's a hard choice." Lauren pretends to contemplate. "But given my earlobes nearly detached when I tried to wear those, yep, I'm going to say the Scrabble set edges out socket earrings." They share a smile.

It's cute seeing how close Josh is to his mom. I know there's an old saying that if you want to know how decent a guy is you need to check out how they treat their mother. And while I already know Josh is a great guy, it's nice to have it confirmed in the way he interacts with her.

There's a bittersweet taste in my mouth as I watch them though, that I'm pretty sure isn't just the lingering aftertaste of the raspberry sauce from dessert. I don't have anywhere near that level of closeness with anyone in my family. I get on okay with my parents but we don't have much in common, and now that I'm living in New York I can go weeks without talking to them or my brothers. I don't go home much to visit either – it feels like I left my life in Oklahoma far behind when I went to college,

As we choose our tiles I can't help thinking what tonight would be like if we were in my house. The TV would be blaring with some sports match right now, and the only game I could ever entice my family into playing would involve sports trivia.

We start playing. I'm no slug, having had an addiction to the online game in my sophomore year at college, but Josh and Lauren are in another league. They know all those obscure little two letter words like zo (a Himalayan cross between a yak and cow) and aa (a jagged lava found in Hawai'ian volcanoes).

Brandon's forehead gets this little crease as he studies his tiles. He takes ages, but eventually spells out the word house.

Halfway through the game Josh reads out the scores. He's at 240 already, Lauren's not far behind with 215, I'm a respectable 195, and Brandon is languishing on only 100 points.

"I'm just here to make up the numbers," Brandon mumbles.

"You provide the nice scenery," I say.

I'm expecting Brandon to retort with his usual speed, but instead he winces, his face flushing.

Oh, shit.

A black hole opens in my stomach. I don't think anyone else noticed, but I'm pretty sure my comment managed to sneak its way through the large shield of Brandon's ego and penetrate something soft underneath.

I dart little glances in Brandon's direction for the rest of the game, but he keeps his eyes firmly on the board like it contains an explanation for antimatter. The black hole turns into a wormhole. Guilt wriggles inside me.

When the tiles are all used up and Josh is declared the winner by a narrow margin over Lauren, Brandon stands up abruptly.

"Dad can take over for me next round," he says. He strides across the room and exits out the French doors to the yard without a backwards glance.

Kevin emerges from the kitchen. He leans over Lauren's shoulder to examine the board, his lips quirking up. "Who put down jezebel?" he asks.

"That was Josh," Lauren says proudly. "But Megan got exorcize."

I smile automatically, at the same time glancing out the door to where Brandon retreated. My stomach still feels squirmy.

"You up for another game?" Lauren asks me.

"Um, I might take a break. I'm just going to get some fresh air." I glance at Josh to see his reaction, but he's already dismantling the board to set up the next game, his brow furrowed as he focuses on scrambling up the tiles.

"Okay." Lauren grabs a thesaurus from the coffee table and starts to thumb through it.

"You trying to get an edge on me?" Josh jokes.

"Hey, I need all the help I can get," Lauren replies.

Their laughter follows me as I head out the same door that Brandon did.

It's a clear, still night. The Seatons' yard is kind of my dream backyard, with perfectly manicured lawns, and paths that weave between garden beds.

It takes me a few moments to locate Brandon in the dim light. He's sitting in the outdoor patio area, where there's a barbecue, pizza oven and fire pit set up. It must be amazing here in summer.

The cold gnaws at me, and I wrap my arms around myself as I head over to Brandon. My sneakers are silent on the dewy lawn, and it's only as I pad onto the patio stones than Brandon snaps his head around.

"Hi," I say as I lower myself on the couch next to him.

"Hey." Brandon's voice is low.

What should I say to him? I want to apologize, because I get the weird feeling I've hurt his feelings.

It's bizarre. Josh and I have so much in common, and I've always thought that one of the things we share is being overshadowed by older jock brothers.

But now, being here with their family, I realize it's actually Brandon who's on the outside. I mean, his parents are obviously proud of him, but they don't quite understand him. He's the odd one out. It's weirdly similar to how I feel in mine. And I can spot that he's putting on a brave face, as I've done so many times myself.

I decide to go for the straight approach. "Hey, I'm sorry.

I didn't mean that the way it sounded earlier. About you just being the scenery."

He runs his hands through his hair and blows out a breath. "It's okay. I've always sucked at Scrabble. Despite being born into a family addicted to the game."

"It's nice to find your Achilles heel. The one thing you don't do perfectly."

Brandon slides a look at me. "You think I'm perfect?"

"Come on, Brandon, you don't need me to boost your ego. You're a multi-millionaire professional sports star who looks like a freaking model. Granted, your personality could do with some work, but most people seem to overlook that."

"How is it that even when you're trying to give me a compliment you still manage to insult me?" he asks.

"Not sure. It just comes naturally to me. Math, science, and insulting Brandon Seaton."

"What a great trifecta."

"It's the holy trinity of skills," I agree.

He grins at me, and I grin back. Even in this dim light, the way his dimples carve out curves in his cheeks catches my eye. You'd think I would have become inoculated to his looks after all the time I've spent with him, but it appears the vaccine isn't fully effective.

"You should come visit my family sometime," I say. "My father and brothers—all they talk about is sport. You'd fit right in."

He quirks an eyebrow. "You're inviting me home to meet your family?"

"Sure, why not? It'll give them a big thrill to meet Brandon Seaton, Football God." I say the last bit of the sentence with as much sarcasm as possible. "I'll find it nauseating, of course, but I'm used to feeling sick to the stomach when I'm around you so I'll survive."

Brandon shifts so his arm is propped up on the couch, and he turns toward me. "I think there's another compliment lurking around in that, but I'm not sure."

I shrug. "Maybe." I pick at the fabric on the outdoor cushion.

"So, how do you cope with a family that's obsessed with sports?" His dark eyes study me.

I screw up my nose. "Not particularly well. I used to try really hard to fit in, but then it became too much of an effort —you know?

"Yeah, I know." The weariness in his voice tells me he really does understand.

We sit in companionable silence for a few minutes. It's funny how sitting on a couch with Brandon has become my comfort zone. I guess we've spent quite a lot of time over the past month in this position.

"You seem to fit in with my family pretty well anyway," he says finally.

"Your family is great."

"Yeah," Brandon says, but he accompanies his words with a frown, shifting slightly as if he's uncomfortable. He fidgets with the arm of the outdoor couch before raising his gaze to meet mine. "Josh is a good guy." There's something hesitant in his voice.

My muscles lock, and suddenly breathing becomes a challenge. Shit. Has Brandon worked out that I'm interested in Josh? "Um...yeah, he is," I agree, trying to keep my voice nonchalant.

Brandon looks like he's on the verge of saying something else, but I'd prefer to eat my own toenails than talk to Brandon about my crush on Josh. I don't know why. Embarrassment, perhaps? Is he going to warn me I don't have a chance with his brother?

I scramble to my feet. "I'd better get back inside. See who's winning at Scrabble now."

Brandon leans back, and the hesitation on his face clears. "Watch out. When Mom and Josh play against each other it can turn pretty ruthless."

"I'll try to stay out of the blood zone," I promise.

An unsettled feeling filters through me as I walk away from Brandon. I pause at the doorway and tilt my head back to look at the stars. It's overcast tonight, so there are only a few peeking out from behind the clouds. Of course, I know how wrong it is scientifically, since the stars are millions of light years away from the clouds in the Earth's atmosphere. Sometimes our perception is warped.

When I make it back inside Josh glances up and gives me an absentminded smile. The gap between his front teeth is so cute. He's obviously been running his hand through his hair while thinking, because that small tuft of hair is sticking up again. It sends a wave of affection through me. I settle down on a chair and return his smile.

I inspect the Scrabble board and notice he's just spelled out the word diplodocus. Which is my favorite dinosaur of all time.

Josh really is the perfect guy for me.

Even his family is perfect. Well, besides Brandon. Yet though I'd never admit it, Brandon is actually growing on me. The way those giant fungi grow on trees, but still...

CHAPTER 14

BRANDON

THE WEDDING CEREMONY is at two o'clock. Because my mother is an avid subscriber to the theory *better late than never* and also *the party doesn't start without me*, we're running late as usual.

We all squash into one car and Mom drives, which is always an interesting experience. Megan's eyes widen as Mom floors the accelerator and we're all sent flying backwards into our seats. I'm pretty sure my mother's driving technique is a direct result of the fact that she's almost always running late.

Megan's crushed in the middle again between Josh and me. Her thigh is pressed against mine, since personal space isn't really a thing when you have three adults in the back of a Toyota Prius. She's all dressed up in a light blue dress, her hair combed neatly into a bun. I can smell her perfume, which reminds me of my favorite vanilla muffins Mom used to make for my birthday when I was a kid.

I have to swallow when Mom takes a corner too fast and Megan smashes into me.

"Sorry." She pulls back, trying to right herself.

"Don't worry, girls fall into my lap all the time. It's a hazard of being me," I say.

"It's probably the gravity pull of your ego, because it's such a large mass."

"You bet it's a large mass." My voice is thick with innuendo.

"Oh, God. Seriously, Brandon?"

I'm being crass to cover my confusion, since apparently my groin is liking it a little too much, having a woman in such close vicinity. It's suddenly decided to remind me exactly how long it's been since I've allowed anyone to get up close and personal with it.

I don't know when dating lost its appeal to me. But I do know I will never live it down if I sport wood in response to Science Barbie.

I shift uncomfortably, adjust my pants and start thinking about the smell of the Goliaths' locker room after training camp.

We arrive at the church only five minutes before the bride is due. Luckily the parking gods are smiling on us, as we find a spot just around the corner.

"I'm now remembering why I always told Mom my games were half an hour before they actually were," I say as we jog in the direction of the church.

Megan stumbles, and I catch her before she falls. "Careful, you don't want to break an ankle."

"I'd like to see you try to run in these," she grumbles.

When we turn the corner and see the church ahead, with some other guests still mingling outside, we relax our pace down to a stroll.

One of the benefits of being a professional athlete is the recovery time. My breathing is quickly back to the normal spectrum while everyone else in my family sounds like black Labradors on a hot day.

I smooth down my suit as I climb the church steps. Ever the politician, Mason's father is greeting people at the top, acting like it's one of his campaign rallies.

He clasps my hand in a firm handshake as I draw close. "Brandon, so glad you could make it. It's so fantastic to see you again. It's been a long time."

"Yeah, nice to see you too, Max."

"I know it means a lot to Adam and Cassidy that you're here today."

Yeah, sure it does. Adam was two years ahead of me at school, and I don't think my existence would have ever registered if it wasn't for football.

"It's great to be here." If there's one thing being a professional sportsperson in the media spotlight has taught me, it's how to bullshit with the best of them.

Max looks at Megan standing next to me. "And who is this lovely young lady?"

"Uh, this is Josh's date, Megan," I say.

"It's so fantastic to meet you." Max's smile bears more than a passing resemblance to the toothy grins of the sharks in the aquarium.

"Nice to meet you too." Megan sounds a bit dazed, but Max has already moved his attention on.

"Josh!" He gives Josh a hearty slap on the back. "Good to see you again. I know Mason's glad to have a chance to catch up with you this weekend. You boys have always been such good friends."

I manage not to snort. I doubt Max would be quite so enthusiastic if he knew exactly how good a friend Josh was to his son.

"Hi, Mr. Bloomfield," Josh says evenly.

Max turns to greet my parents. "Kevin, Lauren, my dear neighbors. I was just saying to someone the other day, we are so lucky to have neighbors like you. We might not agree on everything, but you are decent, God-fearing people. In Romans 15:2 ESV it says, *Let each of us please his neighbor for his good, to build him up*."

Mom plasters on a smile in response. She likes Max about as much as she likes silverfish.

Dad, of course, has never had an enemy in his life, so he responds to Max's enthusiastic greeting with the only genuine smile in the bunch.

Megan's eyes are wide as we get released from Max's clutches and enter the church. "Who is that guy?" she whispers to Josh.

"The groom's father. He's a state politician," Josh replies.

"Good God." She pulls a face.

"I believe that is a blasphemous thing to say in this house of worship, Megan," I say.

She pulls a worse face as we head down the aisle to find a seat in the pews.

Adam, Mason and another groomsman are standing at the altar, dwarfed by a huge arrangement of lilies. I always thought lilies were funeral flowers, but what do I know?

I know the moment Mason sees Josh, because his shoulders stiffen. The one thing that stops me going completely aggro on Mason's ass for the way he treats Josh sometimes is the soft look he gets in his eyes when he sees my brother.

He and Josh stare at each other, and it's like the soundtrack of *The Notebook* begins. Nice one. Because eye fucking each other is a good way to be discreet.

I scan the church. Mason's mother, Julie, and Mason's sister, Brigid, plus a guy who must be Brigid's latest squeeze.

Brigid's always been the rebellious one of the Bloomfields (aka the only fun one), and I'm pretty sure she's chosen her tattooed, dreadlocked date for the maximum annoyance factor of her parents. The saddest thing is that Max would still probably prefer Brigid's date than if Mason manned up and announced he was dating Josh.

It must be hard on Josh, to be here at this family event with his long-term boyfriend but not be acknowledged. Just be treated as the neighbor's son.

I watch Josh now as he takes a seat. He can't tear his eyes away from Mason.

Megan's adjusting the strap on her dress and doesn't seem to have noticed her date's preoccupation with the best man.

I grind my teeth. I came so close to warning Megan not to get too invested in Josh last night, but I couldn't find the right words to say something without breaking my promise to Josh. And as much as I don't agree with him on this, I could never betray my brother.

Mason is talking to Adam, but he keeps flicking glances at Josh.

There's shuffling and clearing of throats as everyone settles down to wait for the bride.

Luckily Cassidy appears to have the opposite of my mom's philosophy toward time. We wait only a few minutes before the organist starts the first notes of the bridal march.

I don't know Adam that well, and he's always seemed too much like a mini-Max for me to ever want to change that fact. But there's something about his face as he watches his bride move down the aisle toward him—a mixture of pride and excitement—that hits me in the guts.

I've never given much thought to marriage. I've never been in a relationship long enough for it to even become a blip on the horizon. But watching Cassidy reach Adam, seeing the smiles they give each other, I can't help thinking about my conversation with Megan at the diner yesterday— about how hard it is now to find someone who likes me for me, not just my celebrity football status.

Cassidy and Adam end up reciting their own vows, which is a surprise given how traditional the rest of this ceremony is. Adam promises to support her in her dreams of starting her own nutrition company and nailing her favorite karaoke song, while she promises to do what she can to help him cut his golf handicap. It strikes me that this is what a relationship should be all about. Supporting each other. Always having each other's back. Being able to be yourself and in return getting not judgement, only acceptance.

I sneak a look at Josh.

His eyes are glued to Mason, and the longing and adoration on his face is impossible to miss.

I nudge him. He startles, then turns to look at me and I raise a pointed eyebrow. A flush spreads up his cheeks.

Megan glances over at us, her gaze seeming to stick on Josh's blush. She flashes a smile at him, and the affection in her eyes causes my stomach to hollow.

Shit. Megan definitely has feelings for Josh.

Why does that knowledge make me feel like I've been winded in a tackle? Am I just worried about her getting her feelings crushed when she finds out the truth?

I have an awful suspicion there might be another reason.

CHAPTER 15

MEGAN

OKAY, tonight is the night.

The wedding was lovely, a really traditional ceremony with just a few personal twists to make it feel intimate rather than contrived.

I've never been one of those girls who's planned my own wedding day, but if I did I'd want a ceremony with a similar vibe to Cassidy and Adam's. Although I'd go for some quirkier readings, like one on friendship from *Winnie the Pooh* and the one about the roots of the tree growing together from *Captain Corelli's Mandolin*. And I'd probably just have some simple daffodils as my bouquet rather than fancy flower combinations, which means I'd have to get married in springtime...

Okay, so it appears maybe I'm becoming one of those girls who plans their wedding day.

Of course, to get married you need a groom. And generally, unless you're into the whole arranged marriage thing or finding someone desperate for a green card, the first step toward finding a groom is securing a boyfriend.

Which leads me back to Josh. And tonight being the

night where I hope we progress our friendship into something more.

Nerves hum inside me as we arrive at the reception venue. My stomach is obviously a good breeding ground for them as they appear to be growing on an exponential growth curve. Although there is the chance that the weird feeling in my stomach is due to Lauren's driving on the way here.

Adam and Cassidy are holding their reception at a stunning country hotel in the middle of nowhere. Every guest has been given a room to stay in so no one has to worry about driving home afterwards. When we check in, I'm a little disappointed they've allocated me a separate room from Josh. Just my luck that the one time I'd like the hotel staff to have a mix-up they prove to be nothing but efficient.

"See you soon," Josh says as he disappears into the room next door to me.

"See you soon," I echo and unlock my door.

The room is beautiful, full of antique furniture, but I don't have time to admire it. I'm more focused than a microscope on maximum power.

I quickly slip into the dress I borrowed from Ashley and stand in front of the mirror, adjusting the waist. It's a peacock blue, matching my eyes.

Okay. That was the easy part.

Now for the tricky bit.

I'm still on a learner's permit when it comes to makeup, but I concentrate hard on keeping my hand wobble-free as I draw on eyeliner. Then, channeling everything I can remember from kindergarten about coloring within the lines, I attempt some lip-liner and fill in the rest with lipstick.

Standing back and squinting slightly, I evaluate the results.

I look...okay. And since an okay grade is about the pinnacle my appearance ever reaches I'll take it.

Do I look okay enough to make Josh see me in a new light?

That remains to be seen.

Brandon's already in the hallway when I step out of my room. He turns, and I inhale sharply. He's dressed in a sleek suit with a killer slate grey shirt, his dark eyes brooding. No matter what else Brandon Seaton is, I can't deny he's incredibly handsome.

I need to cover up my reaction before his ego expands even more. "Nice to see you in a suit that doesn't have sea lion slobber on it," I comment.

"Yeah, I decided to go for the non-slobber suit today." He glances down at himself then up at me.

He runs his eyes over me, and I can't help seizing up. This is a guy who dates actresses and supermodels, some of the most genetically blessed people on the planet. And although I shouldn't care what he thinks of me, it's not nice to know that I'm severely lacking compared to the women he usually associates with.

But when he lifts his gaze to mine there's heat in his eyes that takes me aback.

"You look...nice," he says.

A beat passes between us when neither of us says anything. We just stare at each other. For some reason my heartbeat decides it's a good time to relocate to my ears, because suddenly all I can hear is thudding.

"Nice?" I screw up my nose and adopt a joking tone. "Really going all out with the compliments there, Brandon."

His mouth quirks in amusement. "Sorry. Is my word choice not up to your standards?"

"No, not really."

He grabs his phone out of his pocket, a lock of blond hair falling into his face as he stares at the screen. "You look stunning. Radiant. Sensational."

I raise an eyebrow.

"Online thesaurus," he explains, and a grin carves up his cheeks.

For a moment my breath leaves me. Because, okay—handsome doesn't actually come close to describing Brandon sometimes. It's like describing the universe as big. Technically correct, but really an understatement that doesn't acknowledge the amazing scope of the phenomenon.

Josh emerges out of his room, fiddling with the cufflinks on his shirt, and I tear my gaze away from Brandon to appreciate Josh. He's good-looking too, but in a softer, more understated way.

Josh smiles at me. "You look lovely."

"Thanks. You don't scrub up half bad yourself," I say softly.

As we walk toward the elevator I notice Brandon's smile has gone, his jaw now clenched. What's up with him?

He pushes ahead of Josh and me to stab at the elevator button. "Let's get this over with."

The grand ballroom of the hotel is filled with tables covered in ivory tablecloths and decorated with flickering candles and vases of white roses. I'm so glad I borrowed Ashley's dress, because nothing I own would have been flashy enough to fit here. I'd have been the Honda of outfits, trying to blend in with Ferraris and Lamborghinis.

"This is incredible," I breathe.

"Do you want to come outside? There's a beautiful garden and a lake," Josh says.

"Have you been here before?" I ask him, surprised. He hadn't mentioned it when we were driving here.

"Um...yeah. Once."

Brandon mutters something about finding the bar and wanders off as Josh and I head outside together.

It's getting dark, and the whole porch and lawn area has been covered with twinkly fairy lights. At the bottom of the lawn there's a tranquil lake glinting in the dying light, with a pier that stretches out into the water.

"I love fairy lights," Josh says, inspecting the string of lights that's wound up the railings of the porch.

"Did you know that Thomas Edison was actually the person who invented fairy lights?" I ask.

"Really?"

"Yeah. They used to have candles in Christmas trees before that."

Josh snickers. "Because fire and dry wood are a match made in safety heaven."

"I know, right?"

Josh goes to say something, but then gets distracted by the laughter coming from a couple standing on the porch just along from us. His shoulders stiffen as they come toward us.

It's the best man. I would happily bet my year's salary that he's the groom's brother, because he has the same dark hair and lanky build. His date is a pretty redhead in a stunning little black dress that makes every other little black dress wilt with shame.

"Oh hey." The guy pulls up short, his eyes darting between Josh and me.

"Hey." Josh's voice is casual, but his smile has a forced element that I'm not used to.

There's a moment of silence as Josh and the best man stare at each other.

The guy quirks an eyebrow. "Are you going to introduce us?"

"Um...sure. Megan, this is Mason. We grew up next to each other. Mason, this is Megan, my roommate." Josh seems to have developed a fascination with adjusting a strand of the fairy lights, avoiding eye contact.

"Nice to meet you," Mason says, shaking my hand. His skin is warm, but he lets go after giving me a perfunctory handshake. "And this is my date, Carly." He pulls the pretty redhead into his side.

Carly gives us a wide smile. "Nice to meet you both."

Despite Carly's friendliness, there's awkwardness in the air. Mason's wearing a smooth smile but there is a weird vibe radiating from Josh that makes me take a closer look at the groom's brother. He's really good-looking in a classic dark-and-handsome way. Maybe I'm projecting, but he strikes me as one of those guys who's charming and friendly up until the point where someone does something to annoy him. I wonder if he picked on Josh when they were growing up?

"I was just going to show Megan the lake," Josh says finally.

"It's nice this time of night," Mason says. "Really peaceful."

His words are benign, but Josh flushes. He raises his gaze to Mason, and the air seems to crackle between them.

"Yeah, it is," Josh says.

"See you around." Mason takes Carly's arm and they stroll past us toward the ballroom.

Josh's mouth is fixed in a firm line as we head across the lawn to the path that leads to the lake.

"Are you okay?" I ask.

"Yeah."

"That guy, was he horrible to you growing up?"

Josh almost trips. "Oh no, we were friends," he says when he's righted himself. "I mean, we're still friends now. We actually hang out together a lot when he comes to New York."

"Oh, okay." His words surprise me. The vibe between him and Mason didn't exactly have *good friends* stamped all over it.

The lake is a deep, inky blue in the early twilight. Three cabanas stand guard over the beginning of the pier. There's a slight breeze whipping off the lake, and I shiver because Ashley's dress definitely wasn't designed to optimize warmth.

Josh is fine in his long-sleeved shirt and suit jacket, of course.

It's one of the less logical traditions in a wedding, the fact women and men's outfits are so different in terms of what temperature they are suitable for. In practical terms, it means one person is always going to swelter or the other is going to freeze. It would be interesting to research how the tradition arose.

Suddenly I realize I'm in a potentially romantic situation, and I'm engaged in anthropological musings about the cultural traditions of weddings. Good one, Megan.

I flick a glance at Josh, but he hasn't noticed my distraction. He's a few feet further along the pier, staring out over the lake.

What can I say? How can I turn this into a romantic moment, have Josh look at me and not see just Megan his roommate, but Megan potential girlfriend? Should I pretend to be really cold, in the hope that he offers me his suit jacket? But the thought of playing the damsel in distress card has my feminist side rebelling.

Should I do something? Say something? Hesitantly, I shuffle closer to him.

I only make it to a foot away when he finally raises his gaze to mine. His dark eyes are almost black in the half-light.

"You want to head back?" he asks.

I swallow my disappointment. "Sure."

By the time we get inside, most people are seated for the meal. Josh and I find our places at a table, our names written in calligraphy in golden ink on crisp ivory cards.

I glance around, spotting Brandon a few tables over. A blonde sitting next to him leans toward him, saying something, and he gives her a cocky smile, looking every inch the celebrity football star. The brunette on the other side deliberately drops her napkin then makes sure she *accidentally* brushes up against him as she picks it up. He swings his attention to her.

My mouth falls open. I can't believe that woman's... what? Confidence? Audacity? And I don't know why something is twisting inside me as I watch her flirt with Brandon.

"Are you going to have the beef, chicken or vegetarian?" Josh indicates the menu.

"Um...." I tear my gaze away from Brandon and do a quick scan of the options. "Maybe the beef."

The food is delicious. Josh and I chat to the couple on one side of us. The woman, Abigail, majored in nutrition at college with Cassidy, so Josh and I have an interesting discussion with her on the evolution of human food preferences.

"How long have you two been together?" Abigail asks at the tail end of our conversation.

I feel my face heat up, but it's nothing on Josh. He's gone redder than Rudolph's nose.

The fact we've been mistaken for a couple is a good thing, right? Although I'm not quite sure what to make of Josh's reaction.

"We're not together. We're just roommates," he says quickly.

"Oh," Abigail says, rocking back.

Luckily any awkwardness is avoided by the MC standing up and announcing it's time for the speeches.

Mason does a perfect best-man speech, with lots of brotherly mockery but real affection too.

Josh twists his napkin as Mason speaks. He smiles at the jokes but doesn't laugh out loud like everyone else. I glance at him. There's something about the way he reacts to Mason that I don't quite get. Despite what he said earlier about the two of them being friends, I can't help wondering if Mason is more of a frenemy—someone who doesn't treat Josh well but whose orbit Josh can't escape.

The father of the groom speaks last. Max is an accomplished speaker, but he likes the sound of his own voice and he talks for far too long. He singles out some guests of prominence, mostly local politicians from the state senate. "And of course we can't forget our dear family friend Brandon Seaton, the New York Goliaths quarterback."

Brandon smiles as applause breaks out and the spotlight turns to him. But it's his fake smile. I can tell from here.

Max thankfully rounds up soon after that, and dessert is served.

I can't help throwing glances at Brandon throughout dessert. The blonde and brunette are practically having a talent pageant as they try to compete for his attention. I'm surprised one of them doesn't climb on the table and start a tap-dancing routine.

"What are you staring at?" Josh asks as a waiter clears our plates. He turns to follow my gaze, raising his eyebrows when he spots Brandon in the cross hairs.

"Oh, you're looking at Brandon." I hear amusement in his tone, but I start to panic.

Okay, so the dynamics in their family are different to what I suspected, but I guarantee Josh has spent his life having girls pay attention to his brother over him. I don't want to be lumped into that category.

"I've just been watching those women compete for his attention," I explain. "It's getting to the point where I think someone should remove the silverware as a precaution. Although my money's on the blonde."

"I guarantee you could wipe the floor of both of them," Josh says.

"What? Oh no, it's not like that." My cheeks flame, while Josh gives me a skeptical look.

Shit. Shit. Shit. I don't want Josh to think I'm like 98% of the girls in the world and interested in Brandon. It's Josh I'm interested in, not Brandon. What can I do to convince him?

Taking a deep breath, I put a hand on his forearm. "I'm really glad you invited me here this weekend."

Josh looks at my hand. His Adam's apple bobs furiously. "I need to go to the bathroom," he says, and bolts from the table.

So it appears my flirting skills need a little work. Because sending a guy running away at the speed of light isn't exactly the desired response.

With Josh gone, I slump forward, eyeballing the candle which is spilling drops of wax down the side.

Josh and I together make sense. We get on well, we're interested in the same things, I fit in so well with his family. What can I do to make him see that too?

I'm aware I'm approaching this thing with Josh in a rational, logical manner, and a little part in the back of my brain whispers that maybe love isn't supposed to be about executing a plan. I squash that thought quickly. Josh and I respect each other and have so much in common. I don't need sparkly butterflies turning my insides into a lepi-dopterist's playground. I want solid and dependable.

"Megan!" Lauren swoops toward the table with a large smile on her face. Kevin and another couple trail behind her.

"These are our friends, Carol and Nigel. This is Josh's date, Megan."

"Nice to meet you," I say.

We stand and chat as people come to move the tables away to clear the floor for dancing.

Josh still hasn't come back from the bathroom.

Brandon arrives at my side. Somehow, he's managed to detach himself from both women, which I have to admire him for. It probably required some special type of sorcery.

"Enjoy your dinner?" I murmur to him.

Brandon gives a mock shiver. "I always thought Adam didn't like me much but placing me between two single women was downright cruel."

"From what I saw, you looked perfectly in your element," I say.

"Yeah, if that element is fire. I was getting scorched."

I can't help but snicker, and Brandon grins at me.

"A science metaphor," I say. "I'm impressed."

"I've obviously been hanging out with you and Josh far too much," he says.

I suddenly realize I haven't actually heard Brandon mention going on a date in all the time I've known him. Why not? Maybe it's due to what he was talking about the other day at the diner—how hard it is to find people who don't just see him as a dating prize, who actually like him for him. I feel a little pang of ...something flutter inside me. Because underneath all those layers of ego, Brandon actually is a decent guy. He deserves to date people who appreciate him for the person he is, not just the fact he plays football well.

Thinking about dates, I really need to track down mine.

"Have you seen Josh?" I ask Brandon.

He shakes his head, folding his arms across his chest.

"I'm going to go look for him." I make my excuses to Josh's parents and their friends, but as I turn to leave I notice Brandon watching me with a tight expression. I shoot him a puzzled look and he glances away, his jaw muscles working. What's his problem? Whatever it is, I don't have time to worry about it now.

Pushing through the crowd, I head outside onto the porch. Maybe Josh went to get some fresh air?

The porch is empty, and I pause next to the railing. It's a beautiful night, and the twinkling fairy lights add to the atmosphere. Although, when I look closer, I see that poor confused moths are fluttering around them. Moths evolved to use the moon to navigate, ensuring they travel in a straight line. But now moths get it wrong, flocking to artificial light instead.

As I'm contemplating moth transverse orientation, a movement catches my eye. There's a figure heading across the bottom of the lawn. It's Josh. I recognize him from the way he moves, although right now there's something almost furtive about his steps. He reaches the first cabana, but instead of walking past he ducks inside.

Unease balloons inside me.

Maybe Josh just wants some peace and quiet away from the noise in the ballroom? But what is he doing in the cabana?

My curiosity gets the better of me. I walk down the steps and gingerly tread onto the lawn, trying not to stumble as my high heels sink into the damp ground.

I reach the cabana door and hesitate. Should I knock? I don't want to scare him. But something stops me. A weird feeling grows in my stomach. One I can't put a name to.

Instead of knocking on the door, I tiptoe over to the small window at the side. There's a blind blocking out the window, but it hasn't been pulled completely. There's a crack of around an inch at the bottom. Feeling more like Harriet the Spy than I ever have in my life, I duck down and peer through the gap.

My eyes take a moment to adjust to the dim light. And then my brain needs a few more moments to adjust to the scene in front of me.

Josh is up against the wall on the other side of the cabana. But he's not alone. He's so entwined with someone else it's not easy to tell where Josh ends and the other person begins. They're kissing, although kissing probably isn't an intense enough word. They are consuming each other's mouths with desperation.

The other person turns his head toward me and I cringe

back, although his eyes are shut as Josh kisses down his neck.

Mason.

Mason, the best man.

The realization hits my stomach first, constricting and twisting it.

I stagger away, hoping Josh and Mason are so intent on each other they won't hear the sound of my footsteps. My high heels combine with my jelly legs to make walking across the lawn my own personal Mount Everest.

There's a strange choking sound, and it takes me a few moments to recognize it's coming from my throat.

I make it to the other side of the lawn before I sink down onto a bench, Ashley's beautiful dress puffing out around me.

The disappointment that stabs at me is swift and sharp. My perfect guy is never going to be interested in me. My cheeks catch fire as I think about how close I came to humiliating myself epically.

But there is another emotion rising up through the cloud of embarrassment and disappointment.

Hurt.

Why didn't he tell me?

I thought we were more than roommates now. I thought we were friends. The fact he's gay, the fact he's obviously in a relationship—they are vital facts to share with someone.

Tears prickle my eyelids. Have I completely misinterpreted our friendship?

"Megan." A deep voice calls my name from the other side of the lawn.

At first I think it's Josh. My active imagination goes into hyperdrive and, incredibly, a stupid flicker of hope blooms in me. Is Josh coming to tell me that what I saw wasn't what it looked like? I try to imagine what kind of explanation would make sense. Mason needed an emergency medical procedure that involved Josh sticking his tongue down his throat? They were just practicing some form of advanced mouth-to-mouth technique?

But when I look up I realize it's not Josh who's come after me at all.

It's Brandon.

CHAPTER 16

BRANDON

FUCK MY LITTLE BROTHER.

I mean, he's a great guy and everything, but his stupid vow of secrecy—his nothing-is-more-important-than-keeping-Mason's-sexuality-hidden stance—has claimed a victim.

I don't know what Megan just saw, but I can take an educated guess. It's like Clue—Josh and Mason in the cabana, although I don't want to think about what kind of weapon analogy works in this situation.

Shit. This whole weekend has been like watching a movie based on an historical event that you know didn't end well, yet you can't help hoping Hollywood decided to change the ending. But in this case there's definitely no ending change from the one I predicted to Josh at the start.

And now I'm dealing with the aftermath.

Please don't let her cry, please don't let her cry, I silently beg. I'm not an asshole, so I don't say it aloud. But Megan must be able to see the fear in my eyes as I stare down at her.

I suck at dealing with female tears at the best of times.

When they're coming from Science Barbie, I don't know how I would cope.

Megan's pale in the dim light and she's blinking rapidly.

I drop down to sit on the bench next to her. "You okay?" My voice comes out rough.

"Yeah. I just came across something...unexpected," she manages to choke out.

I feel absolutely no satisfaction in being right about guessing Megan has feelings for Josh. Feelings I'm assuming have just been shredded by the truth. "Let me guess—the unexpected thing involved my brother and the best man?"

She looks up at me, her eyes wide. "You know?"

"Oh, trust me, I know too much about that particular situation."

"Why didn't he tell me?" There's something plaintive in her voice that digs at my heart.

"It's...complicated. Mason is paranoid about anyone knowing and Josh buys into that paranoia. I don't get it myself."

Silence seeps between us, and I sense the mood hangs in the balance, teetering on the edge of plunging into a depressing abyss.

"I should have guessed. He dresses way too well to be straight." She sniffs.

I breathe out a sigh of relief. This is the Megan I know; this is the Megan I can handle. "Stereotype much?" I say. "Besides, I'm a good dresser and I'm straight. Fashion sense just runs in the family."

"You're not a good dresser," she retorts.

"Um, I don't think you can actually say that to someone who's currently wearing an Armani shirt. I think it's illegal."

"Just because you can go into a department store and

hand over your credit card for an expensive shirt does not make you a good dresser."

I bristle at that, but our conversation has done the desired thing. Her lips have turned in the opposite direction. Insulting me has cheered her up.

I hope Josh appreciates how I've taken one for the team. Well, one for his team anyway. For the record, my shirt totally rocks.

"Come on." I get to my feet and reach down, offering her my hand.

She looks suspiciously at it, like it's a viper about to make a quick dinner of her flesh. "Where do you want to go?" she asks.

"Come dance with me."

"I suck at dancing."

"So what? I'm good enough for both of us."

She rolls her eyes.

I don't think I've ever been so grateful to see an eye roll in my life. "And you don't know anyone here. Who cares if you look stupid?" I continue.

"I kind of care," she says quietly. But she takes my hand, and I pull her to her feet. Her hand is soft in mine. She withdraws it quickly, but obediently follows me across the lawn and up the porch steps.

Inside, I find us an empty space on the edge of the dance floor. The band is playing a pretty decent version of Billy Joel's *Uptown Girl*, so I find my groove pretty quickly.

Megan finds her groove too, but it's not a smoothly worn one—more a rough stutter. She was right. She's a terrible dancer. She shuffles her feet from side to side in what is a spot-on imitation of awkward middle-school boys.

"You need to loosen up," I say.

Megan starts flopping her arms and legs around like they have no bones. "Is this loose enough?"

"Almost."

"I never know what to do with my arms," she confesses as she pulls them rigidly by her side.

"When in doubt, go for a set move."

She eyes me skeptically. "Like what?"

"Like the swimmer." I start doing breaststroke actions.

Megan's face folds into a smile.

Spurred on, I continue, "If you need to vary it up a bit you can always go for the snorkel move."

I put my hand on my nose and shimmy down in a perfect snorkel.

"So that's what I've been doing wrong all these years. I haven't been getting my dance tips from *The Little Mermaid*," she says, straight-faced.

"It's a serious mistake. *The Little Mermaid* musical numbers rock," I deadpan back.

Which leads us to a whole new game of trying to come up with under-the-sea dance moves.

Megan invents the Octopus, which involves wildly flailing limbs. I almost double over, I'm laughing so hard.

I reply with the shark, holding my palms pressed together on top of my head, humming the theme song to *Jaws*. *Dum-dum. Dum-dum.*

Megan shakes her head at me. "How do you still manage to look coordinated when you're doing something so stupid? You just can't do uncoordinated, can you?"

"It's a curse I have to bear," I say.

A slow song comes on. Ed Sheeran's singing about loving someone until they're seventy. Megan stops dancing and looks suspiciously at me.

"Come here." I grab her hand and pull her toward me.

"What's this move called?" She takes a reluctant step, putting one hand tentatively on my shoulder and the other on my waist.

"This is called the limpet," I say as I tug her closer.

I feel her laugh vibrating against my chest.

We shuffle around the dance floor as Ed croons about how people fall in love in mysterious ways. And I discover having Megan's feet so close to mine is actually hazardous.

"Sorry," she mutters when she treads on my toes.

"That's okay, I didn't need that foot. I have a spare one."

She pulls back to look at me, her lips quirking in a smile. "Um, you're a professional athlete. I'm pretty sure you need both your feet."

"Let's not start arguing about the merits of professional sport right now, okay?"

I'm expecting her to argue, but instead she just shrugs. "Okay."

She rests her head back against my chest, and I catch a whiff of her perfume. I'm right, it's vanilla, but there is something else floral in there as well, along with a sharply sweet smell of hairspray. Suddenly I'm concerned about what she's hearing in my chest, because I'm pretty sure my heart is thudding like I've got a killer whale bearing down on me.

Shit. As long as the action doesn't spread to my groin we're all good.

But I'm quickly aware there are no guarantees. Because there's something about holding Megan this close that is stirring stuff throughout my body. My fingers are lightly touching her at the curve of her waist, and I can feel the heat of her skin through her dress.

Having her in my arms like this, something clicks perfectly into place. The closest I've ever felt to this has come on the football field, when I've thrown the perfect pass, the type that cuts through the air like a blade and lands with a satisfying thud in the hands of the receiver.

I look down at her. My gaze snags on the little patch of bare skin behind her ear. I have a sudden urge to press my lips to it.

My breath catches in my throat.

She pulls back and raises her eyes to mine, a half smile on her face. Whatever she sees on my face causes her smile to fade.

She stares at me, her blue eyes impossibly wide, her lips partially open. Her bottom lip is pink and full and inviting.

It would be so easy to lower my mouth to hers, to kiss her.

I take a deep breath. She's vulnerable. She's just had whatever hopes she had about my little brother dashed tonight. I can't kiss her now. It would potentially be taking advantage of her emotional state and I never, ever want to be that guy.

But damn, there's no denying I want to kiss her.

I release her and step back, running my hands through my hair. I immediately feel the absence of her body pressed up against me. It's like stepping from a warm room into a cold freezer.

"Uh, I should call it a night."

Megan stands there blinking like she's woken up from a dream.

"Um...yeah. You do need your beauty sleep," she says finally.

For a moment we stare at each other. Her brow is furrowed, like she's trying to make sense of what just happened.

"Goodnight." I do a pivot my coach would be proud of,

stalking away through the table and chairs. I need to get as far away as possible, so I'm not tempted to go back.

I make it out to the side corridor that leads to the kitchen. Waiters are scurrying back and forth with dirty plates.

There's a small room off the corridor, where all the presents have been set up on display. The door is open, and I slump against the wall across from it, staring unseeing at a floral dinner set.

Fuck. Fuck. I rake my hand over my face, trying to get rid of the images that are flying around my head.

The idea of kissing Megan. The way it made so much sense in the moment.

The way it still makes sense.

Fuck.

A movement catches my eye, and I look up. Josh is coming down the hallway toward me.

Shit. He's pretty much the last person I want to see right now. Unfortunately, the feeling isn't mutual. He spots me and veers toward me.

"Have you seen Megan?" he asks.

Anger flares inside me, igniting swiftly and sharply. I don't think I've ever felt as mad at Josh, not even the time his attempt at a homemade rocket burned down our treehouse.

"Yeah, I have seen Megan, actually," I grind through clenched teeth. "I've just spent the last hour comforting her after she discovered you making out with the best man."

Josh's eyes widen. "Where did she see us?"

"In the cabana."

Josh bites his lip. "Shit."

"You're right. That's a good description of this whole situation."

I go to push past him, but he grabs me by the arm and pulls me into the present room. The door at the other end must lead to the porch, and it's obviously open as the white curtains down there billow like they are doing some ghostly dance.

"Did you ask her not to say anything?" Josh asks in a low voice.

The anger that stabs inside me now is so sharp it's painful. There's a chance I might deck my brother. I shake myself loose from his grip.

"Fuck off, Josh," I growl. "No. Surprisingly, my first priority wasn't protecting the fact that you're Mason's dirty little secret. It was actually comforting the poor girl you lured here under false pretenses."

Josh tips his head to one side. "I never thought I'd see the day when you'd go into battle for Megan."

I cross my arms. "She's a decent person. And decent people are difficult to find, which is why you shouldn't fuck them over."

"I like Megan too. But not as much as I think you like her."

I draw back. "What the hell is that supposed to mean?"

Josh obviously sees something feral in my face, because he backtracks quickly. "Nothing."

"You owe her an apology. Big time," I continue unrelentingly.

"I know. I'll apologize to her. I didn't mean for her to find out like this." Josh reaches down and fiddles with the bottom of his shirt that has come untucked.

"I told you bringing her this weekend was going to be a disaster. You've just got your head so far up your own ass on this that you can only see you and Mason. You don't see how this whole thing impacts on everyone else. Do you think it's fair to Mom and Dad that they have no idea you're in a relationship?"

My voice softens when I see my words are hitting home. "I know you've always said it's worth the sacrifice, but do you actually realize what you're sacrificing? How long are you planning on keeping up this charade?"

"I don't know," he says quietly. He rubs the back of his neck. "It's hard."

"You need to think about what you're doing here Josh. Because you and Mason can't continue this indefinitely."

Josh meets my gaze, and I see pain flickering in his eyes. Which I hate, because ever since I was three and Mom came home from the hospital with him, my instinct has been to protect my little brother.

But I can't protect him from himself.

Something breaks in his face. "I gotta go," he says. He avoids my gaze as he turns and walks away.

I stare after him. Fuck. I don't know if I've made things better or worse.

I'm still trying to regain my composure when a movement by the curtains draws my attention.

The curtains continue to move as though they're buffeted by the wind. But it's not the wind that is causing them to move right now. There's an outline of someone behind them.

My heart pounds. Was someone right there on the porch listening to our conversation? Have I accidentally exposed Josh and Mason's relationship to a random guest? Fuck.

But the person who emerges is not a random guest. It's my mother. Her eyes are wide as she approaches me.

Oh, holy crap, no.

"Josh and Mason?" she croaks.

I rake my hands through my hair and don't reply.

"How long?" she whispers.

I don't want to answer, but she stares me down, determination and pain flickering in her eyes.

"You need to ask Josh," I say finally.

She shakes her head, as if she can physically get the ideas inside to fall into some kind of order and make sense. Her eyes are welling up with tears. Her treasured son has been keeping something so important from her for so long.

"Mom..." I begin. But I really don't know how to finish the sentence.

"You're a good kid, Brandon," she says quietly as she slips past me.

CHAPTER 17

MEGAN

I WAKE up the next morning in a hotel room with sunlight streaming across the bed, a shard of light that pierces straight onto my pillow. It appears in my haste to bury myself in my covers last night, my curtain-pulling skills weren't up to scratch.

I slam my eyes shut, but the light flickers behind my eyelids as flashbacks rampage through my head like stampeding bulls.

Josh and the best man tangled together.

Brandon coming after me and being uncomfortably sweet about everything.

Dancing with Brandon, making up all kinds of stupid moves.

Oh, God. And then there was the moment when I thought Brandon was going to kiss me.

Hurt and humiliation take turns to stab at me.

I stick my head under the pillow and breathe in the feathery goodness for a bit, half hoping I will accidentally smother myself.

I must have been oxygen deprived last night, plunging

into the territory of hallucinations, that the idea that Brandon Seaton might want to kiss me entered my head. Did he realize what went through my mind? Is that why he backed away so abruptly? I had Seaton men fleeing from me on multiple occasions yesterday. Freaking them out might be something I can add to my list of skills on my resume. It appears I'm naturally talented at it.

I didn't hang around at the reception last night after Brandon left;, instead I sent Josh a message that I wasn't feeling well and retreated to my room. I really didn't want to face him last night.

Unfortunately that just means I've delayed the unpleasant task until today.

Eventually, when the protests from my stomach have become too much to ignore, I emerge from my cocoon of covers and seek out some breakfast in the dining room.

I try to let normal noises—the low murmur of voices, the clinking of cutlery and plates— along with the routine of helping myself to the breakfast buffet soothe me into not thinking about last night.

Which is all very good, until Josh finds me at the table in the far corner where I've retreated to. Not for the first time, I find myself regretting that my seventh birthday wish for Harry Potter's invisibility cloak didn't come true.

My hurt flares back into life and my stomach decides to send the pancakes I've just eaten on an amusement park ride.

Josh scans my face, his brown gaze intent. "Can I talk to you for a second?"

"Um...sure."

Josh puts his plate down. He glances around to make sure we're not going to be overheard while I try to decide what natural phenomenon I would like to hit right now to prevent this conversation from taking place.

A tornado? No, not devastating enough.

Maybe an asteroid. One on the scale of the Chicxulub impactor, the asteroid that wiped out the dinosaurs, because then it would wipe out all of humanity, and my discussion about my non-reciprocated crush with my gay roommate would be wiped out by, you know, the end of the world.

Josh shifts like someone left a pinecone on the seat. "Brandon said you...uh...came to the cabana last night," he begins.

"Yes, I did." I tuck a piece of hair behind my ear and force myself to meet his gaze. I shouldn't be ashamed. After all, I didn't do anything wrong.

"I'm sorry if I...didn't make it clear...I was inviting you just as a friend..." Josh scratches the back of his neck.

Despite myself, a blush ignites my cheeks. "Um...yeah, it would have been nice to get a heads-up."

"I'm sorry. I shouldn't have put you in that position." Josh lowers his voice to a whisper, although the nearest people are twenty feet away. "Mason...um...he's my boyfriend, but he's not out, and so I can't be either. I never meant to lead you on."

This has to be the world's most cringe-worthy discussion. My mind skips to what other conversations could potentially be this awkward. The ghosts of Mother Teresa and Hugh Hefner discussing sex education?

I'm tempted to just tell Josh it's fine so we can move quickly past this awkwardness. But I need to be honest. Josh and I are still roommates. I still want him as my friend.

"I guess I'm hurt more than anything," I say finally. "You could have trusted me."

Josh huffs out a breath. "Yeah, I know." He studies his

scrambled eggs and I realize how exhausted he looks. It's like he has charcoal smudged under his eyes and I'm not sure he's bothered to brush his hair this morning because the tuft at the back sticks up even more than usual.

"So, who else knows about the whole situation?"

Josh's eyes dart around, but there's still no one in earshot. "Only Brandon. He's known since the start."

"It must be hard on you, this whole weekend," I say tentatively.

He toys with his fork. "Yeah, it's not the easiest. I've never known anything different, but it does actually suck." He raises his gaze to me. "Brandon told me I should tell you before you came here. He's pretty annoyed with me."

I try to hide my surprise. Brandon's mad at Josh on my behalf? "As much as it kills me to say it, Brandon's right. You should have told me when you invited me here," I say the words gently, but Josh recoils slightly.

"Yeah, I know." The tips of his ears turn pink, but he meets my gaze steadily. "I don't usually get the hard word from Brandon, but he was looking out for you this weekend. He's a good guy."

A week ago I would have disagreed with Josh automatically. But he's right. Brandon really does have some serious nice-guy traits. Which somehow makes the fact I thought about kissing him last night even worse. Brandon was looking out for me this weekend, and I repaid him by having inappropriate thoughts toward him.

Speaking of Brandon, it's like talking about him has summoned him. Suddenly he's in the buffet line, spooning food onto a plate but keeping his eyes zeroed in on our table.

Oh, brilliant. Looks like he's planning to sit with us too.

On the breakfast menu today—eggs with a side of awkwardness.

Brandon carries his plate over, weaving between the tables with his usual coordination. As he moves, I have a sudden flashback to dancing with him last night. The way his arms felt around me. Then the way he pulled away so abruptly.

After the debacle of Josh's last roommate, he's probably worried I'm developing a crush on him.

"Good morning," he says cautiously. He slides a look between us, his brow furrowed.

"Morning," I force brightness into my tone. I'm going to brazen this out. Pretend nothing weird happened.

After all, Brandon doesn't know for sure that I was contemplating kissing him last night. As long as he hasn't developed mind-reading skills we're all good.

Brandon settles himself into a chair, his gaze continuing to flicker between Josh and me.

"Dude, I've already apologized to her. You can stop giving me your Superman glare," Josh says.

"Superman?" I raise an eyebrow. "Brandon? Do you really think that's a fair comparison?"

"Why? What character do you think I should be, Megan?" Brandon sprinkles pepper onto his eggs.

I narrow my eyes in thought. "The Joker."

"The Joker? Is that because I'm so funny?"

"No. because you're freaky looking, just like him."

"You seriously know how to compliment a guy."

"Thanks. It actually requires a lot of effort to find a way to compliment you."

Brandon throws me a grin and something inside me unclenches. We're back to our normal interactions. Great..

Josh and Brandon start debating the best superhero villains while I try not to notice the fact that Brandon obviously hasn't shaved this morning, the stubble on his cheeks giving him a slightly disheveled look, which somehow amplifies his good looks.

But so what if I find the guy physically attractive? Brandon is by anyone's definition objectively gorgeous. All it means is that I have functioning eyesight.

I finish up my breakfast and stand up.

Josh glances up at me. "We probably should aim to leave here by eleven to make our flight."

"I'll be ready," I promise.

Hopefully somewhere on the flight back to New York I can relocate my sanity when it comes to Brandon.

CHAPTER 18

BRANDON

FRIDAY NIGHT, and I'm on a date.

Connor offered to set me up with a friend of his new girlfriend, and I found it difficult to turn him down. Because his girlfriend's friend is Harriet freaking Harrison. ——Yes, that's right, the latest sensation in the modelling world— cover model of the most recent swimsuit edition of *Sports Illustrated*.

You don't say no to a date with Harriet Harrison. At least not if you've got a pulse.

But as I sit across from her at The Oakes, enjoying one of the world's juiciest steaks, I realize I'm just not feeling it.

Don't get me wrong, Harriet seems great. She's absorbed in everything I say. She's paying attention, laughing at all my jokes.

And she's beautiful. I mean, that normally goes hand in hand with being a model, but she is truly stunning, with long white-blonde hair, creamy skin, and these giant bright-green eyes that are so large it's like the world is permanently startling her.

I try to work out why I'm itching for the night to end.

Suddenly, it comes to me in a flash.

I'm bored.

Harriet's agreeing with everything I say. She's making pleasant, polite conversation about pleasant, polite topics, but she's not challenging me. She's not mocking me or insulting me or forcing me to defend my opinion, even when I make a stupid comment about profiteroles.

And it's kind of...boring.

Unfortunately, the rest of the world is not finding our date as boring as I am. Some other restaurant diners must have put photos of us on social media, because we have the delight of a handful of paparazzi deciding that the sidewalk outside the restaurant is a good place to camp out despite the pouring rain.

We finish up the meal and head out into the lobby. Harriet stops in the cloakroom where there is only a coat rack to observe us.

"Well, this was fun." She turns to me, giving me a flirty smile.

"Yes, it was," I reply automatically.

She's waiting with an anticipatory smile that fades when I don't add to my comments. Shit. I don't know how to get myself out of this situation. Normally it would be *hot girl, appears to be interested in me, I'll try my luck asking her if she wants to come home.*

Not tonight.

I stuff my hands into my pockets and give her a wan smile.

"You have my number if you want to do it again some-time." She leans forward and gives me a brief kiss on the cheek.

"Thanks for a great evening." I wait a few minutes after she leaves, ordering a car on my phone.

The paparazzi are waiting to pounce on me as I leave the restaurant, cameras frantically clicking as the rain pounds on my face.

"Brandon, are you and Harriet dating?"

"Brandon, have you decided where you're going in free agency?"

"Do you think the Goliaths are going to franchise-tag you?"

I jump in the car and give the driver my address.

Watching the rainy streets of New York blur past me, I wonder what the hell is wrong with me. That was Harriet frigging Harrison. I need to go home and figure out what's going wrong in my life that I'd turn down a woman like that.

But I don't go home. Instead I find myself redirecting the driver to drop me at Josh's apartment—even though I know Josh is out of town for a conference, so I can't even pretend it's my brother I've come to see.

Luckily Megan doesn't challenge me on why I'm there. She's in her pajamas, not wearing a scrap of makeup—I can see the faint smattering of freckles on her nose. Her hair is tied messily up in one of those knot things. Barely looking up from the TV, she shifts over to make room for me on the couch. The *Del* cushion sits like a chaperone between us.

"You smell weird," is the first thing she says to me when an ad comes on.

"It's called cologne."

"But it's not your usual cologne, is it?"

"No, it's a new one."

"Are you trying harder to disguise the odor of fire and brimstone?" She smirks at me.

"Yeah, I'm trying to lure unsuspecting girls into my devil's lair."

Megan opens her mouth to respond, but the ad is

finished, so she decides to ignore me in favor of returning to her program.

I sit there, watching her watch TV, realizing how screwed up everything is. I was just on a date with a super-model, for fuck's sake. And here I am now, in my brother's apartment, watching crap TV with someone who is definitely not charmed by me.

And the craziest thing is, I'm absolutely certain there's no place I'd rather be.

Megan doesn't treat me like a celebrity. She treats me like a normal, everyday human. She doesn't let me get away with anything. It appears a large perverse part of me actually finds that incredibly hot.

When her program is over she immediately switches to an episode of *Naked and Afraid* without even discussing it with me.

"Ten bucks says she complains about both being hungry and tired," I say.

"Twenty bucks says he cries by the end of the episode."

"You're on."

For once, a male comes through for me. The female contestant is constantly whining, but despite injuring his ankle my man doesn't shed a single tear.

"Pay up," I say as the credits start to roll.

Megan leans back on the couch and looks at me. "You're a multimillionaire football player. Surely you don't need my hard-earned cash?"

"Don't tell me you make bets you can't deliver on."

"Fine." She stomps over to where her purse is lying on the counter then stamps her way back to me, twenty dollars in her hand.

"Thanks." I give her my best grin as I tuck the money in my pocket.

"That's my taxi money, you know. If it's still raining like this tomorrow, I hope you'll think of me trudging through the downpour to the subway because I don't have enough money for a taxi."

"Are you using emotional bribery to try and get out of paying your debt?" I waggle an eyebrow at her.

"No, I'm trying to appeal to your heart. I don't know why I bothered."

"Me either. I don't have a heart. Instead I just have a canister where I stuff all my money."

She snorts in a kind of half-laugh and reaches for the remote.

My gaze flickers to her mouth. I still want to kiss her. That insanity from the wedding hasn't passed.

I've never held back from going after a woman before. Normally if I'm interested I charge right in and let them know.

With Megan, it's different. Not just because there's a good chance she'll laugh in my face if I made a move. But also, I really don't want to wreck this thing between us, the strange type of friendship we have. I don't have anyone else like her in my life. Someone who calls me on all my shit. I mean, Josh tries sometimes, but he's too nice. Megan is nice too, but with sharp edges.

Plus, she's Josh's roommate. Which makes it a bad idea for so many reasons. I'm already the reason things went to shit with Josh's last roommate. I don't want it to become a trend.

My phone, which is lying on the coffee table, beeps with a notification. I open it up and discover the message is from this new app I downloaded yesterday. Unfortunately, there's a sound element to the app I didn't realize until my phone starts to speak in a robotic voice.

Crepuscular, relating to twilight. For example, an animal that is primarily active during dawn and dusk is considered crepuscular.

Megan pricks her ears and turns to stare at my phone. "What's that?"

I try to stop the heat flooding my cheeks. "Oh, it's just a vocab app thing. It sends you a new word a day."

I'm bracing myself for an abrasive joke, but Megan just nods. "Cool."

"That's it? Cool?"

"What do you want me to say?"

"I was kind of expecting to get a whole lot of mocking."

"I'm never going to mock someone for wanting to expand their knowledge," she says. "It goes against everything I believe in. Although not mocking you also goes against everything I believe in, so I hope you appreciate my moral dilemma."

I can't help the grin that edges up my face. "I'm sorry I've made you struggle."

CHAPTER 19

MEGAN

I'M IN THE STAFFROOM, unwrapping my sandwich, when I feel the disturbance in the force.

Damn it.

Ashley has been home sick for the last few days, which has made evading her interrogation easier. This morning she was hovering around my desk first thing, but I dashed to the bathroom to avoid her.

I thought she was out on an interview now, so it was safe to sit in the staffroom and eat my lunch.

But apparently not. She's sitting down across from me and leaning forward, anticipation gleaming in her eye. "So...?"

"So what?"

"So you need to tell me all the gossip about your weekend. Rather than just that noncommittal *It was good* message you sent me."

"It was good. Josh's parents are great. The wedding was beautiful."

"And...?" Ashley is the queen of leaving a word hanging and waiting for me to fill in the gaps.

I refuse to fall for her masterly tricks though. "And...what?"

"Well, did your roommate suddenly see you interacting with his parents and realize you are the piece that's been missing from his life?"

Oh, God, Ashley has really missed her calling in life. She should be writing soap opera plots. Or Ed Sheeran songs.

"Surprisingly, that didn't occur. It was a nice weekend," I say evasively.

Actually, Ashley, I discovered my roommate is in a long-term committed relationship with the groom's brother.

Of course I'm not going to say that. I've joined the circle of trust people who are never going to out Josh.

It's surprising how things haven't been awkward with Josh so far. Once I'd gotten over my shock I realized I wasn't actually that upset about things not progressing between us. I think I liked the idea of Josh and me together more than I liked Josh himself in that way.

And I can't help feeling bad for him. It became apparent before we left the next morning that his mom had somehow found out about him and Mason, and she was upset he'd never told her, so things were kind of tense. I've never imagined what it must be like to know that people in the world are going to judge you for who you love, so you've got to keep those parts hidden. It must suck.

"Or perhaps you met your roommate's brother's gaze across the crowded church as the vows were being spoken and realized the unspoken feelings between you." Ashley's voice breaks through my reflection, and I almost choke on my sandwich.

Actually, it was on the dance floor where I met Brandon's gaze, not in the church.

I force my mind to fly past the almost-kiss or, as it has become known in my head—*the moment we shall never speak of or think about again.* The Voldemort of kisses.

It's so embarrassing that I even entertained the thought that Brandon Seaton might want to kiss me. Like, if I ever revealed to anyone that the thought had flitted across my mind I'd be the laughingstock of comedians everywhere. Or else I'd feature at a psychology conference talking about delusions. I can imagine it now—they'd just put up a photo of me next to a photo of him, and the audience would have a massive laugh at how far someone's mind could leap from reality.

The crazy thing is, I don't even want Brandon. Sure, my attitude toward him has definitely changed over the weekend. I got a glimpse of another side of Brandon; a more vulnerable side, where he's not this celebrity football player who acts like he owns the world, just a guy who's afraid of heights and sometimes struggles to fit in with his family.

And I can't forget how nice he was to me after I discovered Josh and Mason together.

But although I might have re-evaluated Brandon on some levels, it's not like he's someone I could ever see myself in a relationship with.

I've got to ask myself what's wrong with me—the fact that I went from wanting a relationship with my roommate to thinking about kissing his brother within the space of an evening. There must be something in the Maryland air that sent me into some kind of momentary crazy land.

Luckily Ashley doesn't push me for more details. She just gives me a knowing smirk. Which I manage to ignore, although it's about the size of the hole in the ozone layer.

When I get back to my desk I can't shake the unease that our conversation has unearthed. I'm googling *regional temporary insanity* just to see if it's a thing when my email chimes. I glance at it almost absentmindedly.

My breath almost stops when I see who it's from.

It's Dianne Marshall's PA.

With trembling a hand I open the email.

It's a brief, matter-of-fact email confirming that Dianne Marshall would be interested in an interview with *The Science Journal* and listing some suggested times when she would be available. The dates are over a month away, but still!

I stand and do some kind of weird waggle thing that is my version of a happy dance. If I was going to categorize it according to Brandon's and my sea creature dance moves, I would be some kind of undulating eel.

I'm aware my colleagues around me are giving me looks you normally reserve for people wearing aluminum foil hats, but I don't care.

I get to interview my heroine! One of the most amazing people on the planet. And for an hour or so her brilliant mind will be focused totally on me.

That night I'm rewarding myself for landing the Dianne Marshall interview with some Ben and Jerry's Cookies and Cream ice cream when Brandon comes into the apartment. Josh is still at work, so I'm a bit embarrassed to be caught standing at the counter spooning ice cream straight into my mouth from the carton. At least it's only Brandon.

He stops still, his brows knotting together. "That's your celebratory ice cream," he says. "What's the occasion?"

"I just lined up an incredible interview. With Dianne Marshall." I spoon another mouthful into my mouth.

Whoever decided to put cookie dough into ice cream deserves a Nobel Prize. The metal of the spoon is cold on my tongue as I lick away the deliciousness.

"That's the scientist who does the work on the brain, right?" Brandon asks as he comes into the kitchen.

My mouth gapes open, and I have to grab at the spoon as it starts to fall out.

"I do listen, you know," Brandon says, leaning up against the counter with a smirk.

"You mean you eavesdrop."

"Maybe I just hang around with you and Josh so much I pick up stuff by osmosis."

My jaw muscles still haven't recovered from Brandon knowing who Dianne Marshall is, and they go slack again when he uses the word osmosis *in the correct context*.

Brandon watches my reaction with an amused grin. He leans forward and whispers in my ear. "Does me using sciency terms do it for you?"

His voice is husky, and his breath tickles my earlobe.

"And you just ruined it," I say. My heart rate speeds up in response to Brandon's proximity, causing me to step back to put some distance between us. "All those cool points you amassed just vanished in an instant."

"I'll have to work hard to get some more cool points then." The dimple in his cheek has a wicked tilt to it.

Stupid heart. It's obviously superficially affected by a cute guy, just like the rest of my body. Luckily my mind is a stronghold in this particular battle.

I roll my eyes because eye rolling and Brandon go hand in hand in the same way thunder and lightning are a thing. Plus it puts me back on familiar ground.

Brandon's now looking speculatively at my small

container of Ben and Jerry's. "Come on, if we're going to celebrate we can do better than ice cream," he says.

I swallow my mouthful. "What are you thinking?"

"I've been craving some of Little Mama's cheesecake all week. This seems like a good excuse."

I rinse my spoon under the tap. "I'm glad one of the highlights of my career serves to provide you with an excuse to eat cheesecake."

"I'll even pay for it," he offers.

"Okay." If I have a personal philosophy in life, I'm pretty sure never turning down free cheesecake is part of it.

We walk the few blocks to Little Mama's and find a booth near the back. The restaurant's interior is dated, with wooden-backed booths and cracked brown-vinyl tables, but I know from experience their cheesecakes are an orgasmic experience. I order the chocolate cheesecake while Brandon goes for the blueberry one. We then proceed to have an argument about who made the better choice, which involves an intense debate about whether color should be a factor in rating cheesecakes and extensive sampling of each other's.

After we declare a draw, Brandon starts describing some of the crazy themed restaurants he's been to in different cities around the country. He tells me about the Heart Attack Grill in Las Vegas that is hospital themed, where servers are dressed as nurses and patrons wear hospital gowns. As he talks I notice he has a bit of cream on his lip, and without thinking I lean forward to wipe it away, my fingers brushing over the side of his top lip.

Brandon freezes, stopping in the middle of his sentence. His dark gaze captures mine.

"Sorry, you just had...uh...cream on your lip." I withdraw my hand like I've been scalded and wipe it on my napkin, trying to stop the blush I know is fighting for control of my cheeks.

Oh, my God. I can't believe I just did that.

Brandon's still staring at me. I meet his gaze, my chest rising and falling as I try to get my lungs to do their job despite the tightness that seems to be clenching them up in a hug at the moment.

And just like that, I have a flashback to the wedding. Back to that moment when we danced together, back to that insane moment when I thought about kissing him.

"It's lucky I've got you around to clean me up," he says finally.

But his words don't reduce the tension between us. If anything, they ratchet it up a notch. Because we're still staring at each other, our gazes locked up tighter than atoms in a covalent bond.

Am I going crazy? The probability appears to be quite high.

I manage to break our gaze, looking down to study the cracks in the vinyl surface as though I'm going to be quizzed on it later.

What's actually going on here? I mean, from an outsider's perspective, us sitting here together would look like a date. But from Brandon's perspective I'm pretty sure I'm just someone to hang out with when his brother isn't available.

Oh God, I'm growing more and more like Josh's last roommate. Becoming obsessed with Brandon. I'm pretty sure I'm never going to break into his apartment and lie in his bed naked waiting for him to come home to discover me, but the slope does appear to be one lined with layers of slime, over-coated by slippery ice.

I don't know how to break the silence that's growing

between us. Thankfully, it wouldn't be a Brandon outing without us being interrupted by football groupies wanting to immortalize themselves with Brandon on their phones.

One of the guys glances at me then scrunches his face like he's seen something offensive. His friend's eyes skate past me as if I'm not even worth looking at.

A sour feeling spreads in my mouth, offsetting the taste of the cheesecake.

I've been judged and found lacking. By jocks. It could really be the theme of my life.

I pick up my fork and viciously stab at the remains of my cheesecake base. It cleaves in two under my assault, shooting one part across the plate where it comes to rest on the edge.

The guys retreat while my nostrils flare.

When I raise my eyes Brandon's watching me closely.

"You really don't like jocks, do you?" he says.

"No, I don't." My voice is flat.

"No one...hurt you, did they?" His jaw is tight.

It takes me a moment to get what he's implying, and when I do my tongue trips over itself to reassure him. "God, no. Not like that."

Brandon's whole body relaxes.

"I was just the butt of the footballers' jokes a few too many times in high school," I say finally. I don't want to tell him the whole truth.

Brandon's eyes twinkle. "So now you're making sure I'm the butt of your jokes all the time to get some cosmic balance?"

"Well, yeah. Plus you make it so easy."

"Easy in what way?" His voice and the smile on his lips are both playful.

Before I realize what I'm doing, I'm slanting my body forward too.

Crap. I slam on the brakes and lean back.

My body does not appear to be processing the repeated memos from my brain.

CHAPTER 20

BRANDON

WHEN I ARRIVE at Josh's apartment the next night I'm bracing myself to see Megan. I've spent the whole day at the gym going back and forth in my head over what to do about these pesky feelings I have for my brother's roommate. I still haven't come up with an answer.

I flop down on the couch next to Josh. Megan is nowhere to be seen.

"So, Brandon." Josh's eyes sparkle with mischief as he tilts his head at me. "I was thinking the other day that I've seen more of you than usual this off-season. If I was going to plot a trend line it would definitely be an exponential increase."

I shrug. "You always have more food than me."

Josh gives his *bullshit-Brandon* cough, which I choose to ignore.

"Where's Megan?" I ask casually.

Unfortunately, my question prompts an annoying smirk to bloom on my brother's face. "She's on a date," he says.

His benign words cause the hairs on the back of my neck to stand on end. "On a date?"

"Yeah, some guy's taking her to dinner. I think that's generally called a date."

I try to keep my tone light. "Who's the guy?"

Josh shrugs. "Some guy she met through work."

Shit. My mood plummets off a cliff.

Josh raises an eyebrow. "Do you have a problem with Megan being on a date?"

I scoff, "Of course not."

I can see Josh about to tee up his *bullshit-Brandon* cough again, so I quickly continue. "Anyway, it looks like the Goliaths aren't going to franchise tag me."

Josh's mocking expression disappears and he leans forward, elbows on knees, fully engaged. "How do you feel about that?"

I shrug. "In some ways, if they'd used a franchise tag it would have made everything so much easier. Because then I wouldn't have to make a decision. But I guess now I'm completely in control, which is a good thing."

"Does Frank think their decision not to franchise tag you means they're not going to want to re-sign you?"

"Nah, he says everything he's hearing suggests they want me to re-sign. But they won't be able to offer me anything close to a max contract."

"That's not surprising, considering the rest of their roster," Josh says. "What are you going to do?"

I shrug. "Not sure. I can't really re-sign without seeing what else is out there. I have no idea how long I'll get to play in the NFL, so I've got to maximize my earnings. There are so many random factors that can affect your career—you've got to take your chances when you get them."

"Don't let Megan hear you say that," Josh says.

"I'm pretty sure she hasn't bugged the room just in case I say something incriminating."

"I don't know." Josh's eyes twinkle. "I wouldn't put it past her. She takes one-upping you very seriously."

"Don't I know it." Talking about my ongoing battle with Megan has made me smile, but it fades as I contemplate the uncertainty around my future. I run my hands through my hair. "Let's face it, I don't really have a wide range of marketable skills to fall back on."

"You could always coach," Josh says.

"Yeah, I looked into that a while back. But generally you need a degree in sports science to coach, and I barely made it through a bullshit communications degree."

Josh looks awkward. We've never really talked about how much I struggle with the academic stuff that comes easy to him.

"You might find it easier if you did some college papers now," he suggests.

I snort. "I don't think so."

Josh goes to say something, but the noise of a key in the lock distracts him.

It's Megan. She slips her coat off, revealing a dress with a sweetheart neckline. While it could still feature in a catalogue of prom dresses approved by conservative Christian ministers, it's showing a lot more skin than what she usually wears. My heart suddenly starts pumping a whole lot faster than normal.

"Hey." She stops suddenly when she sees me and eyes me warily.

I can't help myself. "How was your date?" I ask, trying to ignore the reemergence of Josh's smirk, and my goodwill for the conversation we've just had quickly fades.

"It was good," Megan says. She puts her keys and purse down on the counter and turns to face us.

"What's the guy's name?" I ask.

"Fraser."

"How did you meet him?" I'm aware I've asked the question a tad aggressively, and I force myself to take a deep breath.

"He's an astrophysicist. I interviewed him a few weeks ago for a story I was working on."

I press my lips together. "And he asked you out? Isn't that unprofessional?"

"Are you going to see him again?" Josh asks before Megan has a chance to answer. Given the death glare she'd fixed in my direction, that's probably a good thing.

"Yeah, he invited me on a second date this Friday."

"Oh, where's he taking you?" Josh asks.

"He suggested The Estate."

The Estate is a place that features in nearly every guide to New York's fine dining scene. Pain flashes through my jaw, and I realize I'm clenching my teeth hard enough to shatter granite.

"Wow, he must really like you." Josh gives an encouraging smile.

"Or he's a pretentious asshole who needs to show off in order to get laid," I interject.

Josh and Megan raise matching eyebrows at me.

"What? That could equally be true," I say.

Megan's death glare returns in full force. "I think I prefer Josh's interpretation."

I shrug, pretending not to care. "Suit yourself."

CHAPTER 21

MEGAN

I DON'T THINK I've ever been to a restaurant as expensive as The Estate before. The chairs are covered in red velvet, and chandeliers offer subdued lighting. Everything reeks of money and taste.

You know how you sometimes have those moments where you mentally pinch yourself? Sitting across from a good-looking astrophysicist in one of the ritziest restaurants in Manhattan (and despite my feminist principles I'm totally planning on letting him pick up the check for this), I'm giving myself mental pinches that must leave a massive lesion on my brain. It's a long way from Applebee's in Tulsa, Oklahoma, that's for sure.

Fraser's talking about his work. The one downside of Fraser, as I discovered on our last date, is that his favorite topic of conversation appears to be himself. But hey, he has an interesting job and I'm learning plenty about cosmic rays, so it's all good.

We're tucked away at an intimate table for two in the back corner, and Fraser's positioned himself facing the rest of the restaurant, which I think was a strategic thing since twice he's interrupted his narrative to whisper to me about a famous person he's spotted. I don't think I'm impressing him, because both times my response has been, "Who?"

Hey, at least I can impress him with my knowledge of cosmic rays, right?

Suddenly Fraser's eyes widen. "Oh, my God, don't look now, but you'll never guess who just walked in."

"Who?" I brace myself for not recognizing yet another name.

"Brandon Seaton."

Okay, my brief flush of triumph that I actually know who that is, is quickly replaced by a swamp of confusion. What's Brandon doing here? I'm pretty sure it's not a coincidence that he's turned up at this particular location.

Fraser carries on narrating the action going on over my shoulder. "He's coming this way."

I bet he is.

Part of the reason I accepted the first date with Fraser was to try to get my brain to move past this...weirdness with Brandon. And now he's here? What the hell? Is this Brandon just thinking it would be amusing to crash my date? Is it some kind of game to him?

I summon my nastiest expression and look up as Brandon reaches our table.

He does the worst double take known to man. Seriously, an acting career is not in this guy's future when he retires from football.

"Megan, hi! What a surprise to see you," he says.

"Such a surprise," I reply through gritted teeth.

He looks over at Fraser. "Hi, I'm Brandon." He offers his hand.

"Hi," Fraser squeaks as he shakes Brandon's hand. "I'm such a big fan."

Brandon gives a shark-like grin. "Really? You follow the Goliaths?"

"Yeah. Avidly. I watch every game."

"Oh, it's always great to meet a superfan," Brandon says.

I watch Fraser melt from intelligent guy into football-groupie goo and start peppering Brandon with questions, mostly about his free agency. Brandon deflects them all with the skill of someone who dodges tackles for a living.

As they talk I fidget with my cutlery, incidentally evaluating which utensil could cause the most bodily harm. The knife would be most people's go-to, but I actually think the bluntness of a spoon has overlooked potential.

"We should probably stop talking about football—it's not really Megan's thing," Brandon says finally.

Fraser sends a startled glance at me, like he's just remembered I'm here. "You don't like football?"

"Ah...no."

"So, how do you two know each other?" Fraser's studying me with a whole lot more interest than he has up to now.

"Brandon's brother is my roommate," I say shortly.

"Our relationship is a bit more than that. It's fair to say Megan and I have had a...special connection since we first met," Brandon says.

I almost swallow my tongue as Fraser raises his eyebrows. Brandon's eyes are twinkling. Yep, this is definitely a game to him. Anger flares in my stomach.

"Is 'special connection' the right terminology?" I ask. My voice is sweet, but it's like one of those candies where the sugar on top hides the sourness beneath.

"I think it fits," Brandon says.

I plaster a placid smile on my face. "At the moment I'm thinking of ways to sever the special connection. Violently."

Brandon laughs, a deep chuckle. "Megan has such a great sense of humor, doesn't she?"

"Um...yeah." Fraser looks like he'll agree to anything Brandon says.

My smile is gone, and I just scowl at him.

The waiter sweeps past Brandon to deliver our appetizers. My mouth immediately starts to water at the smell of my broccoli and cashew nut soup.

Brandon takes a step back. "Anyway, it looks like you're having a nice dinner so I won't keep you. I just wanted a quick bite to eat and had a craving for the lobster here."

Yeah, because you come to The Estate for a quick bite. It's similar to McDonald's in that way. I resist the temptation to roll my eyes.

"Do you want to join us?" Fraser asks. He bites his lip as soon as he says the words, looking like he's asked the most popular boy in school to sit at his lunch table.

"It's okay," I say quickly. "I'm sure Brandon would prefer to sit somewhere else."

Brandon gives me a smirk. "No, actually, there's nothing more I'd like to do than join you for dinner."

Oh, God, seriously?

I watch in disbelief as he goes and smiles charmingly at the people at the next table over and returns holding a chair. The Estate is not the type of restaurant where you rearrange the seating to suit yourself, but none of the waiting staff challenge him.

Of course not. He's Brandon Seaton.

Our intimate table for two wasn't designed to have a 250-pound footballer added to it, but with much clinking and clunking we shift our plates and silverware so there is room for the plate that our waiter whisks over to us.

"This is great." Brandon grins broadly once he's set himself up and extracted his elbow from a near miss with a bread plate.

That wouldn't be my first choice of words right now.

"What do you think about your new draft picks?" Fraser asks.

And so the evening proceeds.

Brandon tells lots of funny anecdotes about the Goliaths, which Fraser laps up more than a dog laps water on a hot day. Some of them are amusing. Although I get the feeling he's selected ones that could feature on a *footballers-behaving-like-idiots* channel because he knows the only way to keep me entertained is to support a theme I'm invested in.

This is Brandon in his element. Cocky grin on his face, basking in Fraser's admiration. Watching him, you'd think he'd never had a moment of insecurity in his life. But I've had a chance to peer under his mask, and I know there's a real person lurking there beneath his persona. I don't know if that's why my irritation grows even stronger as the evening wears on. If I'm going to spend time with Brandon, I want the real Brandon, not his public face.

Or maybe I'm just annoyed at how he's completely monopolized my date. There's no chance for me and Fraser to develop any kind of connection. Although to be fair, Brandon does keep trying to turn the conversation back to me at various points in the evening.

"Has Megan told you about the interview she's got lined up with Dianne Marshall?"

"Being from the Midwest, I know Megan will have an

opinion on the importance of small-market teams to their local economy."

And that's the thing about Brandon. He might disagree with me a lot of the time, but his interventions show he's really been listening to me. Not just waiting for his turn to talk.

"Megan, why don't you show Fraser your *Fraggle Rock* impression?"

I send him a glare at that last one, because this was something that was never supposed to leave the walls of the apartment. But I obediently don my Ma Gorg persona.

Fraser appears more confused than amused at the end, though.

As we finish up dessert Brandon gestures to our waiter for the check. "I've got this one," he says.

"Oh, you don't have to do that," Fraser says.

I remain silent. Because Brandon owes me big time after this—much more than even a free dinner at The Estate could ever equate to.

"It's the least I can do, given I crashed your date," he says.

"Oh, that's no problem. You're welcome to crash our dates anytime," Fraser says.

I try to pull my lips into a smile, but I get the feeling it's more of a grimace. My anger and annoyance, which have been simmering away inside me during dinner, spike again. This evening was supposed to be about me getting to know a nice, attractive, smart guy. Instead, it's been all about Brandon. Again. It feels like all my free time recently has been hijacked by Brandon.

Brandon signs the check, then turns to me. "You going home now?"

"Yes. I'll see you back at the apartment sometime." I

keep my voice calm and even, but I leave no room for nego-tiation.

"I'll walk you back," Brandon offers.

"Fraser and I are going to walk in a different direction. Take the scenic route."

Fraser's gaze shoots between us, and he fiddles with his wallet as Brandon and I stare at each other.

Brandon suddenly seems to deflate, his shoulders slumping. "I'll leave you to it then." He gives me one of his fake smiles.

Why does my victory feel strangely like a defeat?

"Okay," I say evenly.

Brandon stands up abruptly. "See you later." He doesn't meet my eyes as he pushes the chair away.

"Great to meet you," Fraser calls after him.

CHAPTER 22

BRANDON

I STOMP the walk back to Josh and Megan's apartment.

She wanted to be left alone with him. Is she going to kiss him? Is he going to invite her back to his place? Are they going to become an item? Boyfriend and girlfriend?

The thought makes the lobster in my stomach churn, like the creature's come back to life and is getting its revenge by turning somersaults.

What the hell does she see in the guy? He didn't even laugh at her *Fraggle Rock* impression. She can't be with someone who doesn't get her.

When I get back to the apartment Josh has already gone to bed. I'm left alone with my swirling thoughts, only the scientists staring down judgmentally from the walls keeping me company.

I turn on the TV, but nothing holds my interest. I don't want to watch replays of basketball or a documentary on the submarines of World War II.

The relief that surges through me when I hear Megan's key in the lock only ten minutes later is almost overwhelming.

But it only lasts until I see the look on her face. Her lips are curled to reveal her teeth, but it in no way resembles a smile. It's the snarl of an animal.

A wild, rabid animal.

"What the hell was that about?" Megan says, pulling up a few feet from where I'm sprawled on the couch. Her voice is loud and a bit shaky, like she's struggling to contain all the emotions that want to come out.

"What do you mean?"

"You crashing my date like that! What were you thinking?"

I shrug, trying for a nonchalance that's so far from what I'm feeling. "I thought it was fun."

Her eyes glint, and I'm pretty sure if they could spit fire they would. "It was presumptuous. And so, so arrogant. Like you can't imagine anyone would not want to spend time with you."

"Your date didn't seem to mind."

"Well, I minded." She's breathing heavily, and her nostrils flare.

"Why did you mind so much, Megan?" I challenge.

"Because I'd been looking forward to getting to know Fraser better, and you completely hijacked that by talking about football all night!"

I snort. "Why do you want to get to know him? What do you even see in that guy?"

Her eyes narrow into slits. "You mean, what do I see in that nice, polite, good-looking, intelligent guy?"

My insides shrivel, but I blunder forward. "He didn't seem smart enough for you. I mean, he didn't even get your *Fraggle Rock* impression. He's not exactly a rocket scientist, is he?"

"He's an astrophysicist. So he's actually the precise definition of a rocket scientist," she spits.

Fuck.

I change tactics. It's one of those things I'm renowned for on the field—the ability to switch things up when something isn't working. "Well, maybe you need to rethink how you choose a date. Because that guy might be smart on paper, but he was duller than dishwater."

Megan's face is flushed red and she crosses her arms. "So now you think you can tell me who to date?"

"No, I don't think that."

But Megan's on a roll. "It's so typical of you. Thinking you can charm the whole world—do whatever the hell you like."

"That's fucking unfair, and you know it," I say, standing up.

"You're so big-headed you can't entertain the possibility that maybe your presence wasn't welcome."

"Excuse me for looking out for you." Like I looked out for her during the whole Josh debacle—something she's never actually acknowledged.

"Looking out for me? Because I need you to vet my dates now, do I? Because I can't handle my love life by myself. Thank you, oh great savior."

"I'm out of here," I say, stalking past her to the door. I'm not going to stay here and let her throw this shit at me.

Megan whirls around. "We haven't finished this conversation."

"Well, I'm finishing it." I leave the apartment, banging the door behind me.

Great. It appears I royally fucked up.

I stomp for about a block before I get out my phone. My hands are still shaking in anger as I order myself an Uber.

When it arrives I throw myself into the back seat. The driver doesn't recognize me, thank fuck, because the last thing I feel like doing now is talking about football. My brain is barely functioning because it keeps getting snagged on Megan.

Why can't I shake her from my head? Why am I interested in the one girl who's never going to be interested in me back?

I'm a...what's the word for it? A masochist. Someone who inflicts pain deliberately on themselves. I'm falling for someone who's never going to see me as a potential boyfriend. She hates football, for fuck's sake. And I know nothing about science. She's far too smart for me.

I've got so much shit going on in my life. I should be focusing on what's happening in free agency, not obsessing over someone I can't have.

The Uber drops me off at the door of my building. I nod at Geoffrey at the door, but I'm definitely not in the mood to stop and chat.

When I reach my apartment I'm still too wound up to go to bed, so I jump in the shower. I find I'm aggressively washing myself. There's no denying how much Megan has gotten under my skin. Unfortunately, no amount of scrubbing is going to remove her.

I step out, grab a towel and wrap it around myself. I'm going to have to avoid Josh's apartment for a bit. That's the only solution.

But the thought of not seeing Megan, even after the argument we've just had, makes something shrivel up inside me.

God, this is so fucked up.

My thoughts are whirring like angry bees, filling my mind with bristling and humming.

I suddenly realize it's not just my head that is buzzing. So is my intercom.

CHAPTER 23

MEGAN

BRANDON LEAVES with a slamming door that reverber-
ates around the apartment.

I don't know why I'm so angry about it. But I'm not
going to let him get away with what he did tonight. I need to
confront him, to sort this out now. Which means I need to
find out where he lives.

The thought stops me short.

How is it possible that I've spent so much time hanging
out with Brandon and I feel like I know him so well, yet I've
never been to his apartment? The dynamic between us is so
messed up.

I crack open Josh's bedroom door and poke my head in.

He's asleep. I feel a twinge of guilt, but not enough to
stop me. Hey, Josh invited me as his date to his boyfriend's
brother's wedding without giving me a heads-up. It's the
definition of owing me one.

"Josh." I shake his shoulder gently.

Josh stirs, half-opening his eyes. "Whassup?"

"It's just me, Megan. Can you give me Brandon's
address?"

Josh attempts to open his eyes more fully. "Why do you want that?"

"I just need to see him." Even as I say the words I'm aware of how ridiculous I sound. It's almost eleven at night.

"What the hell is going on between you two?" Josh mumbles sleepily as he pushes himself up on his pillow.

His words make me pause. What *is* going on between us?

I'm seething with anger that he sabotaged my date like that. But Fraser didn't mind. He'll spend the next year gloating to everyone he meets that he had dinner with Brandon Seaton. Even if he doesn't really like me he'll probably continue to date me just on the off chance he'll see Brandon again.

It gives me a glimpse into what Brandon's talked about. How difficult it is to find people who actually like you for you.

Josh is still watching me expectantly.

"He crashed my date tonight. I just need to talk to him," I say.

Josh studies me for a moment, his forehead scrunched.

"Please?"

Whether it's me using my manners or something about my tone, his expression suddenly clears. "Okay." He reaches for his phone on his bedside table. "I'll forward you his contact details. But don't kill him, okay? I don't want accessory to murder on my resume."

"I'll try to restrain myself," I say stiffly.

When I get to Brandon's apartment building, his doorman won't let me up.

Of course he won't—I'm a strange girl randomly requesting to see a famous football star. I'm sure it's literally written in the doorman's contract that he needs to get rid of people like me.

"Just buzz him, please," I plead.

"It's eleven-thirty at night."

"He's awake, trust me."

"I'm sorry, miss."

I suddenly have a brainwave. "Look, I'm a friend of his. I've got his number." I open my phone and show him Brandon's name in my phone. Along with the string of messages we've sent back and forth.

The doorman frowns, and he taps on his tablet. He checks my phone, and his frown lines deepen. "That is Brandon Seaton's number," he says slowly.

"I know. I told you—I'm a friend of his."

The doorman gives me a suspicious look but presses the buzzer.

"Hello?" Brandon's deep voice stirs something in my stomach.

"Good evening, Mr. Seaton, it's Geoffrey from the front desk. I'm sorry to disturb you, but I've got a girl here wanting to see you. She's not on your approved list."

"It's Megan," I call out in a loud voice.

"She says her name is Megan," Geoffrey repeats. "Can I let her up, sir?"

There's a long pause. Finally he replies, "Yeah, send her up."

I let out a breath I didn't know I was holding as I walk to the elevator. Gnawing on my bottom lip, I press the button for the penthouse apartment, and the elevator starts to glide upwards.

The fight has drained out of me, and now uncertainty

fills the space left behind. What am I doing? Why have I come all this way across town just to continue my argument with Brandon? Why does it matter so much to me?

The elevator doors open into a fancy foyer area. My reflection in the large gilded mirror increases my uncertainty. Even though I'm still dressed up for my date, I don't look like the beautiful people who usually grace apartment buildings like this.

My high heels are muffled by the plush carpet. I reach the door to Brandon's apartment and stop, hesitating. Maybe I should just go home, talk to him tomorrow when we've both calmed down.

But knowing Brandon is right through the door, possibly only a few feet away, I can't back down now. Summoning my anger so I can wear it like a protective shield, I rap sharply on the door.

He answers on my first knock.

I barge in past him then spin to face him, my breath leaving me when I realize he's dressed only in a towel.

Seriously? This is the body that caused so many accidents in Times Square they had to take the billboard down. It's not exactly playing fair.

I narrow my gaze. "Why are you dressed like that?"

Brandon closes the door behind me and leans against it. "Because I was in the shower."

"Well, go put some clothes on."

He folds his arms over his chest. "Why, Megan? Why do I have to be fully clothed for you to insult me?"

He's close enough that I notice the water droplets that drip from his wet hair onto his shoulder then run down the smooth, golden skin of his chest. Really, anatomy students should be using Brandon to learn their muscle groups.

I divert my attention away from his chest to his face. He

looks tired. Not just late-at-night fatigue, but a kind of bone-weary exhaustion. When he speaks again, his voice is steeped in the same tiredness. "You're right, I was an asshole tonight. I'm sorry, okay? Now you can go home with your apology, and I can get some sleep."

There's something defeated on his face. Something vulnerable.

The seconds tick by as I just stare at him.

He's apologized to me, but it's not enough. It suddenly dawns on me the real reason I've stalked Brandon across town isn't to win our argument. There's a pressing question that I want answered. That I *need* answered.

"Why?" I ask finally, my voice quiet.

"Why what?"

"Why did you hijack my date like that?"

He's watching me closely. "I don't know."

"Liar," I say. The words fall out without meaning to, channeled from some black hole in my brain.

Brandon's eyebrows fly upwards, and annoyance flickers across his face. "Well, if I'm lying, Megan, then I'm pretty sure you're also lying. To yourself."

His words loom between us. They've created a challenge, forcing me to face something I've tried to pretend doesn't exist. It's like how the flat earth supporters cling to their theory despite all the evidence to the contrary.

My breathing has picked up under the weight of Brandon's brown eyes challenging me. My chest rises and falls rapidly as the last few months of our interactions fly through my mind.

All those nights watching television with him. The Barbie and Ken saga. The close dancing with him at the wedding. The way when I'm not spending time with him I'm looking for excuses to talk about him.

And then there's the reverse. How he's always at our apartment instead of his own. The way he looked at me at the wedding and at Little Mama's Cheesecakes. The way he stood up to Josh, tried to protect me from getting hurt. Even how he crashed my date tonight.

It's like one of those optical illusions you've been staring at for so long, sure you know what you're looking at, when suddenly a completely different picture is revealed to you.

Oh.

Right.

For a few weeks I've been worried that my body is missing the memo from my brain. But apparently it's my brain that hasn't been processing the data correctly.

"I'd say it's more like I'm in denial." I say the words slowly, but at the same time my pulse increases in speed, like I'm on a rollercoaster that's just about to take the plunge.

He squints at me. "What?"

"I'm not lying to myself—I've just been in denial. There's a difference."

Brandon's face relaxes, and he lets out a low chuckle. "You're point scoring now?"

"I'm always going to keep score. You, as a sportsperson, should understand that."

Our gazes stayed locked together. It's like the air has ignited between us.

He takes a step toward me, his eyes dark and mysterious.

My whole body is trembling. I try to control my breathing, because fainting right now probably isn't the best etiquette.

He takes another step to be right in front of me now, and I can almost feel the heat radiating from his skin.

I try to think up something to say but I don't get a chance to formulate a sentence before Brandon lowers his head and presses his mouth against mine.

There's a moment where disbelief runs rampant in my brain. The holy-shit-Brandon-is-kissing-me bit is so loud there's no room for anything else.

But quickly the input from my other senses flood in.

His lips are soft and warm. There's just a graze of stubble. One of his hands comes up to cradle the side of my face; the other falls to my waist, tugging me closer. He smells like soap, but underneath is another scent, something uniquely Brandon—masculine and addictive.

Our kiss stays chaste and sweet for a few seconds, before my lips part.

Then it happens.

It's like one of those exothermic chemical reactions. When you combine two ordinary substances that are normally benign but combust the instant they are put together. Because I barely have a chance to register the taste of minty toothpaste before his tongue touches mine and it's all on. We're used to battling each other, but this time the battlefield is far more pleasurable. His tongue slides against mine in a way that sends a shudder through my whole body.

He pulls me even closer as we try to consume each other. My skin tingles at all points where our bodies collide. His hands move into my hair, and I slide mine down his back, stroking his golden expanse of skin over rippling muscles, my hands splayed so I can touch as much of him as possible.

Brandon gives a soft groan, and I've never heard a sexier sound.

When I eventually pull away he just stares at me, his pupils dilated, his lips red and swollen.

"Holy shit," he says finally.

For once I am in total agreement with him. Because that is by far the best kiss I've ever had.

Before I have time to process anything, he kisses me again.

It's even hotter than before. Hotter than the surface of the sun. Hotter than a Supernova explosion.

We stumble backwards together. It turns out moving when your mouths are fused together isn't the most efficient way to travel, but neither I the scientist nor Brandon the athlete decide to stop and point that out. Instead, we continue to move in fits and starts. I'm kind of propelling us to begin with, but I quickly realize I don't know what direction I'm heading.

My mind staggers like my feet.

That's right—my first time in Brandon's apartment and it appears I'm heading straight for his bedroom.

But then my brain shuts down thinking about that, because it's too busy processing all the sensory data that's coming in. Brandon is stroking my back, his mouth still against mine.

Oh, my God, that feels so good.

It's not until we reach just inside his bedroom and Brandon starts kissing down my jaw and I catch a glimpse of his bed that panic swells inside me.

I wrench away from him.

Brandon's chest is heaving. "Are you okay?" His voice is wrecked, deep and husky. A jolt of lust manages to briefly penetrate my panic.

Somehow his towel has stayed in place, but the fact that this half-naked gorgeous football player is standing there, looking at me with desire burning in his eyes, triggers something in me.

I try to wrestle my panic under control. But it's like trying to grapple an anaconda into a straitjacket.

I take deep breaths. This is Brandon. Brandon who would never pretend. Because deep down, under all that bravado and ego, I know Brandon is a decent guy.

"What's wrong?" His head tilts to the side.

"You really want me?" The words leave my lips without permission, channeled from the seventeen-year-old version of myself. I cringe, because I know there is nothing as unsexy as lack of confidence.

But Brandon grabs me and pulls me to him so I can feel him pressed against me. The whole of him pressed against me. Including some very hard parts.

He whispers into my ear. "Is this not scientific proof enough about how much I want you?"

"Um, yeah. There's definitely some large proof going on there."

I can't stop myself reaching down to touch him, and his breath catches.

His dark eyes are smoldering. "I know how much you like your scientific proof," he gasps.

I can't help the beginnings of a smile creeping up my cheeks. "I might have to investigate further."

"Please do."

As I caress him I still can't shake my disbelief. This is happening. I'm here in Brandon's bedroom, and he wants me.

When he drops his towel, my disbelief grows to epic proportions. Because epic is the right word.

Brandon stands there naked, seeming completely at ease.

"I believe you're overdressed for this particular occasion, Megan," he says huskily.

He unzips the back of my dress, letting it fall to the ground, then kisses me again.

If I'd had any premonition this morning that tonight I'd be in bed with Brandon I'd have spent the day researching some fancy moves. Or at least thought more about personal body hair.

In some ways it's probably good I haven't had a chance to obsess over this. Cringe-worthy self-consciousness has always been an extra companion in the bedroom with me. Like one of those frenemies undermining and questioning everything so you end up doubting your every move.

But today my companion doesn't make it onto the bed.

Because this is Brandon. Brandon knows me. I know him.

And then there's the fact that his eyes are firing with so much heat and passion as he reaches out to stroke my skin that I can't focus on anything except how good he's making me feel.

And when he finally slips inside me, he kisses me so deeply that I'm on the edge incredibly fast, and then I'm flying over it, but instead of plummeting down I discover the laws of gravity have been suspended and I'm heading for intergalactic space exploration instead.

Then watching his face as he comes apart is equally mind-blowing.

Did I ever think I'd see an expression like that on Brandon's face? And that I'd be the one to cause it?

As he lies there, his face nuzzled into the crook between my neck and shoulder, I wait for my panic to return or awkwardness to set in.

He pulls back to stare at me. I'm trying to think of something lighthearted to say, something to reset us to our usual dynamic, but my brain is blank.

I'm braced for him to do it instead—crack a joke, get us back to our normal interactions.

But instead he leans down and kisses me gently. Tenderly.

He tugs me into his arms, curling his body around mine like it's the most natural thing in the world.

"What if I'd wanted to be the big spoon?" I grumble.

He laughs, his breath tickling the skin at the back of my neck. He plants a kiss in my hair, and a weird feeling flows through me. It's something that until now I've never felt when I've been in bed with a guy, a feeling I didn't even realize was missing.

I feel safe.

CHAPTER 24

BRANDON

I WAKE UP, and there she is, her hair sprawled all over the pillow. Hogging the duvet, of course. I wouldn't have expected anything less.

I can't explain the feelings bubbling up inside me.

Normally when I wake up beside a woman I have this tiny surge of panic. No matter how great things were the night before I'm always worried they'll want more from me than I can give.

But this time I can't wait for Megan to wake up. Not so we can have a repeat of last night (although I'm definitely up for that, in all the meanings of the word). But because I want to talk to her. I want to hear her voice, hear her laugh.

"Staring at people when they sleep is borderline psychopathic, you know," she says without opening her eyes.

"I'm actually just admiring my pillowcase," I say. "I have good taste in linen."

Her eyelids lift and her blue eyes pierce me. There's amusement there, along with caution.

"I have good taste in women too," I continue, because

nothing is more important in that moment than dimming that hesitation in her eyes. I don't want Megan to regret last night. I don't think I could stand that.

"Is this where you say 'present company excluded'?" Her brow is arched, but vulnerability flickers on her face.

If I was in usual Brandon-Megan mode I'd go for a mocking comment right now. But instead I go for the truth. "Present company is definitely not excluded. In fact, present company is the best evidence of my good taste there's ever been."

A smile toys with her lower lip, and I can't help but lean over and gently kiss her. After a pause, she kisses me back. Our kiss doesn't stay gentle for long. It tumbles quickly into furious fumbling territory.

Which I'm totally onboard with.

Afterwards I start to make Megan breakfast. She sits at the counter in an old T-shirt of mine, her hair tumbling in all directions.

Here's the thing: conversation with Megan is so easy. There's none of that awkward next-day thing where you're struggling to find something to talk about—where things seem weird because only a few hours ago you were pressed up naked together, and now you're finding out that your bed partner is leading a petition to have Sean Hannity awarded a sainthood by the Pope.

I know Megan better than anyone I've ever slept with before.

And I'm not worried about saying anything that's going to put her off having a repeat. Because A, we've already had a repeat this morning, and B, Megan is already familiar with all my bad traits, so she could provide a complete list of them faster than I could.

She's watching me make pancakes. "Are you sure you've put in enough flour?"

I pause in my sifting to look at her. "You just can't help yourself, can you?"

"What?"

"Second guessing what I'm doing."

"I can so help myself," she argues.

"Okay. Let's see if you can get through me making you breakfast without you questioning anything or insulting my pancake-making technique."

"I can do that, no sweat."

"Sure you can." My tone is full of laughter.

Watching Megan biting her lip to restrain herself from saying anything brings back a memory of last night. Which is not a bad thing. Because they're probably the hottest replays in the history of flashbacks.

I've been with women who've turned themselves into gymnasts with all their fancy moves in the bedroom. But I've never had sex that's so...intense before. That wasn't just about getting off. Instead it seemed to be about building something.

Though what it's building, I've got no idea.

Does Megan see this as a one-time thing? Or is it something she'll want to continue? I know where my vote's going. I mean, it's probably stupid to start something now when I'm on the countdown to free agency—where I could be signing anywhere in the country and be relocating before the start of next season. But I definitely want more of this.

I crack an egg into the bowl, and because I'm not paying enough attention I manage to get some eggshell in the mixture.

Shit. I grab a spoon out of the drawer to try and fish it

out. Megan produces a noise that sounds like what a constipated goose would make.

"How's that not giving instructions or insulting me
thing going?" I ask.

"Fine," she says in a strained voice.

She does manage admirably to keep her mouth clamped
while I extract the shell and then finish adding the rest of
the ingredients.

I deliberately turn the hand mixer on too high when it's
time to beat the mixture, and droplets whip from the bowl
and cover the surrounding area.

Megan wipes a few spots where they've landed on her
face. "Seriously, you'd do that just to try and win a bet?"

"You know me, Megan—anything for the win."

She throws a tea towel at me as I laugh.

The pancakes turn out fine, if a little odd looking.

"They taste pretty good," Megan admits with obvious
reluctance.

"That compliment must have cost you."

"You have no idea." She finishes a bite, and then absentmindedly reaches up to rub her lip. "Oh, my God, I think I
actually made my lip bleed when I bit it so hard before."
She dabs at it with a napkin.

"Do you want me to kiss it better?" I ask.

I'm expecting Megan to banter back, but instead her
eyes heat up.

"Okay." She puts down her fork.

We don't make it past the table. That time, anyway.

"I've really got to get going," Megan says a few hours later.

We're back in my bed. I watch her stand up, my heart

starting to race as she pulls on her dress. Her date dress, from last night when she was on a date with another guy.

Shit. I've really got to sort out where things stand between us.

Does Megan want this to turn into something real? How can I ask? I mean, I know Megan probably won't mock me on something like this—she'll probably let me down gently—but rejection is still rejection. It's been a long time since I've faced rejection from a woman. Chloe Parker ripping up my Valentine in sixth grade is the last one that springs to mind. I'm suddenly aware of how much I really really want this to continue.

"You don't want to stay for lunch?" I ask.

Megan's hunting around for her shoes. "I've got an article I need to edit for tomorrow. And Josh will be wondering where I am."

"Yeah, talking about my brother when I'm naked in bed isn't my usual thing."

She rolls her eyes. "Maybe you should get out of bed then."

I obey her, quickly pulling on boxers and a T-shirt before following her out. She grabs her purse off the kitchen counter and turns to face me, her expression wary. There've been lots of times in my life when I've wished I could read minds, but nothing like this moment.

I rake my hands through my hair. "So, um, tonight..."

Her shoulders stiffen. "Yeah?"

"Are you going to be finished with your article by then?"

Megan fiddles with the strap of her purse, not looking at me. "I should be."

"Are you up to anything?"

"My usual Sunday night involves Netflix and maybe folding laundry. You know that."

"You want to come here, hang out? I can cook you dinner if you want."

Megan hesitates.

Oh, shit. She's going to say no. She's trying to think of a way to let me down gently.

Finally she asks, "What's wrong with hanging out at our apartment? Given you've been almost surgically implanted on our couch for the past few months, why mix it up now?"

I blow out a breath I didn't know I was holding. "I'm thinking the things I want to do with you on the couch tonight I don't really want my little brother to witness."

A grin blooms on her face and she struggles to control it. "Yeah, okay."

We stand there, looking at each other for a moment, and I try to wrestle back the happiness and relief coursing through me. I really don't want to scare her off by coming on too strong.

"Awesome," I manage.

I move toward her and give her a quick kiss on her mouth. After everything we've done over the last twelve hours, a small peck shouldn't feel like a big deal. But somehow it does.

"See you then," I say.

CHAPTER 25

MEGAN

DOING the walk of shame anytime is bad enough. It's far, far worse when you were last seen hightailing it toward your roommate's brother's apartment the night before.

And it's even worse when you're not doing the walk of shame until lunchtime the next day. Because it's pretty obvious what you've spent the morning doing.

I unlock the door to our apartment and compromise my atheist principles by sending a quick prayer to every god I can think of that Josh is out somewhere. But apparently the gods are not pleased by my opportunistic conversion. Josh is in the kitchen, making himself a sandwich.

"Good afternoon, Megan," he says, his voice bright.

"Afternoon," I say grudgingly.

"Did you sort everything out with Brandon?" Josh's smirk is large enough people can probably spot it in Boston.

"Um...yeah," I mutter.

Josh is silently laughing at me, and I can't blame him.

"I'm going to sort my laundry." I slink off with as much dignity as I can muster. I close the door to my room and lean against it for a second. So that wasn't embarrassing or anything.

Okay. Focus, Megan, focus. Laundry. If I'm going to Brandon's tonight, then I need to put in a load of laundry and then get started on my article.

But my focusing ability isn't that great as I haul my load of laundry down to the communal machines in the basement. Because my brain keeps flickering back to what happened between us, which also could be titled The Best Sex of My Existence.

Of course, it would be with Brandon Seaton. The universe likes to play those kinds of games with me.

I'm halfway through putting my load into the washing machine when my phone beeps with a message.

Hey, just wanted to say I had a great time last night (and this morning too). Looking forward to tonight.

I swallow. Twice. There's a rush through my body, which I'm pretty sure is most of my organs doing a happy dance. Definitely all the fun organs and body parts anyway.

I quickly tap out my reply.

Are you looking forward to tonight because there's a new episode of Naked and Afraid *to watch?*

Brandon's reply comes back almost immediately. *I'm actually looking forward to doing my own show titled* Naked and Horny.

I groan, my fingers speeding as I reply. *That's awful. Truly, truly awful.*

But it made you smile, didn't it?

Damn. I can't deny there's a large smile on my face

Maybe. But that says more about my automatic smile reflexes than your sense of humor.

Let's talk more about some of your reflexes tonight.

Seriously, I'd say quit while you're ahead, but you've been behind for a while now.

Suddenly I realize that putting the words 'head' and 'behind' into a conversation with Brandon is never a safe thing, so I quickly tap out another message.

And if you manage to turn my last comment into something suggestive I refuse to come over tonight.

I'm not saying anything then ☺

I can't help the flutter of happiness that goes through me. Which is then followed by the twins of wariness and cold, hard reality clapping me over the head.

What am I doing?

If I was smart I'd stop this thing right now because it's never going to lead anywhere. Brandon and I make absolutely no sense together as a couple.

But maybe this is what I need to help me recover from my past? A quick fling with a hot football player. It's probably worth a few sessions of therapy, at least.

And why shouldn't I? I'm young. I'm single. The sex was amazing. I know Brandon well enough to trust he's not going to hurt me. He's made it obvious he wants this thing to continue.

All those are reasons why I should go to Brandon's apartment tonight.

And what's the negatives? It could turn awkward between us? The football season starts in a few months anyway, and then he won't be around nearly as much.

No, my concern isn't about any potential awkwardness in the future. It's the old familiar standby that I feel any time I'm starting something new with a guy.

I'm scared of getting hurt.

But actually, my chances of getting hurt here are less than if I started a relationship with someone like Fraser.

With Fraser, I'd immediately be invested and planning out our future together. But with Brandon, I'll be able to keep my expectations of happily-ever-after under control, because ultimately I know Brandon and I are just too different to ever make it as a couple long-term. So, if I know from the start that Brandon is just Mr. Right Now and treat him as such then I'll be fine. Right?

I finish loading the washing machine and switch it on. The machine starts to whirl. Just like my head.

I manage to finish editing my article that afternoon. Then, ignoring the knowing smirks from Josh, I head to my room to get ready.

What do I wear to go to Brandon's place? Do I get dressed up? What's appropriate attire in this situation? Does Google know?

Eventually I settle on jeans and my cream sweater. A little more dressy than normal for a Sunday night for me, but given Sunday nights are usually a sweatpants zone the bar isn't that high.

Josh is sitting on the couch as I go to leave.

"You off somewhere?" he asks.

I fiddle with my keys. "Yeah."

The silence and Josh's smirk both grow in a linear relationship.

"Are you going to make me ask?"

"I'm going to Brandon's place," I mutter.

"So, this thing with Brandon is continuing, is it?"

"It appears so."

Josh's smirk is back. "Don't worry, in the history of surprises it's not ranking that high up there."

"I'm so glad I'm providing you with amusement," I say as I head to the door.

"Tell my brother that he and I need to have a little chat at some point," Josh calls after me.

The doorman at Brandon's apartment is the same one as last night. He greets me with a raised eyebrow. "Good evening, Megan," he says in his smooth voice.

"Um, hi...I'm here to see Brandon Seaton again."

"I know. You've been added to his approved list. Go on up." He gives me a knowing smirk.

"Oh...thanks."

I'm feeling awkward as I ride up in the elevator. I wipe my palms on my jeans.

Have I made the right decision coming here tonight?

I knock lightly on the door. It's so different from my knock last night, when I was demanding entrance so I could argue with him. This time my knock is tentative, with a what-the-hell-am-I-doing sentiment built in.

Brandon opens the door. His smile is a slow burn, starting in the center of his lips but spreading out until it's engulfed his entire face. It's a smile that slays all the concerns and doubts inside me.

"Hey," he says.

"Hey," I reply.

He doesn't allow any time for my doubts to replenish. He leans down and kisses me deeply, crushing his body against mine in a way that has me breathless when we pull apart.

Okay, it was totally the right decision.

CHAPTER 26

BRANDON

THERE IS one downside to this thing with Megan, and I discover it when I stumble out of her room on the fourth morning we're together—and come face to face with my brother.

So far we've been hanging out at my apartment and I've been avoiding Josh like I normally avoid getting sacked behind the line of scrimmage.

But last night, Megan decided she was sick of having to wake up extra early so she could make it to work on time. And given I'm the one who has a much more flexible schedule I couldn't really argue.

Josh wasn't home last night when I arrived at the apartment late, and I had a wild hope he'd sleep in and I'd manage to avoid him. No such luck.

And now the full implications of sleeping with my brother's roommate are coming home in the judgmental stare of my brother.

"Hey," I say cautiously.

"Hey." Josh's tone gives nothing away. He's bleary-eyed and his hair sticking up at the back in a way I'm all too familiar with as he pours himself some cereal at the counter.

Megan's in the shower and I was planning on making her breakfast. After all, I bear quite a bit of responsibility for the fact she's running late this morning. I decide to continue with my plan, stepping past Josh to retrieve bread from the pantry and putting it in the toaster. I'm concentrating on getting my timing right with the temperamental toaster so it cooks it enough but doesn't burn it, which requires the reaction speed of an air-traffic controller, when Josh clears his throat.

"Are we going to talk about this?"

"Talk about what?" I'm not stupid enough to believe the playing dumb strategy is going to work, but I'm willing to give anything a try at this point.

If Josh tells me he's not comfortable with Megan and me, what am I going to do? I mean, I haven't even had a conversation with Megan about where this is heading yet.

"Um...maybe talk about the fact you're hooking up with my roommate?"

It's funny, but part of me instantly wants to argue with him when he uses the term hooking up. Because it feels wrong to dismiss this thing like that. Sex with Megan continues to blow my mind. Up until now, sex has always felt like a performance. An incredibly enjoyable performance, don't get me wrong, but still something where I'm thinking about my moves, making sure I'm at the top of my game. I've always felt expectations, like it's completely up to me to make sure my partner is having a good time.

But sex with Megan is totally different. With her, half the time it descends into laughter. I never realized humor was such a turn on.

"Are you officially together now?" Josh presses.

I busy myself putting some more bread into the toaster. "Um...we haven't really talked about it."

His eyebrows shoot up again. "You haven't talked about it? What have you been doing in all that time you've been spending together?" There's a layer of laughter in his voice.

"How have I never realized what a jackass you are?" I give him a withering glare as I butter the toast.

"So, is it just hooking up, or is it actually something more?" I can see Josh isn't going to leave this alone.

I'm trying to work out how to answer him when Megan comes in.

Shit.

Her face doesn't show if she's heard Josh's question. Or my lack of response to it.

"Here's your toast." I hand the plate to her.

"Thank you—you didn't have to do that."

"You know me, I live to please."

"If that's the case, then I suggest you need to work harder to achieve your life mission," Megan chips back.

I grin at that, but the grin fades slightly when I see Josh watching us with the same focus he usually has when he's reading about a new scientific breakthrough.

Megan takes a bite of her toast and chews it. The toaster pops again and I turn my attention to making my own breakfast. The sound of my knife scraping across the toast only seems to amplify the silence in the kitchen.

"So, what's on your agenda today? Still doing your Dianne Marshall prep?" I ask Megan, keeping my voice casual.

"Yeah, but I also need to pitch some more story ideas for the next issue. Dan has been big about us doing some more popular science stuff—you know, articles with broader appeal that explain the science behind everyday life. They think they need to grow readership. That's why he was so enthusiastic about my idea on the animal training stuff. I need more ideas like that."

"What about something about the difference between people's microbiomes," Josh suggests.

This is good. This is the three of us having a normal conversation, just like always.

"Yeah, maybe. Although, I don't know if that's going to be mainstream enough," Megan says.

"Why don't you do something on the science behind athlete training?" I ask. "You should see the high-level analysis my trainers do that goes into my conditioning. I can get you an interview with the Goliaths' head trainer if you like."

Megan's eyes widen. "That is actually a really great idea."

Triumph rushes through me but I school my face. "You don't need to sound so surprised," I grumble. "I'm pretty sure you've liked some of my other ideas recently."

Megan tries to restrain her laugh. "You do occasionally raise some concepts worth investigating," she admits, scrunching up her nose in a cutesy smile.

I can't help winking in return.

When I look at Josh, his brow is furrowed as his gaze darts between us.

"Actually, I think that could really work," Megan continues to muse. "I could do a whole series of articles looking at how the different sports use science for their training. Dan's a big sport fan, so I think he'll go for it."

"Dan is obviously a man of impeccable taste."

Megan rolls her eyes at that. She glances at her watch. "I'm running late. I'm just going to brush my teeth."

"Yeah, your breath is a little rank," I say.

She shoulder nudges me as she goes past. "You didn't seem to mind this morning."

"I definitely didn't mind anything this morning," I reply. Her gaze heats, and we have one of those little moments that are fast becoming a Megan-Brandon specialty.

Josh clears his throat.

Oh shit.

Megan's face flushes as she heads to the bathroom.

I start to stack her dishes in the dishwasher. It's weird how I'm into all this domestic shit now. But I enjoy the day-to-day hanging out with Megan almost as much as I enjoy what happens in the bedroom.

"Okay, so I guess I'm shelving my 'don't mess around with her' speech," Josh says finally.

"What do you mean?" I grab the dishwasher powder and sprinkle a liberal amount in.

"I mean, you've just answered my question."

"What question?"

"About how serious you guys are."

"What?" I look up at him in surprise.

He doesn't have a chance to elaborate because Megan comes back.

"See you guys later." She raises her eyes to me.

"Tonight?" I ask.

"Yeah, okay." She puts her bag on her shoulder then hesitates, her eyes flashing to Josh.

"You're actually thinking about leaving without kissing me?" I ask.

She rolls her eyes as she comes forward and gives me the world's quickest kiss on my cheek.

I trap her against the counter before she manages to retreat. Blocking out my brother's presence, I focus solely on Megan. "You can do better than that."

"So now you're grading me on my kissing ability?"

"No. You've already received top marks for that. You're the champion of champions. I just want you to give me a masterclass demonstration."

She puffs out a laugh. "And what Brandon Seaton wants, he gets, right?"

"That does seem to be the way the world works," I agree, mock-seriously. "Please Megan? I really need your tutorage."

She shakes her head. "I honestly can't believe the stuff that comes out of your mouth sometimes." But there's a grin on her face as she closes the distance between us.

She lingers slightly longer this time, although it's very much still a PC, doing-in-front-of-someone kiss.

"Satisfied?" she asks as she pulls away.

"Very." I say and Megan rolls her eyes.

"I almost feel I need disinfectant after witnessing that conversation," Josh says.

"Right, some of us have jobs to get to," Megan says.

"See you tonight."

I avoid my brother's gaze as I close the dishwasher and turn it on.

When I finally look up, he's staring at me like I'm some alien species.

"I didn't think I'd live to see this day."

"And what day is that?"

"When you're gaga over a girl."

"Gaga? What level of gaga? The Lady kind or the stuck-in-a-retirement-home kind?"

Josh snorts. "Seriously though, I mean it's obvious you're into her. Don't you think you should talk to her about it?"

I don't tell Josh that I'm trying to avoid having that

conversation with Megan. Because I get the feeling she's taking this thing a whole lot less seriously than I am. "Yeah, maybe," I mumble.

"You need to be honest with her about what you want out of this."

Yep, Josh preaching to me about honesty in a relationship. That's got to be a new low point.

"I don't know what I want," I say.

But Josh gives me his little brother I-know-when-you're-talking-bullshit stare. "Yeah, I think you do. Just talk to her about it. Make sure you're both on the same page. Especially with your free agency decision coming up. Have you guys talked about that? About whether you'd stay together if you move to another city?"

I shrug. "It probably won't matter. I don't know yet if anyone else is prepared to offer me more than the Goliaths."

"What will you do if you get a huge offer from another franchise?"

His words make me feel like I've been tackled and winded, and I struggle to keep my face neutral. "I guess I'll worry about that if it actually happens."

CHAPTER 27

MEGAN

I PITCH the idea of doing an article on the science behind athlete conditioning, and my editor loves it. Between beginning my background research on that plus preparing my interview questions for Dianne Marshall, I have a fruitful and productive morning. I love my job, and times like today it's hard to believe I get paid to learn about such interesting stuff.

"You killed it in the editorial meeting today," Ashley tells me at lunch.

"Thanks. I really like your idea about doing an article on plastics in the food chain." I fork another piece of spinach into my mouth. "Some of my contacts from my Great Plastic Garbage Patch article might be useful for you."

"That would be fantastic," Ashley says. "Do you want to go to a bar tonight, discuss it over drinks?"

"I can't tonight. Sorry. I've already got plans." I concentrate on my salad.

When I look up, Ashley's studying me with a curious look. I don't know how she does it, but she has a knack for identifying anything I'm trying to conceal and zooming in on it.

Sure enough, the next words out of her mouth are, "What are you up to?"

"I'm hanging out with Brandon." I mumble the words in the hope that she won't understand them. No such luck.

Amusement flickers in her eyes. "So, those sparks between you are still flying then?"

"Um...you might say that those sparks have kind of ignited." My face flames as I say the words. "It's just a casual thing," I add quickly as her eyes widen. "We're too different. It's never going to be anything more than fooling around."

She spoons some yogurt into her mouth, still studying me. "You know the science behind casual sex, right?" she finally asks after she swallows.

I crease my forehead. "What science are you referring to?"

She shrugs. "It offends my feminist principles to say this, but the science ain't all that pretty for us women when it comes to hookups. Oxytocin screws around with us. Look it up."

I follow her instructions and do a quick Google search on my phone. She's right.

Orgasms release oxytocin into the bloodstream, which is a bonding hormone. So often people enter into a casual relationship, only to find themselves catching not-so-casual feelings. Apparently a third of all friends-with-benefits arrangements ends with one of the partners falling in love.

But the article points out that not everyone is affected the same way, and knowing the biology means you can protect yourself against the most unpalatable STI —emotions.

Ashley watches me read everything, an eyebrow cocked. "It's just casual," I say firmly. "I can keep it casual."

I have to remind myself of the fact that I'm keeping it casual when I see Brandon that night. Even if Brandon and I are only having a quick fling, I'm enjoying being flung.

Sex with Brandon continues to be the most spectacular of my existence. There is one massive advantage to dating a professional athlete. Stamina. That's all I'm saying.

But it's not just the duration that makes it so good. Brandon is surprisingly sweet in the bedroom. Always focused on what I want. And he's interested in talking to me afterwards in a way that no other guy has ever been.

We're lying in my bed after just having finished an epic encounter. He's got his arms around me and is stroking my hair. "Let's play twenty questions," he says.

"Because we're having a sleepover at summer camp?" I mock.

"Nope, because it'll mean we'll find out stuff about each other that we don't already know."

I'm not sure why my pulse has quickened at the thought of being interrogated by Brandon, but I'm looking for an excuse not to play. "We already know lots of stuff about each other." It's true. I know Brandon way better than any of the guys I've slept with.

"Indulge me."

"Didn't I already do that?" I smirk. God, now I'm making comments laced with innuendo. I really have been spending too much time with him.

He leans forward to plant a kiss on my forehead, his

breath warm. "Yes, and you did it very well. But I want to know more about what makes Megan tick."

I force my muscles not to tense. "Fine. What kind of stuff do you want to know?"

"Who was your first kiss?" Brandon asks. My breath catches at his line of questioning, and I take a few seconds to steady it before I answer.

"Zac Adams. Space camp. I was fourteen. It was a bit of a disaster."

"Why was it a disaster?"

I risk a glance over at him. "Uh...because we both had braces, and the wires caught together."

Brandon loses it, laughing so hard that I think he's going to do an injury to himself.

I scowl. "Let me guess, you never had braces?"

"Nope, perfect teeth." He shows off those teeth in a smile, still chuckling.

I roll my eyes. "Of course. So who was your first kiss? Was it perfect, to match your teeth?"

He snorts. "Not really."

He tells me about kissing Veronica Lambert at the middle school dance and how he thought it was great, but she ran back to her friends and complained he hadn't used his tongue, and he was confused because he had no idea why you would use your tongue to kiss someone.

I listen and smile in the right places, but my stomach is clenching. I'm bracing myself for his next question. Are we going to move from first kiss stories to discussing who we lost our virginity to? Will I share that story if he asks? I'm pretty sure he's not going to laugh if I tell that particular tale.

I decide to head him off at the pass. "I've got a question for you," I say after he finishes.

"What?"

"What's really your biggest fear?"

"My biggest fear?"

"You know how you told me on the first night that your biggest fear was heights? And yeah, I know you don't like heights, but there's something you fear more—right?"

He props himself onto an elbow. "How do you know that?"

"I have supreme psychic powers."

He continues to stare at me. Brandon's got this intense stare that's the definition of skeptical. I've seen him use it on Josh a few times, and now I feel its full power. It makes you want to confess everything.

"I did an article on body language last year on all the ways you can tell someone is lying," I admit.

"Oh. Right." He flops back down and looks at the ceiling. "I guess my biggest fear is failure," he says finally. "And looking stupid."

"That's so normal."

"What, were you expecting something more exciting? Like an irrational fear of mutant hens pecking my eyes out?" He wiggles his eyebrows.

"Well, yeah, that would be way more original and interesting."

He props himself up on an elbow. "My fear of looking stupid comes from a traumatic spelling bee instance in sixth grade when I forgot how to spell school in front of my entire class. Is that original and interesting enough for you?"

I screw up my nose. "Nah, I'm pretty sure most people have a traumatic spelling bee moment."

"Not you though, right?

"My nickname in elementary school might have been 'Dictionary'," I admit.

"Of course it was." A grin edges up his mouth and around his eyes.

I'm always intrigued by the way the skin by his eyes crinkles up when he smiles. Before I can help myself, I reach out and brush the creases with my fingertips.

Brandon freezes under my touch. "Um...what are you doing?"

"I'm feeling your eye smile," I say, withdrawing my hand like I've been scalded.

"Feeling my eye smile?" He quirks an eyebrow. "That has to be the weirdest thing anyone has ever said to me in bed."

Things women have said to Brandon in bed. My good mood evaporates faster than boiling water.

Yeah, not what I want to spend time thinking about. All the women who have come before me, and all the women who will come after me.

Somehow, Brandon has never made me feel self-conscious about how I compare to the string of beautiful women I'm sure have been in his bed before me. He's never said anything like "Wow, I've never been with anyone whose breasts flop like that" or "Actually this position isn't such a great idea—I mean, it would be great if you were taller but I'm going to do myself an injury if I have to stretch that far."

But I don't want to think about how I'm just another notch on a jock's bedpost. A unique notch, though. Misshapen compared to the other notches.

I pull the covers up around me, tucking the soft cotton across my shoulders.

What am I doing?

This is supposed to be about the sex. I'm supposed to just enjoy the chance to be with a super-hot guy, not worry about where I fit in the succession through his bed. And that super-hot guy being a jock—a professional football player no less—is supposed to be helping me exorcise some demons that linger from my past.

Worrying about Brandon's other hookups is definitely not part of the plan.

Is this what Ashley was warning me about? After a few orgasms, am I now starting to become too attached to Brandon? It appears I need to consult with the patron saint of casual sex.

I've gone too quiet, and Brandon's eying me with concern. "What are you thinking about?"

"Nothing."

"Uh-oh, you've gone into Megan lockdown mode."

He reaches out to stroke the side of my face then trails it down my neck and sneaks under the covers.

My breath starts to quicken.

"Luckily I know the secret code to unlock a Megan lockdown," he whispers as he moves closer and brushes his lips over mine.

It would take a force stronger than gravity to stop me kissing him back.

CHAPTER 28

BRANDON

THE FREE AGENCY negotiating window is only a few days away, and I feel like I'm walking around with a ticking time bomb inside my guts.

I can't go near the internet or TV without stumbling across a multitude of talking heads speculating about what I'm going to do. It occurs to me that instead of switching off quickly, maybe I should actually tune in and see what the experts are predicting. After all, I've got absolutely no idea what's going to happen. Maybe they could give me an insight?

Up until now everything has been straightforward in my football career. Choosing colleges was easy, because Penn State had a great program and offered me a full scholarship. Then, declaring for the draft after college was a no-brainer, and while getting drafted to the Goliaths was awesome I didn't actually have any control over it.

Both with college and professional football, I just needed to do what I've always done—put my head down, work hard, and let the rest work itself out. In some ways I love the simplicity of football. You follow what your coach says in training, play your hardest, and follow the plays in the game. Just do your best. It's all the off-field bullshit that does my head in. Especially now, with the biggest decision of my career so far looming.

I head to Frank's office, hoping a discussion with him will help soothe my nerves.

"Here he is!" Frank ushers me to his couch as soon as I walk in. "Not too long to wait now."

"Yeah, I know."

Frank's eyebrows bunch together as he studies me. "You holding up okay? I know it's an anxious time—but remember, you're the one in control in this process."

"I'm only in control if teams want me," I point out.

Frank waves away my comment dismissively. "Oh, trust me, you're going to get more offers than an ice cream vendor in the Sahara."

"We'll see."

He leans back, giving me a quick onceover. "You're looking good. I take it you've been keeping up condition in the off-season?"

"Yeah, I've been working out lots." Both in and out of the bedroom, but Frank doesn't need the finer details.

Frank snaps his fingers. "Before I forget, ABS Studios have just called me, wanting to know if you would participate in a celebrity quiz show they're filming."

"A quiz show?" My heart starts to beat faster. "It's not really my thing."

"They'll donate the money to a charity of your choice."

I hesitate. Shit. I don't want to say no when I know how much the Active Coaches organization could use the extra money. And it's not just the money—the extra exposure they'll get if I'm on TV talking about them will be priceless.

"Okay," I say reluctantly.

"Great. I'll let them know."

I feel like I've just agreed to wrestle a *T. rex*.

I might not be smart, but I know some people who are. Megan and Josh will help me practice. It'll be just like football, right? You put in the training, you get into the right condition, and you succeed.

And to be a success in this I don't need to win the thing. I just need to not embarrass myself on national television.

Frank is looking at me with a contemplative look on his face. "So, you know I'm not officially allowed to talk to teams until Monday..."

"Yeah, I know." From the way he's trailed off, I'm guessing he's got more to say.

"But I was wondering how you'd feel about a bit of California sunshine?"

I widen my eyes.

"Lots of rumors coming from credible sources that the Bighorn front offices are seriously interested," Frank explains.

"Really?"

"They've got the second biggest cap space this year. They're looking to secure some serious talent. I'm hearing rumors they're also looking at Deek Taylor as receiver."

I blow out a breath. Deek Taylor is probably the number one receiver in the league. He'd be amazing to play with.

"We'll know in a few days' time what numbers they're prepared to throw around. Potentially it'll be more than the Goliaths can match, so you might have a big decision on your hands."

"Shit...I mean, wow."

"I tell you, kid, now's the time to cash in." Frank claps me on the back. "Have your phone with you at all times on

Monday. I'll let you know the moment I have anything concrete. I get the feeling my phone is going to be buzzing like an angry wasp on Monday morning."

I leave Frank's office, my mind swirling.

I should be fucking ecstatic, I know that. A top team potentially wants me. They're prepared to pay me what I'm worth. And it's a major-market team too, with championship prospects. Every professional sportsperson fears being stuck in a small-market team that's bottom of the league when they're in the prime of their career.

If Frank's right and the Goliaths want to re-sign me plus other top teams are interested, then I'm sitting pretty—in complete control over where I go.

So why does the prospect of another championship contender being interested in me make me feel like a giant squid has wrapped itself around my chest and is slowly squeezing the life out of my lungs?

The truth is simple. I don't want to leave New York.

A few months ago I didn't care much one way or the other. My preference was to stay with the Goliaths because it's familiar, but I was prepared to go wherever was best for my career.

But now...now things have potentially changed.

CHAPTER 29

MEGAN

I'M TRYING REALLY REALLY HARD NOT to think about things with Brandon. Just go with the flow—enjoy the experience without analyzing it to death.

Unfortunately, successfully doing that means undergoing a complete personality transplant, but hey, I'm trying.

Like this afternoon. Brandon turned up to hang out at the apartment and we ended up in bed together. But I'm not thinking about how we've seen each other every day for the last few weeks. I'm not thinking about how good it feels to be curled up in his arms, making each other laugh by coming up with our own reality TV show concepts.

I'm not thinking about any of that.

Brandon eventually detaches himself from me and heads for the shower. I get up and go to the kitchen to grab myself a drink of water. Josh is in the kitchen and greets me with a knowing smirk. I can see some smart-ass comment brewing on his lips. It's cut off by a knock on our door.

"You expecting anyone?" Josh asks.

"No. You?"

He shakes his head.

I eye the door suspiciously. People don't generally turn up unannounced in this city. I do what any good New Yorker would do and put on the safety chain as I open up the door a smidge.

"Surprise!" I recognize my mother's voice before I have a chance to focus on the couple standing there.

Mom has this thing about surprises. Which was cool when she threw me a surprise pool party for my seventh birthday.

It's not so cool right now. Especially with a naked Brandon in the shower only ten feet away.

"Mom, Dad." I open up the door and stand there, blinking to make sure my eyes are working properly. "What are you doing here?"

Mom wraps me up in a large hug. "Dad's just finished a conference in Boston. We decided to come here afterwards and surprise you!"

"I'm definitely surprised," I say weakly.

"Aren't you going to invite us in?"

"Um...sure, come on in." I back out of the way. Mom bustles into the apartment, Dad trailing after her.

Even though my parents are dressed in their sophisticated "city" clothes, they still look out of place in my apartment. Dad's jeans have been ironed so a crease up the back is still evident. Mom's hair looks freshly permed, because our neighbor Janice who does Mom's hair is still stuck in the 80s when she did her hairdressing course.

I feel a squeeze of affection for them. My parents never change. They may be different from me, but all science experiments need constants. It's a nice thing in my life that I get to have my parents as a constant.

Josh is standing at the kitchen, looking like a startled vole.

"Mom, Dad," I say in a loud voice, hoping Brandon will hear from the bathroom. "This is my roommate, Josh."

"Hi, Josh. We've heard so much about you." Mom smiles.

I manage to suppress my groan. In the early weeks after moving here I'm sure I spent a disproportionate part of my phone calls home talking about my great new roommate, and I'm not surprised Mom jumped to the obvious conclusion that I liked him.

And now I'm hooking up with his brother. Fantastic. That's going to be a fun one to explain.

Mom exclaims over how cute the living area is, while Josh and I exchange a frantic conversation with our eyes.

Have you told your parents about what's going on with Brandon?

Hell, no. I don't even know what's going on with Brandon, so I'm not about to start trying to explain it to my parental unit.

Will they recognize Brandon when he comes out of the shower?

Given my father is the biggest football fanatic in the state of Oklahoma, and possibly the world, then yeah, I think there's a chance he'll recognize the starting quarterback of the Goliaths.

It'd just be like Brandon to come out of the shower wearing a towel, drop it, and proposition me. He'd see it as a double win, being able to gross Josh out and get my girly bits going at the same time.

As Mom moves her inspection to the kitchen, my eyes slip to the counter.

Oh, shit.

Josh has decided over the past week that it's funny to

arrange Science Barbie and Football Ken on a center spot in increasingly lewd positions.

When Brandon saw this particular one earlier he'd raised his eyebrows suggestively and said, "Hey, that's one position we haven't tried yet." Which led to more comments from Josh about bleaching brains etc. and us making a quick exit to my bedroom.

I move quickly to the counter and *accidentally* knock the dolls onto the ground, then reach down to pick them up. When I straighten back up, Mom's eyeing me curiously.

"Why do you have Barbie and Ken dolls?" she asks.

"Um...inside joke."

There's the sound of a door opening and feet padding down the hallway.

I seize up, sending a panicked glance at Josh. *What the hell am I going to do?*

I haven't come up with any answers when Brandon appears in the living room. He's wearing only his tracksuit pants but no top, his sculptured body on full display, his hair still damp.

"Hey, Brandon, look who's here—it's Megan's parents," Josh says quickly.

"Oh, hi." He comes to an abrupt stop, his eyes darting to me.

"This is Josh's brother, Brandon," I say reluctantly.

My dad is standing close to him, so he goes to shake his hand. I can see the exact moment when my father realizes he's shaking the hand of the starting quarterback for the New York Goliaths.

"Hang on a sec, you're...." He trails off, looking at me in bewilderment, like he wants independent confirmation that his eyes are seeing what he thinks they're seeing.

"I'm Brandon."

"Brandon Seaton," Dad squeaks. I haven't heard his voice that high-pitched since the day my brother Keaghan accidentally smacked him in the balls with a baseball bat.

"Um...yeah." Having dropped Dad's hand, Brandon now runs his own through his hair, sending another glance at me. I don't know how to interpret that glance. Is he freaked out that he's having to meet my parents? Especially since it's merely minutes after he was in bed with their daughter?

Mom's standing next to me in the kitchen, her eyes widening. "You never told us Josh's brother is Brandon Seaton," she says in a stage whisper.

"Didn't I?" I say weakly.

"I mean, you told us all about Josh, but you failed to mention that one fact."

Oh, God. If I had a button to make my mother stop talking I would be pressing the thing as hard as possible now.

"Is this part of your vendetta against football?" she continues.

"I think she's slowly working her way past that vendetta," Josh says with a hint of a smirk. "There're some aspects of football you now like, aren't there, Megan?"

"Some," I mutter, throwing him a glare.

The room is suddenly infected with awkward silence. Brandon and Josh both seem to be looking at me, obviously expecting me to break it, but I have no idea what to say. How are you supposed to introduce your parents to the concept of your celebrity hookup? Are there etiquette books that cover this?

"Well, as nice as it is to meet my brother's roommate's parents, I'd better get going," Brandon finally says.

"You might want to put on a shirt before you leave," Josh suggests.

Brandon looks down at his bare chest in surprise. "Oh, yeah. Right."

I seize up. His shirt is in my room. He doesn't look at me as he heads down the hallway, his expression schooled into neutral.

My parents stare after him then turn to look at me, their faces still the definition of incredulous.

"Anyway, what are your plans while you're in town?" I ask brightly.

Mom shakes her head, seeming to need to mentally adjust before she answers me. "We thought we'd take you out to the theater. We've got tickets to *Hamilton* tonight."

"Sounds great," I reply a tad too enthusiastically.

Brandon comes back wearing one of Josh's shirts. The shirt is tight across his chest, but I'm not sure if that is why his shoulders seem stiff. Luckily my parents don't think to ask why Brandon showered at his brother's apartment.

"It was really nice to meet you," Brandon says to my parents. He flicks a glance at me, and there's something in his expression that cuts at me. Deeply.

"So lovely to meet you too, Brandon. We can't wait to tell the folks back home all about this. They won't believe us!" Mom says.

"See you later, Brandon," I say brightly, avoiding eye contact.

I don't want to see whatever it is that's in Brandon's gaze.

∽

It's nice to go to the theater. It reminds me I don't take advantage of all the opportunities living in New York provides. It's so easy to get caught up in day-to-day living and forget all the cool cultural experiences this city has on offer.

I try to relax and enjoy the visual spectacle in front of me, yet I can't get Brandon's expression out of my head. I get the feeling that not introducing him to my parents properly hurt him some way, and I hate that. But what could I say? *"Mom and Dad, this is Brandon, the guy I've been casually having sex with for the last few weeks."* Because that would have been well received.

It's not helped when at intermission my mother does her interrogation of my love life, while all my father wants to talk about is Brandon's stats and how great he is.

After I get back to the apartment I receive a message from Brandon. *Can I come over?*

Although I'm tired, I'm never going to turn Brandon down. There are parts of my body that would never speak to me again. But I also have a deep urge to see him—to still that thing squirming away inside me every time I remember his expression earlier.

I'm already in bed when he arrives. "Hey," I say softly. I've turned the lights off, so Brandon appears silhouetted against the light from the hallway. I can't see his expression.

"Hey." Brandon moves into the room. He strips off into his boxers and climbs into bed. He leans over to give me a kiss, and I find myself relaxing against his lips.

But I've barely started to enjoy the kiss when he pulls away from me.

"What's wrong?" I ask.

"I just wanted to talk to you about something."

My stomach clenches. "What?"

He hesitates for a few heartbeats. "Why did you introduce me to your parents just as Josh's brother?" he finally asks.

His question startles me. "What do you mean?"

"I mean, why didn't you introduce me as your boyfriend?"

At his words, some strange feelings start establishing a home in my chest. Happiness and fear appear to be moving in together. "Boyfriend?" I splutter.

"Yes, boyfriend." He bites his lip, and there's a flicker of vulnerability on his face.

I find my voice. "I didn't really think we'd put a label on whatever this is."

"Megan, we've spent every single waking second when you're not at work together for the past two weeks. I've stayed every night. I've watched an entire series of *The Universe* with you, cooked you pancakes every morning when you felt like them, and brought you Advil when you had your period. You don't think that qualifies as a boyfriend?" There's an edge to his voice.

"But we've never really talked about it," I argue. "It felt presumptuous to call you my boyfriend when we haven't had that discussion yet."

"We're not in tenth grade anymore."

"For all I know I could have introduced you as my boyfriend and you would have freaked out, said 'I thought it was just casual sex' and bolted."

Brandon's face relaxes into a grin. "I definitely wouldn't have said that. Okay, Megan, let's do it your way. Would you like to be my girlfriend?"

I look at his smiling face and the fear flickers out, leaving behind only happiness. Because he's right. The way we are together, it's already into boyfriend-and-girlfriend territory. Somehow we've stumbled there without discussing official labels. Yet everything in the last two weeks between us has been so easy, so...right.

"Um...let me just weigh up the pros and cons of that idea." My tone is teasing, and I put on an exaggerated thinking face. My hesitation lasts for so long that Brandon tackles me, and then we're doing things that boyfriends and girlfriends usually do to each other.

"Yes," I gasp out at an opportune moment. "Yes, I'll be your girlfriend."

Late night booty calls are all well and good, but it means sleep is often deprived. Which means you tend to oversleep the next morning to catch up.

Which isn't a good idea when you agreed the night before to have breakfast with your parents.

I'm jolted back into consciousness by a discreet knocking at my door. It's Josh.

"Um...Megan. Your parents are here," he says through the wood.

My parents are here. I run that phrase sleepily through my head a few times before the analysis is complete and I sit up with a jolt.

Shit.

I look over at Brandon. He's on his side of the bed, still asleep, doing this squinty-frowny thing in his sleep, one side of his hair sticking up like it's spent the night doing the friction thing with the pillow.

He's my boyfriend.

My boyfriend, the celebrity football player.

Yeah, I don't have time to unpack that now.

I frantically throw on jeans and a T-shirt, running my hands through my hair to get the waves into some kind of order.

Josh is being a fabulous roommate and entertaining my parents in the living room when I emerge.

"Sorry. I overslept," I say.

"You've never been a morning person," Mom says with a smile. It's funny how she can think affectionately of that trait now, given the amount of time she used to spend bellowing up the stairs for me to get out of bed when I was growing up.

"Are you ready to go for breakfast?" Dad asks.

"Sure."

We move toward the door and I'm just starting to relax, when Mom suddenly ducks back.

"Oh, you didn't show us your room last night."

She goes to push past me into the hallway, but without thinking I move to stop her. We end up playing a kind of game where she's trying to get past me but I'm preventing it. Brandon would have been proud of my blocking technique.

She pulls back in confusion. "What are you doing?"

"Someone is in there, okay?" I hiss.

"What do you mean, someone is in there?" Mom's brow is furrowed. Then realization dawns. "But," she splutters, "we left you at eleven o'clock last night. Please don't tell me you went out to a club and met some boy and brought him home after that."

My mother has always had an overinflated view about how exciting my life is in a big city.

I roll my eyes. "No, Mom, I didn't go out and hook up with some random guy. My boyfriend came over."

There it is. That word. Boyfriend.

Mom's eyebrows threaten to fly off her face. "You have a boyfriend?"

"Um...yeah. Kind of. Yes."

"Well, can we meet him?"

Shit. Shit. Shit.

"Um...well...you've kind of met him. It's just that..."

"I think she's trying to say that you met me yesterday. She just didn't introduce me properly." Brandon's voice interrupts my stammering.

He's leaning against the door frame of my room. He's pulled on a T-shirt, but he's still in his boxer shorts, looking every inch a hot jock. There's a reason why companies use him to sell underwear.

My father's mouth has dropped open. Forget flies, he could catch bald eagles in that thing.

Mom looks equally bewildered. "You're Megan's boyfriend?"

She looks around, and I'm sure she's trying to find the *Punk'd* or *Candid Camera* crew.

"Yes, I am," Brandon says.

There are a few moments of silence while my parents relocate their ability to talk.

"Oh, that's nice," Mom says finally, faintly. "Do you want to come to breakfast with us?"

I'll give my parents credit. They at least pretend that this is within the normal scope of their existence. Although I'm willing to bet if someone had told them before they left home that on this trip that they'd be having breakfast with their daughter's new boyfriend who was also a famous football star, they'd have been edging for the phone to report an escaped maniac to the police.

"So, Brandon, I guess we don't have to ask what you do," Dad says as we arrive at the restaurant.

It's a beautiful early spring day so the waitress shows us to a table outside on the sidewalk and hands over the menus. It's a full-day menu, which is good because my father has this thing about eating burgers and fries when he's out. He doesn't trust anything more advanced than that.

"No, I guess you don't." Brandon says, rubbing the back of his neck.

It occurs to me that he's nervous. Which is probably natural when you're doing the meet-the-parents thing. However, given the fact that my dad is looking at him like he's a cross between Babe Ruth and Muhammad Ali I think he's all good.

"But maybe we should ask who you're planning to work for?" Dad leans forward, his eyes glistening almost as much as his bald forehead.

"Dad," I groan.

"I'll look at the offers on Monday," Brandon says. "Hopefully I'll have some good ones on the table."

"You'd prefer to stay here though?"

Brandon flicks his gaze to me. "Yeah. New York is home."

I stare back at him. I haven't given much thought to the idea that Brandon might be signing with another team and moving. I haven't thought of the consequences if he decides to move.

Now we're officially in a relationship, maybe that's something I should be considering?

"What do you think of the commissioner's decision on the draft picks?" Dad asks.

"It'll be interesting to see if it helps small-market teams."

My father's face is alive with interest as he and Brandon discuss the news.

I start to relax, because maybe my parents can play this cool and not overreact.

"I can't wait to tell Keaghan you're dating Brandon Seaton. He'll be so excited," Mom says the moment their conversation lulls.

Brilliant. Great job of keeping it normal and low-key, Mom.

"Megan's brother Keaghan is really into football," Mom explains needlessly to Brandon. "So is her other brother, Mike, but Keaghan is obsessed."

"I already told him that," I mutter.

"Oh, so you've told him stuff about us yet never thought to tell us about him?" Mom shoots right back.

Luckily the waitress choses that moment to interrupt us to take our orders.

My parents and Brandon chat about football throughout the meal. My mom's not rabid about football like Dad and my brothers, but I think she figured early on in their marriage that if she wanted to spend time with my dad she had to become a sports fan.

Even though I knew Brandon would fit in perfectly with my family, it's still odd to observe it in real life. Seeing my parents laugh and joke with him does something funny to my insides.

I tune out of the conversation and instead watch as people scurry by on the sidewalk. This is what I love about New York—the constant pace and bustle, the feeling that things are always happening here. And spring happens to be my favorite season. The weather is warming up but not too hot, and the trees are just beginning to bud. Okay, so sitting here I get a whiff of that special New York street scent, where the predominant odor is car exhaust and garbage, with perhaps a hint of urine mixed in, but you can't have everything.

Brandon shoots a few glances at me during the conversation, as if he's worried about me being left out. I'm used to it though—this was pretty much my life growing up.

"Has Megan told you about the interesting article she's doing on athlete conditioning?" Brandon asks.

"Really?" Dad looks at me for the first time in five minutes.

"Yeah, I'm investigating the science behind their training regime. I've got interviews with some of the medical team at the Goliaths."

Interest is sparked in Dad's eyes. I try not to care too much that he's actually engaging in something that matters to me.

"If I didn't know better, I'd think she was using me for my contacts," Brandon says.

I stir my yogurt. "But you do know better," I point out. "I've made it perfectly clear I'm using you for your body."

My father splutters on his mouthful of coffee.

Oops. Things not to say in front of the parents, number one.

"I'm joking. I'm joking," I say quickly.

"She's only dating me until she invents her perfect man. Isn't that right, Megan?" Brandon says.

"Yes, I really should speed up the process," I say.

Brandon flashes his dimples at me and I scrunch my nose back at him.

Mom looks between us, eyes widening.

Brandon checks his watch. "I'd better dash. It's time I hit the gym."

"That's right. If you don't start exercising by midday your muscles will spontaneously combust, right?" I say.

"That's right. And no one wants to see that," he deadpans back.

He stands, shaking Mom's hand first and then Dad's. "It was so nice to meet you. I now know where Megan gets her intelligence, looks and charm from." He kisses me on the head. "I'll see you tonight."

"Okay." Great. I might as well tattoo a sign on my forehead in case my parents missed the subtext that their daughter is getting laid tonight.

As he leaves, he's stopped by some fans. We all watch as he poses for a picture with them, laughs, and then keeps on going.

Once he's left the restaurant my parents turn their attention to me.

"So, what do you think of Brandon?' I ask conversationally as I help myself to one of my father's French fries.

My father is shaking his head in disbelief. "My daughter is dating Brandon Seaton."

"Yes, Dad, I'm glad you picked that up."

"He's lovely," Mom says.

"I don't know if I'd go for lovely, but he's a nice guy."

"But I think you need to be careful."

I seize up. Of course my mother is going to warn me. She knows how many women throw themselves at him.

"That man is clearly besotted with you, Megan. You need to be careful not to hurt him."

I almost choke on the French fry I've just stuffed in my mouth. Like, literally. The waitress comes running over ready to give me the Heimlich maneuver and looks vaguely disappointed when she just has to settle for getting me a glass of water instead.

"Besotted?" I manage to get out after all the coughing and spluttering and reassuring is over and my face has changed back from red to somewhere in the peach-white spectrum it normally is. "We're just having some fun together, Mom."

"Fun? What do you mean by fun?"

Yeah, I'm pretty sure that parents don't need to know the intimate details of what constitutes my idea of fun.

"I mean, you can hold off on the wedding invitations. Brandon and I are very different people, so it's hard to imagine that we'd ever be a long-term thing."

I'm saying the words to myself as much as I'm saying them to her. Because it would be so easy to get swept up in this fairytale. After all, Brandon's my boyfriend now. He wants to be my boyfriend. He just did the very boyfriendy thing of charming my parents. But that doesn't change the fundamentals of who Brandon and I are.

Fear stirs in my stomach. By investing in this relationship with Brandon, am I risking getting hurt myself?

CHAPTER 30

BRANDON

IT'S MONDAY MORNING, and the negotiation window has officially begun. Also known as the legal tampering period, it's two days where franchises are allowed to talk to agents about contracts before the league year officially starts and contracts can be formally signed.

I'm holed up in my apartment because I really don't want to do anything to fuel the swirling rumors in cyberspace about where I'm going. If I'm seen eating a taco, some journalist will decide it means I'm going to sign with Texas, Arizona or New Mexico because it means I want to be near Mexico. If I eat a steak they'll think I'm considering the mid-West.

As I make myself some breakfast, I notice there's a book lying on the counter titled *Humble Pi – A Comedy of Math Errors*. It's pretty easy to guess who it belongs to.

Little traces of Megan are starting to appear around my apartment. We spent most of last weekend here because I got the feeling I was starting to wear out the welcome from my brother, especially when we forgot to lock the bathroom door and he walked in on us in the shower together.

There is some stuff that brothers don't need to see, no matter how close we are.

The weekend was incredible. Waking up together, cooking breakfast together, watching TV together. At one stage she was curled up on the couch reading while I watched a game of basketball, and as I gave her a foot massage I couldn't name the feeling that overwhelmed me. Something like peace, with a side order of happiness.

It's just so easy to hang out with her. And fun. Because she's always going to mock me and I'm always going to hassle her back. She makes me laugh. And I make her laugh too. And most of the time now she's laughing with me, not at me. That ratio is definitely improving.

My thoughts about Megan are interrupted by my ringtone.

Frank.

I snatch my phone up, my heart suddenly doing the medically impossible and relocating to my throat.

"Hey, Frank." I try to keep my voice relaxed, but I'm aware it must come across like I'm being garroted.

"Hey. I've just been talking to Simon Nixon."

Simon Nixon. General Manager of the Goliaths.

"Okay. And...?"

"They're offering you a four-year, sixty-million deal to re-sign. I'm doing my best, but with their salary cap I doubt I'm going to get much higher than that."

A surge of adrenaline flows through me. It's good. The Goliaths still want me, and they've offered me decent money.

This is the one contract I can actually sign right now, because they're my current team.

"You there?"

"Yeah, I'm here. That's good news." I give a shaky laugh.

"I was hoping we'd be talking upwards of seventy-five, because I think that's where your value is, but cap space is a big factor."

"I know."

"It's early days yet, though. Good to have this as a starting point, and I'm talking to other teams this morning."

I clear my throat. "Thanks."

"Talk soon." With that, Frank's gone.

My head's buzzing. Despite Frank's reassurances, I was still worried that my lack of playoff success would cost me, and the Goliaths would look to go in a different direction.

I breathe a sigh of relief as I shoot a quick text to Megan. *Goliaths have offered me a good deal.*

She sends me a whole lot of emoji smiley faces in return then quickly follows up with another message.

How good is it? Or do I really not want to know the inflated value our society puts on athletic achievement compared to the monumentally underfunded arts and sciences?

I bite down a grin as I message her back. *You probably don't want to know.*

That's the thing about dating Megan. I definitely will never get an unrealistic view of my own importance.

Okay, well congratulations. Celebrate tonight after the exhibit opening?

I've got tickets tonight to the opening of a new exhibit on bioluminescence at the science museum. Frank offered them to me, and unlike most of the free tickets he's forwarded on to me this off-season I decided to take them. I actually don't have a clue what bioluminescence is, but I'm sure Megan will explain it to me.

I message her back. *I'm sure we can come up with some creative ways to celebrate* 😉

Thanks for that. I'm sitting at my desk trying to write an article about the evolution of whales. Going to be fun to get myself back into that headspace.

I laugh out loud.

As I make myself a cup of coffee, my mind drifts to some of the ways Megan and I can potentially celebrate together. It's not an unpleasant way to pass the time.

When my coffee machine has done its thing I take my mug over to the couch. I can't resist grabbing my phone and scrolling through some of the speculation about what other franchises are interested in me. Now that the Goliaths are sewn up, it's ego stroking to see what the analysts are saying. It's always nice to be wanted.

My phone rings again. Frank.

"I'm just reading on *The Bleacher Report* that both Denver and New Mexico are potentially interested," I say.

"Yeah, they've made contact, but don't worry about that now. Because we've landed the big one."

My heard starts to pound. "How big?"

"I've just been talking to Jason Meyers from the Bighorns. They're talking four years, eighty million."

My breath leaves me, slammed from my lungs like I've been sacked by a three-hundred-pound linebacker.

"That would put you in the top five quarterback salaries," Frank tells me.

I actually don't need the reminder. I'm very familiar with the contracts for other quarterbacks in the league.

"It's big market, and a shitload of money. I don't think we're going to get any better than that."

"Yeah. Right." I swallow hard. "Okay...wow."

There's a pause as I try to get my head around this.

"Gotta admit, Brandon, you're not sounding like someone who's just been offered an incredible contract to play for a championship contender."

I force the words out of my throat. "I'm not sure I want to leave New York."

"I thought you were open to all possibilities?" There's no hostility in Frank's voice, only curiosity.

"Yeah, well, things have kind of changed."

"What things?"

"I've got a girlfriend."

Frank is silent for a few seconds. "Shit, Brandon, you're the last person I thought I'd have to advise not to let personal stuff get in the way of making good career decisions. How serious is it with your girlfriend? Would she relocate to LA with you?"

His questions make my mouth go dry. Because how serious are Megan and I? I'm pretty sure I can answer that question for myself, but I have no idea what Megan's thinking. We hadn't even agreed on our relationship title until the other day.

Don't get me wrong—I know Megan likes me. She definitely likes what we're doing together in the bedroom. And I know she likes spending time with me too. But it comes back to the basics. I'm a professional football player. She's a science journalist who hates football. On paper we have nothing in common.

And while it doesn't bother me, I don't know if Megan can look past that. Maybe she'll think that long-term she needs someone like that rocket scientist douchebag. Someone as smart as her. Someone who can talk about the stuff she's interested in.

"We're not at the point where I can ask her to relocate," I say.

"But you're at the point where you're going to make your decision based on her?" Frank's voice is dripping disbelief.

"I don't know. I've got to think it through."

Frank lets out a breath. "Right. Have a think and touch base with me later. I'll talk to Denver and New Mexico, but they don't have the cap space to offer you anything near what the Bighorns can."

"Okay, thanks."

I hang up. I hate the feeling that I'm disappointing Frank. That twenty million dollar difference is a lot of money.

But it gets to a point where money is just money, right?

I know I need to maximize the amount I earn now, because a football career is short in the scheme of my life. And I have no other skills besides throwing a football.

I follow Frank's instructions and think about it. A lot. I pace around my condo, wearing tracks in the carpet. I contemplate calling my parents for advice. But I haven't even told them about Megan and me yet. And although they've tried to hide the fact, I know deep down they agree with Megan that it's ridiculous how much I get paid just to throw a football. I could try talking to Josh, but he's going to ask me some hard questions my mind is currently shying away from.

Megan and I could potentially stay together even if I relocated. But it would place a lot of pressure on our relationship, especially at this stage. And she's already talked about how much she loves New York, how she fits in here. Imagining her in Los Angeles is like trying to imagine a tortoise living on the moon. I don't think I could ask her to relocate, even if we were serious. I'd be taking her away from the city she loves, a job she loves, to a place where once the season starts I'll be only there intermittently anyway. It just wouldn't be fair.

So what am I going to do?

~

I still haven't reached any decisions when I head out for my date with Megan. Of course she greets me with a huge hug when she sees me, enthusing about the Goliath's contract offer, joking about being scared to touch me now someone thinks I'm worth so much. The paparazzi are equally enthusiastic to see me and yell lots of questions as I usher us through to the museum's front door. Yeah, I really didn't think tonight through.

Still, I'm glad I didn't miss the look on Megan's face. She's practically vibrating with excitement as we show our tickets at the door. It's funny, because the few other girlfriends I've had swooned over flowers and chocolates and jewelry, but for Megan it seems nothing can top an exhibition opening at the science museum.

Inside, there are a few A-list celebrities mingling in the crowd. And a few more who would definitely make B and C lists of famous people.

But Megan's not at all interested in any level of the alphabet soup of celebrities surrounding us. Instead she heads straight for the exhibits.

"So what exactly is bioluminescence?" I ask, trailing after her.

"It's where creatures make their own light." She nods at the photo displays in front of us.

I have to admit, there are some pretty amazing photos of glow-in-the-dark animals. "It's like that scene from *Avatar*."

"Yeah, but these are actual creatures on planet Earth,"

Megan says.

I follow her around the exhibits, but I keep on getting intercepted by people who want to talk to me about football and free agency.

I get so sick of saying the same thing. "As negotiations are currently underway I'm not allowed to say anything at the moment."

I'm intercepted by the mayor, who talks about how next season is going to be the Goliaths' season and what a boon for the city it will be if we manage to bring home a championship, and how he wants me to be part of this.

As I'm listening to him rant my gaze finds Megan.

She's absorbed in reading some of the information attached to one of the exhibits. There's a little crease in her forehead that she always gets when she's concentrating, and she's squinting slightly because her eyes must be tired and she's forgotten her glasses. She has a secret smile playing on her lips though, as if nothing makes her happier than learning something new.

It's so Megan.

For some reason a weird feeling settles in my chest as I watch her. Too many of the people here tonight are just here to be seen. They don't care what the exhibit is about. But Megan is only interested in learning new things. Appearances and mingling are the last things on her mind.

I make my excuses to the mayor and head over to her.

"Sick of talking about free agency?" she asks as I come to stand next to her.

"I'm so far beyond sick I'm in intensive care right now."

"So, when are you going to sign the contract and put everyone out of their misery?"

Her question is completely innocent but it starts my heart pounding.

"Uh...soon..." I splutter. "Anyway, can we talk about something else? Tell me everything you know about bioluminescence."

Her smile shines. "It's actually so fascinating, all the different reasons why animals use bioluminescence. I mean, there are the obvious ones, like attracting prey or mates, but the vampire squid uses glowing ink to confuse predators. How cool is that?"

I have to clear my throat to answer her. "Yeah, that's pretty cool."

I force myself to look away from her and check out the photos. I notice a fish that has a peculiar glowing extension coming down from its forehead.

"I saw that one in *Finding Nemo!*" I say. "It almost ate Dory."

"It's amazing how much of your science knowledge comes from Disney and Pixar."

"Hey, don't knock my movie education," I say.

"You realize most of the creatures who are friends in animated movies would actually eat each other in real life, right?"

"What, you mean a lion isn't usually friends with a meercat and a warthog?" I clutch my chest in pretend surprise.

"Simba would have turned Pumba into pork chops in a New York minute."

"What exactly is a New York minute?" I ask. "I've always wondered that."

"It just means immediately. Because we live in the one city on earth that thinks it can redefine time."

This is one of the things I love about hanging out with Megan. You can never predict where the conversation is going to go.

She moves on to the next exhibit, a tank of jellyfish which are all lit up. Her face lights up even more than jellyfish. "Wow, these are incredible."

She turns to me, her eyes sparkling, and it's like I've been sucker punched.

I don't think I've ever found a woman more beautiful than Megan is in this moment.

I just stare at her.

"Isn't it stunning?" she breathes, turning back to watch the jellyfish again.

"Yeah, stunning." I agree. But it's not the jellyfish I'm looking at.

Stunning is the right word. Because it feels like I've been hit with a stun gun.

My dumbfounded feeling starts to fade, replaced by a certainty sweeping through me. I've only ever felt this sure a few times in my life before. It's always been on the football field when I've somehow instinctively known the perfect play to call, known what is going to get us through the defense and result in a touchdown.

I've got that exact same feeling now. I know the play that is going to win me the ultimate prize.

"I've...um...got to go make a call," I say.

"Okay." Megan's still watching the jellyfish in fascination.

I duck out into the hallway and head out into a stairwell and down a flight of stairs to where I've got complete privacy.

Before I can second guess myself, I call Frank.

"Tell the Goliaths I'll re-sign."

I hear Frank's uneven breathing on the other end of the phone. "You sure?"

"Yeah. I want to stay in New York."

CHAPTER 31

MEGAN

SO, it turns out that when your boyfriend signs a massive contract with the local NFL franchise it's a big deal. Even though I still have my football avoidance thing going on, I can't help some of the buzz around Brandon's re-signing with the Goliaths filtering into my existence. It's hard to ignore his name screaming out on newspaper headlines as I head to the subway in the morning. Apparently to the majority of the New York football-loving public, it's a huge relief that they get to watch him throw a football for another four years. And while I'm secretly as excited that Brandon's not leaving as the rest of New York, it has nothing to do with what happens on a 100-yard field.

"You'd think you'd singlehandedly saved the city from the bubonic plague," I say to him. We're at minigolf and have just endured the woman at the counter recognizing Brandon and spending the entire time she was sorting our clubs and balls gushing over him.

"Something like that," Brandon says. He tugs his cap further down over his eyes as we walk to the first hole. I can only hope the cap will obscure his vision and affect his performance. I'm a little competitive when it comes to minigolf.

"So, I'll give you a shot a hole, okay?" he says as he sets his ball down on the starting mat.

I may have suggested that Brandon has an unfair advantage when it comes to playing golf against me because he's a professional athlete. I've been arguing strongly that he needs to handicap himself in some way.

"Okay." I try not to smile too brightly.

The minigolf course theme is places around the world, and the first hole is Egyptian. Brandon hits the ball into the hole in three.

"Okay. With your extra shot, you've got four shots to get it in the hole to tie my score," he tells me.

"That sounds about fair," I reply.

I line up my shot, then hit the ball into the side, where it bounces cleanly off then comes back and hits the side of a pyramid, angling off at 60 degrees and stopping an inch from the hole. I tap it in for two.

"So, with the shot you're giving me every hole, I'm now two ahead, right?" I ask, looking up to find Brandon watching me, his eyes narrowing.

"How did you do that?"

I shrug. "Would you believe it's just luck?" Unfortunately I can't keep the triumphant look off my face.

"No. Not with you. You're some kind of minigolf shark, aren't you?"

"Minigolf is all about the angles. It's basically just math," I confess.

Brandon shakes his head but can't stop the grin edging up his face. "I should have known."

"Hey, don't mock my genius."

"I'm never going to mock your genius. After all, you're

with me." He pulls me in for a hug, planting a kiss on the side of my head before he releases me to place his ball down at the start of the second hole.

I try to pretend my heart isn't stuttering as I follow up behind him. This is the kind of stuff that sideswipes me about Brandon. These moments when he's affectionate, and it has nothing to do with what goes on in the bedroom.

We go through the first few holes, and I'm up four shots. Brandon's pretending mock disgust at how much I'm thumping him, and we're having an in-depth debate about whether omitting information is the same as cheating. But he can't hide his amusement. It's there in his eye smile. The irregularity of my heartbeat continues.

Unfortunately we're going fast, and soon catch up with a group of four guys in front of us.

We're waiting patiently for them to finish the hole when one of the guys with a mop of curly hair turns and does a double take. He whispers something to his friends, and they all look over. I stifle a sigh.

Sure enough, as soon as they finish the hole they hang around to watch us play through. I beat Brandon again, but it's definitely not my golf performance that the group watching are interested in.

"Hey, can we grab a selfie?" Curly Hair asks when we finish.

"Sure," Brandon says.

"I'll take it," I offer. "Then you can all be in it together."

The four friends smush in together around Brandon, who gives his fake smile.

Curly Hair hangs back close to Brandon after I hand back the phone. "I've just graduated from Penn State. I played ball all the way through."

Brandon's fake smile turns genuine. "Oh, cool. You played under Coach Kelly?"

"Yeah, great guy."

"Totally. He's one of the best. Except his suicides. I could have lived without those."

"Tell me about it," Curly Hair groans.

He and Brandon chat for a few minutes about playing college ball, reminiscing about other members of the coaching staff.

"Why don't you guys play on ahead of us?" Curly Hair offers as he and Brandon finish up.

"That would be great, thanks," Brandon says.

Brandon tees off first, and I follow him. We finish the hole quickly.

I go another shot up, but I'm not trying to conjure up ways to gloat to Brandon. Instead, my mind replays how his face lit up as he talked about his time playing football at college.

It's been easy to ignore the football side of Brandon—it's the off-season. I mean, I know he's still training hard and I've seen plenty of evidence about how famous he is, but I've never really thought about how passionate he must be about the game.

But as long as I'm Brandon's girlfriend I'm going to be around football and meeting up with football players. If we're still together when the season starts I'm sure I'll be expected to go to games to support him. My chest gives a weird squeeze, as it often does whenever my thoughts veer to future plans with Brandon.

"I can tell you're taking this minigolf challenge too seriously," Brandon says.

I drop my ball at the starting mat of the next hole. Looks

like we're now venturing to Antarctica. "How can you tell that?"

"You have that little line on your forehead." He reaches over and lightly brushes the skin between my eyebrows, making it tingle where he's touched it.

"I'm thinking about football, actually," I say.

"*You're* thinking about football?" Brandon's eyebrows rise.

"Yeah. I know. Flying pigs are skating on an ice rink in hell right now."

"What aspects of football are you thinking about?"

I shrug. "I don't know. I mean, it's obviously an important part of your life. And we've never really talked about it. Why do you love it?"

Brandon looks skeptical, but as we play the hole he talks about the first time he ever played football, how he threw the ball so far that his teacher clapped him on the back and told him "'You've got some arm on you, Brandon," and how that little bit of praise kept him buzzing all afternoon.

"With my family, up to that point, I'd never had anything I felt really proud of." He clears his throat as he bends down to pick his ball out of the hole. "It becomes one of those self-fulfilling cycles, you know. The more you practice something, the better you get and the more positive reinforcement you receive, so it motivates you to practice harder."

"I always liked the atmosphere of the games," I say as we move on to the next hole, which has an Amazon jungle theme. "There's just this certain scent of mown grass and cooked hotdogs that you only get at football games."

"So, are you ever going to tell me why you dislike football so much?" Brandon asks the question casually, but there is nothing casual about the way my heart starts pounding in response.

I stare down the course, pretending I'm giving serious consideration to my path through the jungle vines and water hazards.

I could shut down this conversation. Go into retreat mode. But I glance up and see Brandon's steady gaze on me. He's waiting patiently for me to answer, totally focused on me, like nothing else is important. This is how he always is with me. Like what I say really matters. And this makes me want to tell him the truth. The whole, ugly, vicious truth.

I lick my lips. "Tad Morton happened." The bitterness in my voice surprises me. I lean down to place the ball on the mat, trying to school my expression. My pulse is still racing far more than a game of minigolf should warrant.

"Who's Tad Morton?"

"The football captain of my high school." I keep my eyes on my ball, striking it firmly.

When I straighten up Brandon's giving me a strange look. "What, did you have a crush on him or something? I thought you didn't like football players."

"I don't now. I didn't mind them back in high school." I try to keep my voice nonchalant as I walk down to where my ball has finished up trapped behind some vines. "I actually lost my virginity to Tad, so I can't have minded him too much."

Brandon stops halfway through his swing. "You lost your virginity to the football captain of your high school?"

"Yep. Prom night. Are you going to play your shot?" I'm aiming for casual, but everything about me – my voice, my shoulders – feels strung out like an elastic band coiled too tightly.

Brandon obligingly strikes the ball and manages to hit it

straight through all the vines. His ball pulls an inch from the hole. He doesn't brag about it though. Instead he fixes me with an intense look. "What happened?"

I hit my next shot, managing to extract myself from the hazards. When I look up Brandon's still watching me.

I shrug. "There's not that much to tell. Tad was my chemistry lab partner. I thought we got on well. Like, we used to joke around and stuff. So when he asked me to prom ... I don't know, I thought I'd won him over with my personality or something." I snort, because it's hard to think of that version of Megan without derision.

"So you went to prom with him?"

I take the few steps toward my ball, using the chance to steady my breathing. I can't believe I'm about to tell Brandon this. I've never told anyone.

"Yeah, I went. It was great, actually. Afterwards he had a key to a hotel room. And he invited me back. I wasn't drunk. I knew what he was asking. But I liked the guy, so I went."

To punctuate my words, I tap the ball into the hole. My stomach drops like the ball as memories of what came next flit through my mind.

When I glance up after grabbing my ball Brandon's watching me, his eyes deep and dark.

I walk to the next hole with Brandon following me, and suddenly I'm back there. Seventeen-year-old Megan. Geeky, a little naïve, with her head stuffed full of romantic notions about love and first times. I honestly thought it was the start of something between me and Tad. I thought it was like one of those movies or books where the geeky girl triumphs and wins the heart of the football captain.

The next hole is the Sahara Desert. Brandon doesn't make any attempt to start playing though.

"Was it okay?" he asks softly.

I keep my gaze on the sand trap ahead of me. "Yeah, it was fine. I mean, it was my first time and he was a seventeen-year-old guy, so it was what you'd expect. But at the time I thought it was fine."

"What do you mean, *at the time*? What happened afterwards?" There's agitation in Brandon's voice.

I play with the handle of the putter and swallow hard, choking down the emotion that's balling in my throat. I manage to squeeze words past the malignant mass. "The next day I found out the whole thing had been a bet. His friends—all the other football players—had promised to pay him two hundred dollars if he got me to sleep with him."

Brandon rears back as though someone has punched him. Meanwhile memories continue to flash through my head.

At the prom Tad's friends had exchanged these little smirks and were overly nice to me, making sly comments about Tad and me together. At the time I'd thought it was a sign that they were accepting me into the group. I was such a fool.

And nothing—nothing—can ever fully describe my hurt and despair when I discovered the truth. I was the joke for the rest of the school year. Tad avoided me. He switched lab partners in chemistry and lowered his eyes when he saw me in the hallway. But his friends thought it was funny to hound me and make stupid remarks.

"That is one of the most disgusting things I've ever heard." Brandon's voice is low.

I try to hold myself together as I strike the ball. It avoids all the sand traps and bounces into the wall, and ricochets off at a good angle, pulling up within a foot of the hole. I stare at the ball as I respond. "Technically he didn't break any laws. I fully consented. And hey, I got to lose my virginity to the hottest guy in school. Not everyone can claim that." My attempt at levity chokes me almost as much as telling the story.

Brandon runs a hand through his hair. "Shit, Megan, don't joke this away. He broke your trust. He might not have abused you by the letter of the law, but there are different kinds of abuse. And what he did to you is fucked up."

"Yeah...well..." I try to muster a smile. Somehow seeing Brandon so upset about it sharpens the pain.

He drops his putter and reaches for me, tugging me into a hug. I tense for a moment, but then relax with the familiar feeling of Brandon's arms around me, the familiar scent of him. This is one of the most perplexing things about Brandon. There's no logical reason for it, but I've never felt as safe as I do with him. Wrapped in bubble wrap inside a child's safety seat in the middle of a padded room kind of safe.

After a minute I pull back. "I'm over it now. Well, mostly. You know the saying, *What doesn't kill you makes you stronger?* It's true. I used to care what those popular kids thought about me. After they did that I stopped caring."

"No wonder you have a grudge against football players," he says.

I take some time to compose myself before I look up at him. "I recently had a change of heart and decided that some football players are okay."

CHAPTER 32

BRANDON

IT'S FRIDAY NIGHT, and I'm hanging out at my girl-friend's apartment.

My girlfriend. I still can't get over how happy it makes me to call Megan that. Things between us seem to be getting better and better. It's weird, but ever since she told me about what happened to her in high school it's like the final layer between us has finally dissolved. Suddenly her grudge against everything football-related makes sense. And the fact that she can get past that and be my girlfriend has got to mean something, right?

Although currently anyone walking into the apartment wouldn't just see a guy casually hanging out with his girl-friend and brother. It looks more like an intervention. Josh and Megan are on the couch and I'm on the chair facing them. Serious expressions are on everyone's faces. I've just pleaded for their help in preparing for the celebrity quiz show in a few weeks' time.

"They're filming it live," I explain. "And they're going to be taking donations throughout the show. It's a great chance to raise money for the Active Coaches organization."

"So, do you know the format of this quiz?" Josh asks.

"No. I've never watched it."

"What's it called?"

I clear my throat. "Um...I think it's called *Dunk the Dummies*. It's pretty new. This is the first time they've done a celebrity version." I try not to show that even the name has fear shooting up and down my spine.

Josh raises an eyebrow. "*Dunk the Dummies?*"

"Yeah. I think if you get too many questions wrong they end up dunking you in water or something."

"Well, I think the first step is to watch the show and see what we're up against," Josh suggests.

Josh cues it up on his laptop and I gnaw on my lip as we watch. It's pretty simple. For every question you get right you earn cash. For every question you get wrong you're slipped down a notch, until finally the seat you're sitting on overturns and you're dunked in the water.

"Science, literature, sport, geography, history—these are pretty standard categories," Megan says as Josh leans over to press pause.

"So that's what you need to teach me," I say. "Everything I need to know."

Josh and Megan share a look. I feel like I'm back in third grade with Mom and my teacher having a conversation about my math struggles.

"Um...we don't have time to teach you all of that, Brandon. It's pretty broad," Megan says.

"The advantage is the fact it's multiple choice, so that makes it easier," Josh says.

"I've always hated multiple choice," I mutter.

"With multiple choice the right answer is there," Megan says. "You just need to find it."

"But they always try to trick you by having an option that's close to the correct answer."

"I'll make up some cards for you," she suggests. "We can practice your multiple choice technique."

Of all the techniques I want to practice with Megan, multiple choice is pretty low on the list. I decide not to say that though, because then I'll have to put up with Josh's jokes about disinfecting his brain.

Josh doesn't actually seem to be as invested in my multiple choice strategy as Megan. His attention is focused on his phone. I'm about to call him out on it when he lifts his gaze to us.

"Adam Schefter's just talking about the players who left money on the table, and you're top of his list." Josh raises an eyebrow at me.

"Oh...right." I try to send a message with my eyes to Josh. It goes something along the lines of *Shut the fuck up right now.*

Unfortunately Josh stays glued to his phone, scrolling down to read more. "Did you seriously turn down eighty million from the Bighorns?" he asks.

Megan's forehead scrunches. "Eighty million?" she squeaks. "You never told me about that."

Shit. Shit. Shit.

My sentiment is reflected in Josh's face as he looks up from his phone and clocks how badly he's dumped me in it.

"Yeah, they were interested in me," I tell Megan. "It didn't get to an official offer stage though because I re-signed with the Goliaths during the legal tampering period."

I can see from her hurt expression that the fact I hadn't told her about it is a big deal.

"Oh...okay," she says finally.

An awkward silence descends.

"Talking about football," Josh says in a bright voice, "I see they've started promoting the Goliaths' casino night. You two going?"

Awesome attempt to change the topic, little brother.

"What's the Goliaths' casino night?" Megan asks.

Of course Megan wouldn't know about the most talked about social event on the New York football calendar. The Goliaths hold it every year, and all players and their families are expected to be there, hobnobbing with the New York elite and media.

"I've been meaning to talk to you about it," I say. "It's just this thing the Goliaths run every year to raise money for charity. I have to go, and I was hoping you'd come with me. All the other players' girlfriends will be there."

"You'll get a chance to hang out with all the WAGs," Josh says with a snort.

Megan frowns. "WAGs?"

"Stands for Wives and Girlfriends. It's what everyone calls the football players' significant others," Josh explains.

"Oh, so they reduce a diverse group of women with their own interests, personalities and careers down to a simple acronym, do they?"

"Yep, pretty much." Josh grins.

I'm glad he's enjoying this conversation. When he was young I'm sure there were times when he was defenseless and I would have had the chance to amputate his tongue and make it look like an accident. Right now I'm really regretting the fact that I didn't do it.

"It should be a fun night," I offer. "They have blackjack and roulette tables all set up. I mean, I'm not sure if you're into gambling, but it's fun."

"I quite like gambling," Megan says, a glint in her eye.

"In fact, I've always found the statistical probability side of gambling quite fascinating."

"Is this another thing like minigolf that you weirdly turn out to be brilliant at because of some obscure math principle?" I grumble.

"Hey, never mock the power of math."

"I should have picked you for a card counter." Josh grins at Megan.

"So, are you in?" I ask.

Megan hesitates. "Yeah, I'm in."

Megan's unusually quiet as we get ready for bed. It's one thing I'm getting used to, the domestic routine. We brush our teeth side by side in the bathroom. I now have a toothbrush that lives here permanently. And pajamas too, though they were bought by Josh because apparently seeing me clad in only my boxers every morning at breakfast didn't do good things for his appetite.

I slip into bed next to her and switch off the light. It's not completely dark because Megan's curtains aren't actually that good at their one job.

We don't reach for each other the way we normally do. Instead, Megan lies straight as a board on the other side of the bed, like we're one of those 1950s sitcom couples who maintain a foot of distance between them in bed.

A gnawing feeling grows in my stomach.

"What's wrong?" Just saying those words makes me feel like I'm teetering on the edge of a cliff.

Megan takes a long time to answer. "I thought you were the one who wanted to be officially in a relationship," she finally says to the ceiling.

I prop myself up on one elbow to look at her. "Yes, I did. I mean, I do."

"Well, boyfriends and girlfriends tell each other when they get an amazing job offer."

I shrug, trying to keep my face neutral.

"You seriously didn't consider going to LA?" She's still acting like the ceiling is the most interested party in this conversation.

I don't want to discuss my thought process behind why I didn't want the Bighorn offer. I get the feeling if she knew how heavily she featured it would freak her out. A lot.

"Nah. I like my life here," I say instead.

Megan turns to look at me, her blue eyes serious. "You didn't talk to me at all about free agency. I assumed that was because it was really clear-cut. But it's obviously a big deal, and you had to make some tough decisions."

"Sorry. I guess I'm just used to making career decisions by myself—you know?"

"You didn't even talk to your parents about it?"

I shake my head. "My parents have never really cared about that stuff. I know they think I'm stupidly overpaid for what I do."

"But it's your career," she says.

"Yeah, I know."

"Please tell me you didn't avoid talking to me about it because I don't like football."

"No, that wasn't it. There just wasn't much to discuss because it was an easy decision to stay in New York."

"Even with all the extra money that other team was going to offer you?"

My heart starts pounding erratically. "There are other factors more important than money."

We lie in silence. I know stuff is ticking over in Megan's head. I can almost hear the gears grinding.

She's right. And I know she's right. I probably should have told her about it. She's now thinking it's a reflection on how serious I'm taking this relationship, when it's totally not. She goes to speak, hesitates, then plunges on, and I find myself bracing for what she's about to say. But the next words out of her mouth aren't anything to do with my decision.

"So, what do I have to wear to this Casino night? Like, do people get dressed up?"

"Um, yeah, I guess. I wear a suit and tie. Not a tuxedo though."

"I'll have to see if I can borrow something from Ashley again." Worry creases her forehead.

"It'll be fine," I say.

"I don't know." There is an uncertain note in her voice. "I'm not exactly your typical...what did Josh call it? WAG? God, it makes them sound like a dog's tail or something."

The words slip out of me easily. "I don't want you to be a typical WAG. I just want you to be you."

An unreadable expression comes over Megan's face. "Okay, I can probably do that," she says finally. "I've had twenty-four years of being me. I should have it mastered by now."

I huff out a half-laugh and reach out an arm, pulling her in close. She snuggles into the crook under my arm, her cheek resting on my chest.

When we eventually start kissing, it's slower and lazier than normal. We just lie there and make out for ages, neither of us in any hurry to escalate it to something else. Like we have all the time in the world.

CHAPTER 33

MEGAN

IF YOU LOOKED at my work desk right now you'd think I had an obsession with neuroscience that's beyond the point of healthy.

I've printed out every journal article Dianne Marshall has ever published and they're strewn around my desk. A stack of her books is propped up on one corner, along with other neuroscience books I've tracked down for background reading.

It's fascinating stuff. Incredibly fascinating, world-changing stuff.

And yet my mind keeps sliding to Brandon.

God, I'm turning into such a cliché. Sitting here at my desk, daydreaming about my boyfriend. But I can't help replaying last night in my head. I thought things couldn't get better between us in the bedroom. However, last night proved me wrong. A whole new level of wrong.

I don't think anyone has ever touched me as tenderly as Brandon does. Part of me desperately wants to read more into it. In fact, I hate how desperately I want to over-interpret Brandon's actions. I'm another victim of the stupid oxytocin curse.

Then there's his reaction to my story the other day about Tad. In some ways it made me feel vindicated. Deep down I've wondered if I overreacted to the whole thing. I mean, people have a lot worse stuff happen to them, and they seem to get over it without having massive, long-lasting hang-ups.

But seeing Brandon's disgust in response to my story helps me finally accept that it was a really shitty thing that happened to me. And I didn't deserve it.

My phone beeps. It's my brother, which provides a welcome distraction to my thoughts.

Until I actually read his message.

I don't want to alarm you, but I think Mom has gone crazy. I just got back from my hiking trip, and when I called her she told me all about her and Dad's weekend in New York where they met your new boyfriend. Apparently his name is Brandon Seaton. <crazy face emoji>

Great. Not really the distracting-my-brain-away-from-Brandon message I was hoping for. But the childhood part of me that relishes getting one up on my brother can't resist messaging back immediately.

What, you don't think I can land a hot celebrity football boyfriend??

I actually don't give much thought to the type of guy my sister can land. But I can't really picture you and Brandon Seaton together.

Right. I scroll through my phone until I find the selfie Brandon took of us that he sent through to me. He's got his arm around me, and he's leaning in to kiss my cheek while I grin goofily. For some reason looking at that photo for too long does uncomfortable things to my stomach, but it fits this particular purpose so I send it through to Keaghan.

Here's a picture to help you.

My phone rings almost immediately.

"What the hell? It's really true?" Keaghan's raspy voice is full of disbelief.

"Yeah, it's true."

"How did you meet him?"

"He's my roommate's brother."

"Holy shit."

I feel a bit bad about how much I'm enjoying this conversation. Brandon's told me how he feels people are only interested in him because of his celebrity status. And here I am, flaunting our relationship to have a moment of triumph over my older brother, who has always dismissed me as his nerdy little sister.

"Is it serious?" Keaghan asks. "You didn't have anything to do with him choosing to stay in New York, did you?"

For a moment, faced with the eagerness in Keaghan's voice, I wish I could lie and say we're serious and he chose to re-sign with the Goliaths because of me. But how stupid will I feel when it all implodes in my face?

"Um...no. And it's not serious. I mean, we've only been together a few weeks. It's just a casual thing." I go for my standard line, trying to ignore the little tug in my intestines as I say the words. Because this thing with Brandon is starting to feel past the point of casual for me.

Is there a chance our relationship was a factor in his decision? I can't imagine Brandon—or anyone else for that matter—making a major career decision based on me.

"Can I meet him?"

"If you come to New York." I'm joking, but I suddenly hear what sounds like a computer keyboard clattering.

"I could possibly come at the end of July. I think I've got a free weekend then."

"Seriously? You're going to fly here just to meet Brandon?"

"It's my brotherly duty to check out who you're dating."

I roll my eyes, which I'm aware is a totally wasted gesture on a phone call. "You've never cared before. Funny that now you do."

"I've got to do it soon before you guys break up."

A cold feeling sets up camp in my stomach at the factual way he says those words. His tone is absolutely no-nonsense. Like there's no doubt that Brandon and I will not last.

"What makes you think we're going to break up soon?" My words come out as spiky as a cactus, but Keaghan doesn't seem to notice.

"You said it's not serious, right? And I mean—it's Brandon Seaton. He must have girls throwing themselves at him all the time."

Tact has never been something my brother has specialized in. The cold feeling that has made camp in my stomach now constructs a campfire and starts toasting marshmallows. Because Keaghan's words reinforce something I suspect deep down: that Brandon has picked me up like a kid does when they find an unusual toy they're fascinated with for a while, before they lose interest and move on to the next thing.

A tight feeling rises in my throat, choking me.

Keaghan continues on, oblivious. "I'll book a ticket for the end of July. I'll make it a refundable ticket, so that way if you guys have broken up I won't lose any money. Please try to keep him hanging around until then."

"I'll try," I reply, bitterness coating my words.

CHAPTER 34

BRANDON

IT'S WEDNESDAY MORNING, and I'm at the same place I am nearly every morning.

The gym.

Pounding away on the treadmill, I welcome the burn of my muscles. My workout playlist blasts in my ears.

When I step off the running deck, my phone lights up. I get a happy thrill through my body, because eighty percent of my phone action nowadays is Megan. We message each other back and forth all day long, usually just funny stuff we know will make the other laugh.

But this time my phone doesn't contain a witty message from Megan. Instead, there's three missed calls from my mother.

I get a sneaky suspicion I know exactly why she's trying to reach me.

Just as I'm trying to decide if I have enough endorphins flowing in my veins after my workout to handle a conversation with my mother, my phone vibrates again with an incoming call. It's Mom again. She's one of those impatient people who will call you every five minutes until you pick up.

Stifling a sigh, I answer. "Hello?"

"Oh, good, I've finally got you. I really want to talk to you. I can't talk for long now though; I'm just making a lemon cake to take to the church fundraiser Rotary stall. I'm trying a new recipe, and it's proving a bit challenging."

Somehow listening to a few sentences from my mother exhausts me more than a two-hour workout. "What do you want to talk to me about?" I ask.

"Why didn't you tell us about the Bighorn offer?" Typical of my mother. She doesn't waste any time building up to anything. I can just picture her, phone tucked in by her ear as she bustles around the kitchen. She's probably wearing that hideous apron that shows all of the internal body organs, the one Josh gave her years ago.

I'd talked to my parents after I'd re-signed with the Goliaths, and they'd been their usual supportive selves. But I hadn't mentioned any of the other potential offers on the table.

I stiffen. "An offer doesn't really matter if I don't take it. It wasn't a big deal. I'd already decided I wanted to stay in New York."

"Fair enough. I was just curious."

I can't help wondering if her desire to find out why I turned down the LA offer has anything to do with the fact she's going to be at the church fundraiser and people might ask her about it.

"Well, there's no big story. I just like playing for the Goliaths." My tone is a tad defensive.

"Okay, okay. So is there anything else going on with you?" Mom asks chirpily.

Megan floats into my head. Maybe I should tell my

parents about her. Before something leaks out and they find out from the TNT website.

Nerves cartwheel in my stomach at the thought. This isn't something I've ever done before.

"Actually, I've got some other news." I clear my throat.

"What news is that?" I'm pretty sure she's stirring something on the stove now. I can hear the clinking of her spoon against the side of a pot.

"Um...I'm seeing someone."

"Oh, wow, that's great news. Is it Harriet Harrison? I saw a news thing that you and she were spotted on a date."

Damn, I always forget that my mother has a Google alert for my name.

"Ah, no, it's not Harriet." I cough, trying and failing again to get rid of the raspiness in my throat. "It's Megan."

"Megan?"

"Yes, Megan."

"As in, Josh's roommate, Megan?" Mom's voice is laced with disbelief.

"Yes. Her. That Megan."

"Okaaay." Mom stretches out the word a few beats longer than normal. "How long has something been...ah... happening between you and Megan?"

"A few weeks now."

"Right. Okay."

"What's the issue? I thought you liked Megan."

"I do really like her..." She trails off, and my stomach does a plummet.

"But?" I prompt.

"I'm just surprised, that's all. You are very different people."

"You mean she's too smart for me," I say flatly.

"No. Of course not. You're just interested in different things—that's what I was meaning."

"Well, it actually is working out great."

"I'm glad to hear that. I just hope it won't be too awkward for Josh when you break up."

Anger slices through me. Of course that's what she's concerned about. How this will affect Josh.

"Way to show some faith in me."

"Are you telling me you think this could be serious?" Mom asks, her words coated in skepticism.

"Yes. Definitely." The words are out of my mouth before I have any chance to filter them through the don't-share-too-much sieve.

There's silence on the other end of the phone. I'm pretty sure it's a stunned one.

"Well, in that case I'm very happy for you, Brandon. Megan is a wonderful person."

"Yes, she is."

"You'll have to bring her home again sometime soon."

"I'm sure she'd like that. I know she thought you guys were great."

I press the end button on my phone and stare at it blankly as my mind heaves and swirls.

When I arrive at Megan's apartment that evening, I find her burrowed in the couch, surrounded by books and articles. She looks up from what she's reading to give me a distracted smile. She's wearing her reading glasses, and her hair is stuck up in a topknot with some escaping messily around her face.

Something flutters in my chest. It appears I have some

previously undiagnosed heart condition that I only suffer when Megan is around.

"Is that reading for your interview?" I ask redundantly.

Megan leans back and stretches. "Yep. Dianne Marshall is notorious for either giving one-word answers to interviewers or going into incredibly high-level detailed explanations. I want to be really prepared."

"Don't let me distract you."

"No, it's fine. In fact, I've got a surprise for you."

"Do I need to get undressed to get this surprise?"

She rolls her eyes, and happiness skips through me. Because apparently this is my drug of choice: Megan's mockery.

She grabs a stack of index cards off the coffee table. "I made these up for you. I thought this would give you a chance to practice with multiple choice. If there are any questions you get wrong we'll know that's an area you need to brush up on."

There's another squeeze in my heart region as I grab the cards and thumb through them. It's obvious Megan has gone to a lot of time and effort on these cards. And I know she's been really busy preparing for her interview with the brain science lady.

She cares. She really does care.

Or maybe she's just a nice person who doesn't want to see me humiliated on national TV.

Megan seems oblivious to the conflict going on in my brain. "Let's practice," she says.

"Are you sure you've got time to take a break?"

"Yeah, it's fine. I'm just rereading stuff now. It's more a way to cope with my nerves than for any actual benefit."

I hand the cards back over to her, and we begin.

Megan said "any questions" I get wrong. Unfortunately

we start with history, which means I get every question wrong. She's having to stop after every card to give me a brief overview of the time period. We cover American Independence, the Civil War and modern history, progressing through three cards in forty minutes. I learn a whole lot about tea parties, understand the controversy about the confederate flag, while the Battle of Saratoga, Trenton and Fort Sumter enter my vocab for the first time ever.

It's becoming incredibly apparent that the highlight of my academic career was eating the most paste in kindergarten. It's all been downhill from there.

"Um, maybe we should just note down everything that you need to brush up on as we move along," Megan suggests when I get the next card on the dates of World War II wrong.

"You should note down it all then. The entire history of humanity. How about we cover that?"

I'm in a bad mood. There's nothing like having it rubbed in my face exactly how stupid I am.

Megan just gives me a look as she turns over the next card.

Where did the Vikings originally come from?

a) Russia

b) Scandinavia

c) Britain

d) Spain

e) Iceland

This time I actually know the answer is Scandinavia, but only because I spent far too much time watching the TV show *Vikings*.

"Well done," she says enthusiastically when I give her the correct answer.

"Are you going to give me a sticker?" I ask.

Megan's eyebrows pinch together at my tone. "What?"

"Well, you're treating me like a kid."

"I'm not treating you like a kid. But you are starting to behave like one." She turns over the next card.

"I'm sorry if my maturity level isn't to your standard." I rub my forehead. This is not our usual mocking each other in fun banter. This has another edge to it.

Megan twists the cards in her hands, fixing me with a look. "What's the problem, Brandon? In case you haven't figured it out, I'm trying to help you. So how about you quit acting like I'm the enemy?"

I tug at my collar. "I told you, I hate looking stupid. I felt like that my entire childhood, okay? So forgive me if I'm stressed about feeling dumb in front of the whole country." The words burst out of me, and I really want to switch on an extractor fan so I can remove them from the air.

Her eyes widen. "You felt stupid your entire childhood?"

The words hang between us. I feel like a dog when it lies on its back and exposes its underbelly to the world.

I run my hands through my hair. "Yeah, I did. You've seen what my parents are like, right? And Josh learned to read before I did. He was four, and I was six. I was still struggling through those early readers— you know, the ones that go, *The cat sat on the mat*—while Josh was working his way through *Harry Potter*."

"Just because Josh is very bright doesn't mean you should feel stupid," Megan argues.

Her mention of Josh makes something else boil up from inside me where I thought I'd buried it in a deep grave. I can't stop myself asking it now. "If Josh had been straight, do you think you would have picked him over me?"

Megan blinks. "Where did that question come from?"

"From my mouth. And before that, my brain."

"Okay. It's just a weird question."

"And you haven't answered it." My voice is tight.

Megan shuffles the cards in her hands, avoiding my eyes. "I don't know, Brandon, okay? I thought I liked Josh in the beginning, because we had so much in common. It's different with you. You just kind of...crept up on me."

"I 'crept up on you'?" I echo.

"Yeah. Like poison ivy creeps."

I know she's joking; I can tell by the curve of the smile on her face. So I try to match it, but I'm feeling sick inside.

A big part of why I chose to stay in New York was because of her. I'm falling for her, but it appears she doesn't feel the same way about me. And I don't really blame her. I can't help feeling that ultimately Megan's going to want someone more on her intellectual plane. Someone who knows about civil war battles and ancient philosophers and biological theories.

Someone who's not me.

CHAPTER 35

MEGAN

I AM NAILING THIS INTERVIEW.

The time I've spent reading every scientific paper Dianne has ever written is paying off.

Her personal assistant confirmed she would be available for an hour for the interview. It's now long past the hour mark, it's starting to get dark outside the conference room window, and we're still talking.

Not that I'm complaining.

We've branched off from discussing her work on the underlying genetic basis of memory formation in the brain to talking more generally about breakthroughs in science. Which leads us to a conversation about how difficult it can be to be a woman in science.

We discuss Katie Bouman, the woman who was part of a team which wrote the algorithm that contributed toward taking the first image of a black hole. After M.I.T. innocently shared the photo of Katie's delightful reaction to seeing the photo for the first time, the trolls emerged from their rocks to pull her apart with their ignorant teeth.

Dianne also mentions a recent Nobel prize winner, Tim

Hunt, who talked about how the trouble with "girls" in laboratories is that "they fall in love with you, and when you criticize them, they cry." And how his solution was to have sex-segregated laboratories.

Which leads on to us discussing the perception that to succeed in a man's world, you have to embrace typically masculine traits and how this needs to change for women to fundamentally be treated as equal.

"I really want to write an article on the experience of female scientists," I say eagerly. "Talk to a range of top scientists about the challenges they've faced. I'd love for you to be involved." I hold my breath as I say the words. I know if Dianne Marshall agrees to participate, it will help convince other prominent female scientists to become involved too.

She pauses. "I'll consider it," she says finally.

"You will?" I squeak. I cough, attempting to wrestle my vocal cords back under control. "Great, I'll pitch the idea to my editor, but I know he'll love it. It might even be the cover story."

A slow smile spreads on her lips. "I think an article like you've described is exactly what we need in this current climate."

We continue to talk about great female scientists in history and how some of their contributions to science were devalued and underrated, when we're interrupted by a knock on the door to the interview room.

"Yes?" I say, my tone slightly impatient.

When the door opens I'm expecting one of my colleagues, who'll get a pointed glare. *Hey, I'm interviewing Dianne Marshall here. What the hell?*

But it's not another journalist. It's Brandon.

My eyebrows shoot up.

He freezes when he sees I have company. His gaze slides to Dianne. "Sorry to interrupt."

"What are you doing here?" I ask.

Brandon's jaw gives a little twinge, and his shoulders stiffen under the sleek, dark suit he's wearing.

"Um...it's seven-thirty. You haven't answered any of my messages. We're going to be late for the Casino night. One of your colleagues thought you might still be in here finishing off your notes. Sorry. I don't think anyone realized you were still in the interview."

He flashes a smile at Dianne, who stares back at him with a blank face.

"Oh, right." I'm flustered, glancing at my watch. How the hell did it get to be seven-thirty?

"That's all right. We were just finishing up," Dianne says. She gathers up her phone and compendium.

"You must be the brain science lady Megan's told me about," Brandon says with a brash grin.

I close my eyes in horror so I don't have to see the look on Dianne's face. I'm pretty sure she's never been referred to as 'the brain science lady' in her life. At least not in her earshot.

Dianne gives Brandon a flat stare in reply. His grin fades. While Brandon's charm works on most people, it meets a brick wall of resistance with Dianne Marshall.

"I'm Dianne Marshall," she says, holding out her hand.

He shakes it. "Brandon Seaton. Megan's boyfriend."

She narrows her eyes, squinting at him. "You're a football player, right?"

"Yes, that's right." Brandon's smile makes a quick comeback. "Do you follow football?"

"No. But my son does. He has a poster of you in his room."

She glances at me, and it's a quizzical look. There's no judgement in it, more like the data hasn't lined up in the way she was expecting.

"I'll walk you out," I offer.

"Thank you."

I try to match Dianne's strides as we walk to the elevator.

"It was great to talk to you. I really appreciate your time," I say when we reach it.

"It was my pleasure." Dianne seems distracted, checking messages on her phone.

"So, I'll be in touch regarding the women in science article," I say as the elevator arrives, hope tinging my voice.

"Yes, just email my PA with an interview request. That's the standard procedure." Her voice is distant, and she doesn't make eye contact as she steps into the elevator.

I stand until the door closes, trying to stop my stomach dropping like it's going down the elevator shaft too.

After all, Dianne said she'd consider another interview. Just because she grew noticeably cooler after Brandon's interruption doesn't mean she'll change her mind.

Brandon walks toward me. "I'm sorry. I didn't mean to interrupt your interview." He looks so abashed that any anger I might feel is punctured before it begins to swell.

"It's okay. We just lost track of time."

"I guess that meant the interview went well?"

"It went really well." I try to summon enthusiasm. "There's a chance she's going to participate in an article about the experience of women in science. If I could get her and a few other prominent female scientists it could be a really big deal."

I don't say what I'm thinking. That the chance of

Dianne agreeing to the second interview seemed significantly higher before Brandon interrupted us.

"That's great!" He leans in for a hug. "Well done, babe."

Babe? Just like Dianne had undoubtedly never been referred to as 'the brain science lady' before, this is my first experience of being called 'babe'.

"Anyway, are you ready to go? We'll have to head straight to the hotel," he says.

A shiver of fear runs through me. I've been so focused on the Dianne Marshall interview I've deliberately pushed aside all thoughts of the other thing giving my nerves a workout today. The Goliaths' Casino night. Being Brandon's date in public for the first time.

"I'm not dressed for it." I go for the most obvious thing. I borrowed a sleek black dress from Ashley to wear tonight, but it's at my apartment. Ashley was excited at the thought that her dress was going to get to rub shoulders with celebrity athletes.

Brandon scans me up and down. "You can come like that. It's no big deal."

I've dressed in my best work outfit in honor of my Dianne Marshall interview. A light blue shirt and pencil black skirt, with my hair tucked up in a bun. It's tidy and professional. But it's not at all glamorous.

I hesitate. "Are you sure?"

"Yeah, it'll be fine," Brandon says.

CHAPTER 36

MEGAN

IT'S NOT FINE.

In fact, it's so far from fine, we can't even see the fine line in the distance. It's hidden behind extreme embarrassment and total mortification.

Brandon seriously understated the dress code for this thing. Sure, the guys are wearing suits and not tuxedos, but the women are dressed like they've just stepped out of the pages of *Vogue*.

In comparison, I look like I've just stepped out of the pages of *Frumpy Tax Inspectors*.

He also seriously downplayed how big this event is. There's a red carpet leading up to the hotel, for God's sake! I'm having to walk down it next to him with cameras clicking while I blink like a bewildered raccoon.

And because he's recently re-signed with the Goliaths, all of the media is clambering to take pictures and get quotes from him.

Brandon stops at one point halfway down the red carpet to say a few generic words about how excited he is to continue to play in New York, while I hover by his side, trying not to fidget.

When we reach the end of the red carpet there's this place we have to stop and stand, while more cameras click and flashes explode in an epileptic's worst nightmare.

"What the hell?" I hiss at him through clenched teeth.

"Just smile." Brandon pulls me close. Obligingly, I bare my teeth.

He ignores all the calls from the paparazzi asking him if I'm his girlfriend and what my name is. There are also a few others who throw out some different questions.

"Brandon, is that your sister?"

And I'm pretty sure I also hear some wit asking him if I'm his accountant.

Inside it's actually worse. Because Brandon proudly introduces me as his girlfriend to his teammates and coaches, and I get to see the stunned reactions and double takes at close range. Widening eyes, eyebrows almost flying off their faces, mouths falling open.

A weird rage takes over my body. Just an hour ago I was talking to one of the greatest minds in the world, holding my own in a conversation about the fundamental way our brain processes our experiences and how that contributes to understanding ourselves and our world.

Now I'm being judged because I don't meet society's generic standard of beauty. I'm being judged by what I look like and what I'm wearing.

There's a cold contrast to the respect I saw in Dianne Marshall's eyes only hours earlier compared with the judgement I'm now seeing in the faces of all these people.

It's not fair. It's so not fair.

I wish I didn't care.

Brandon introduces me to his teammate, Connor. I

recognize Connor's girlfriend, Karla, from the jeans ad I see on the subway every morning. She's stunningly beautiful, but she at least has a genuine smile as she greets me.

"So, how long have you been together?" Karla asks.

"We've known each other for ... what, three months?" Brandon looks at me for confirmation. "But we've only been dating for just over a month. She's a tough one to catch."

"Do you really think a predator/prey analogy is the right way to describe our modern, equal, feminist relationship?" I ask.

Karla laughs. She has a deep, slightly dirty chuckle that doesn't seem to fit with her angelic appearance.

Connor studies me. "You're the Science Barbie," he says suddenly.

"What?"

"You're the one he got the Barbie doll for, right? I was with him the day he bought it."

"What, you're telling me he doesn't buy Barbies for all the girls?" I widen my eyes in pretend surprise.

"Yeah, Brandon's game definitely needs some work," Connor says loosely. He snags a canapé from a passing waiter and chucks it into his mouth.

"Whatever. That Barbie doll was comic genius," Brandon replies.

My stomach is recoiling from Connor's words. Was he just hassling Brandon, or did he mean Brandon's game needs work because he's ended up with me?

Am I being overly sensitive? Yet it's hard not to be paranoid when I intercept a waiter to grab a glass of champagne and catch him giving me an incredulous side-eye.

I follow Brandon over to one of the roulette tables, sipping on my glass of champagne. As we arrive a woman casually bets my month's salary on red.

We watch as the wheel spins the ball.

It's black.

She shrugs and goes back to chatting with her companion like it's no big deal.

"Is that real money?" I ask Brandon.

"Yep. Tickets for this thing sell for over a grand each," he murmurs.

"People pay that much money just to come and gamble?"

"And to hang out with football players."

It's a completely different world. Brandon could probably drop that kind of money without thinking too. After all, he just signed a contract worth millions of dollars.

Funny, I've never thought about the difference in our finances. Because we pretty much only hang out at my apartment it's easy to ignore how rich he is. But being here is just reinforcing how different our realities are. The beautiful people in expensive outfits and adorned with glittering jewelry, the canapés being circulated by crisply dressed waiters, the enormous floral displays, and the ice sculpture in the corner—everything about this experience is unfamiliar to me.

Although maybe not *everything* is unfamiliar.

Because I spot someone I recognize. For a second relief fizzes through me. I don't immediately place the face of the guy who's watching at the blackjack table in the corner, but he's definitely familiar.

My relief morphs into a corrosive acid and it feels like all my internal organs are being eaten away.

It's Tad Morton. From high school.

Here. In New York.

I've had fantasies about bumping into Tad Morton again. Maybe at our high school reunion, where I'm the guest speaker because I'm a famous journalist and writer and he's some balding, overweight car salesperson who's never made it out of Oklahoma. But not here. Not now.

"Megan? Are you okay?"

I'm suddenly aware that Brandon's talking to me and I haven't responded.

I can't pull my eyes away from Tad.

Brandon follows my gaze. "Who is that guy?" he asks.

CHAPTER 37

BRANDON

MEGAN'S GONE PALE. I didn't think that actually happened to people, but it looks like a vampire's had access to her veins and has had a full banquet.

She's staring at a guy by one of the blackjack tables like she's in a trance. From the look on her face you'd think he was Hannibal Lector, Freddie Kruger and Jack the Ripper all rolled into one.

"Who is that guy?" I ask again.

Megan doesn't seem to hear me. She just continues to stare.

"Megan?"

She finally wrenches her gaze away. "That's Tad Morton." I know she's trying for a nonchalant tone but she misses it by several beats. Instead she's into the strained and frayed zone.

I narrow my eyes. Tad Morton. The name is familiar.

Then it suddenly clicks.

It's him.

The guy who stole her virginity. The guy who tricked

her into sleeping with him, then humiliated her in front of the whole school.

My hands fist into a ball. The rage that overcomes me is impossible to describe. A thick, damp, dark rage that descends like a fog, blanking out everything else.

"He's the guy from your high school." My voice is shaking, but I need to clarify this important point. I need to make sure I'm not about to go aggro on someone innocent.

"Yeah, that's him." Megan says. She finally meets my gaze, and whatever she sees on my face causes her eyes to widen.

"Brandon." She reaches to grab my arm, but I'm a professional athlete. I dodge out of her way.

I stalk across the room, the anger seething in my veins with each pulse of my heart.

I'm known for being the guy who keeps it together on the field. Who never loses his cool no matter what dirty tactics the opposition throws at us. I need to channel every ounce of that now. Otherwise there's a good chance I will deck this guy in front of my entire team, management and owners, plus most of the New York media. Even in my rage, common sense is tapping me on my shoulder to inform me that this is not the best move.

I reach the guy. "Hey, you. It's Tad, right?" My voice comes out like a growl. There's so much fury pounding through it.

"Yep." The guy turns to me with a confident smirk, which fades into a look of astonishment. "Holy shit. You're Brandon Seaton."

"I know I am," I grind out through clenched teeth.

"I'm a big fan of yours," he stammers.

"Yeah? It turns out I'm not such a big fan of yours."

Tad just stares at me. "What?"

"Do you recognize that girl over there?" I give a sharp nod in Megan's direction.

He follows my gaze, his eyes widening when he sees Megan. She's watching this whole thing with her arms crossed and an enormous scowl on her face.

I know the scowl is for me and I'm in big trouble, but Tad doesn't know that.

"That's Megan Anderson," he says slowly.

"You're right. It is. She's my girlfriend. Don't you think you might have something to say to her? Like an apology? For what happened prom night, Senior Year?"

Tad blanches. He takes a step back, potentially trying to get out of the range of my fists.

"Shit." Panic runs rampant on his face.

"You're right. You were a shit. And now you get to apologize for it."

He swallows, his Adam's apple bobbing.

"Come on." I grab his arm and yank him in Megan's direction. Tad doesn't resist me as I pull him through the crowd. Which is a good thing.

"Hey, Megan." I plant Tad in front of her. "Tad has something he'd like to say to you."

Megan gives me her withering-balls death glare. But then she turns it on Tad, who actually deserves it. I can only hope his balls do wither—preferably to the size of raisins.

"You have something to say to me?" She raises an eyebrow.

"Um...yeah," Tad clears his throat, then stumbles on. "I'm...uh...sorry. You know, for what happened...prom night. It was...ah...a...shitty thing to do."

Tad could give lessons on how to stammer your way through an apology. Megan just watches him, her face impassive. When the agony is over she takes a small step forward, and he flinches back.

"What a fabulous unprompted apology, Tad. I've waited such a long time to hear it. It was so worth it." She turns and stalks away toward the bar, leaving us both standing there.

Tad swallows and slides a nervous glance at me. "Hey, man. I tried."

"Yeah, but it's probably a case of too little, too late, right?" I bite out.

Tad stares after Megan. "She's seriously your girlfriend?"

"Yep. And she's incredible." Something clogs in my throat as I say this, so I veer in a different direction. "And you should be grateful I don't tell all my buddies here tonight about what you did. I mean, I don't condone violence or anything—" I hold up my hands in an innocent gesture "—but a whole bunch of these guys do crunch people for a living."

Tad pales.

"I'm going to leave you to crawl back under whatever rock you came from." I turn and head after Megan.

A hollow feeling engulfs me as I plow through the crowd to where she's standing by the bar. Ultimately, it doesn't matter what happens now. It doesn't matter if Tad grovels at her feet. It doesn't matter if I'd followed through on my impulse to smash his face open. No words or actions can ever undo what was done. Nothing can give Megan back what was taken from her.

All I can do is try to prove to her now how desired she is and how much she means to me.

If she'll let me.

When I reach the bar, Megan doesn't look like she's in

the mood to hear me express my feelings. Instead, she looks like she's in the mood to cut off my balls and offer them to the chef to fry up.

"I can't believe you did that," are her first words. And not in the I-can't-believe-you-brought-me-a-diamond-necklace-for-my-birthday tone. More in the I-can't-believe-you-killed-the-dog-then-ran-over-the-kitten-on-the-way-to-the-vet tone.

"I just thought you deserved an apology from that guy."

"So, what I thought—what I wanted—wasn't at all relevant?" she hisses. "Was this all about Brandon being the avenging hero?"

Shock and anger flare in my chest. "No. It was about you getting the apology you deserved."

"That's the thing, Brandon, I can fight my own battles. I could have told Tad Morton exactly what I think of him for what he did. I don't need a guy—especially not you—to defend my honor."

What the hell? "I know you don't need me to defend your honor. But I wanted to make that asshole accountable for what he did. Is that such a bad thing?" My voice is tight.

Emotions war on her face.

"I need some air," she says, pushing past me.

I let her go.

CHAPTER 38

MEGAN

I NEED to get away from the crowd. I need to process everything.

Tad Morton. Here.

He's become such a giant figure in my mind. I'll always remember the way he used to saunter around the hallways wearing his letterman jersey and confident smirk. The way all the girls wanted to be with him and all the boys wanted to be him. He was this mystical, untouchable figure.

It was an other-worldly experience seeing Tad next to Brandon just now. Dwarfed by him in every sense. Stammering out an apology.

Yet I hate that part of me liked the fact that I have a hot celebrity football boyfriend to stand up for me. I shouldn't need a man's validation to be seen as a worthy human. Tad should feel terrible about what he did to me regardless of whom I'm hooking up with now.

Brandon's bewildered expression tells me he has no idea what he did wrong. I don't know if I have the words to explain it to him. I can hardly explain it to myself.

I stumble toward the door to the balcony. Only one of

the glass doors is hitched back to let people in and out, so a small queue of people have lined up waiting to get through.

I wait next to a huge floral display, which probably cost the equivalent of what you could feed an average neighborhood for. Snatches of conversation float out from the other side.

"Great turn-out tonight."

"Yeah, all the rich and famous are here."

"A few surprises too. Did you see Seaton's girlfriend?"

I seize up. My breathing becomes shallow as I wait for the next words.

"Yeah. Not what I was expecting." There's amusement in the voice.

"Maybe she has a sense of humor?" a female voice offers.

Another deeper voice says, "I'm pretty sure it just illustrates Brandon has a sense of humor."

"I heard Brandon's agent told him he needed to keep himself out of the tabloids to get a good contract. You reckon the girlfriend is part of that? Although he possibly went too far, don't you think?"

"Brandon's always been an overachiever," Deep Voice snickers.

My breath leaves me like I've been punched.

The backlog of people waiting to get out on the balcony has cleared. My eyes unseeing, I stumble my way through the door.

Outside, the cold air greets me like a slap. It's as if the night is trying to knock some sense back into me after all these weeks.

I battle my way through the crowd, heading over to the railing. Clinging to the smooth top, I take a few deep breaths. But getting air into my lungs helps gives clarity to my thoughts, which is not what I actually want right now.

Because it's becoming obvious that Brandon and I make no sense together. Everyone can see it. It's like with Tad in high school—I'm the butt of the joke again. The big giant joke that everyone gets a good laugh out of. The girl who thinks she can land herself a popular jock boyfriend, the girl who thinks she's good enough to keep him.

Brandon's agent told him to stop playing around, to get out of the tabloids, and then he started to date me. I know it wasn't a calculated move—I know Brandon well enough to know that he wouldn't ever do something like that.

But maybe, subconsciously, part of his attraction to me was because I fulfilled his agent's criteria? After all, I definitely won't lead him astray by binge drinking and misbehaving in nightclubs.

I grab my phone, looking for any distraction. But going on Twitter is the wrong move, because there are a few hashtags trending for Brandon, including *#whatthehellisBrandonthinking*. The first thing that comes up is a photo of him and Harriet Harrison together on a date, leaning in toward each other. It's side by side with a picture of him and me that a photographer obviously snapped on the red carpet. I've got my mouth open and my eyes half shut, looking like I'm doing an impression of a constipated llama.

Oh, my God. My face suddenly feels hot, and I cross my arms across my chest.

I look up to see that Brandon has followed me out onto the balcony. He heads toward me, cutting through the crowd like a knife slices butter. People melt away from him, sending him admiring glances as they give him room to move.

I doubt he notices the reaction he gets from other

people. For him, it's built in to the experience of being Brandon Seaton. He doesn't understand that it's not like that for everyone.

I try to control my breathing, to see the situation objectively.

Gorgeous guy dressed in an expensive suit carving through the crowd. Even the way he moves is attractive, with the same kind of coiled-up power combined with gracefulness that you see in a tiger.

He's gorgeous, but I hardly spend time thinking about his looks anymore. Because I know the person who exists under that good-looking jock façade now. And that person is even more attractive than his exterior.

That thought makes me blink in shock, just as Brandon reaches me.

He pulls up a foot away, his expression wary. "Hey," he says cautiously.

"Hey," I reply.

Apparently having tested the waters, Brandon decides to plunge right in. "I'm sorry. I was so angry at Tad for what he did. I wanted to do something to make it better. I didn't mean to upset you."

"I know you weren't trying to upset me," I say wearily. I can't process this now. I can't even attempt to articulate my mixed feelings about his altercation with Tad, why it left me so unsettled.

Brandon studies my face closely, but he doesn't say anything. We stand in silence for a few moments, a stark contrast to the laughter and chatter of the crowd around us.

Brandon shifts a little closer to me. "Do you want go play blackjack? Show me your awesome probability skills?" he asks.

A weird kind of tiredness has gripped my body. "Okay."

We head back inside together. Brandon grabs my hand like he normally does.

Normally I love the feel of his hand in mine. But tonight it just feels wrong.

Because there are eyes everywhere. Eyes looking in judgement at us. Eyes following us as we move through the crowd. And mouths turning up in smirks, mouths laughing, mouths talking about me. People are on their phones, and I can't help thinking they're reading what people are saying about me on social media.

Panic pushes down on my chest, and something breaks inside me.

I come to an abrupt stop. "I can't do this," I whisper.

"You can't do what? It's just blackjack, Megan."

I look straight into his brown eyes. "I can't be with you."

Brandon flinches like I've sucker-punched him. He just stares at me, and this awful silence fills the space between us.

A muscle in Brandon's jaw works. "Why not?" he asks finally.

I fumble in my mind how to explain the certainty that's overcome me. How to sum up the fact that I don't belong with him—that I will never belong with him.

"We're just too different," I manage.

Brandon blanches. "We're good together," he says quietly.

"It's just...seeing you with Dianne Marshall tonight, and then coming here. It's just shown me our worlds are too far apart."

The pain that shoots across Brandon's face cuts at me. I hate it. I hate hurting him.

But I know I'm saving us both pain in the long run.

Saving us from getting deeper into this thing that's never going to last.

"I'm sorry," I say.

He doesn't say anything as I turn on my heel, pushing through the crowd, trying to put as much distance between Brandon and me as I can before I change my mind.

The crowd seems to part for me now, like it did for Brandon earlier. But this is a different kind of parting. All these beautiful people are moving aside so the outsider doesn't contaminate them—so I can be expelled quickly.

I make it out onto the street and keep moving as I fumble on my phone to organize a ride.

I'm trying to outrun the feeling rising inside me like damp rot.

Grief.

CHAPTER 39

BRANDON

SO NOW MY brother's apartment has become a no-go zone for me. Awesome. Call the press: Brandon Seaton manages to screw something else up.

When Josh comes over he nicely doesn't mention that this is the second time I've managed to exile myself from his apartment because of issues with his roommate. At least he hasn't had to be interviewed by the police on this one, like he had to with the restraining order debacle.

Dunk the Dummies is being filmed tomorrow, and Josh is helping me with some last-minute cramming. The way I'm feeling right now, I totally belong on a show with dummies in the title. After all, I turned down a great career opportunity for someone who broke up with me a few weeks later. Someone who never actually saw us as something serious.

It's the very definition of dumb.

I'm trying to cling to my anger because I know once it goes I'm not going to like what's left behind. The last few days have been hell. I've missed Megan. A lot. Not just physically—being in bed with her or on the couch together

—but talking to her, messaging her, laughing with her, getting to see her expressions. Just *her,* period. So many times I've reached for my phone to message her before remembering we're not together anymore.

I know I'm making it hard for Josh to concentrate on teaching me because I'm alternating between scowling and huffing out big sighs.

He finally lowers the trivia book he's been quizzing me from and leans back on the couch, fixing me with a look.

"What?" I demand.

"I'm trying to stay out of this, because the last thing I need is to play romantic counsellor between you and Megan. But I don't get it. You're miserable. She's miserable."

I snap my head up. "She's miserable?"

"Well, she's eaten her weight in Oreos and has been binge-watching *Parks and Recreation* in her pajamas, which I'm pretty sure is Megan's definition of miserable."

Despite myself, my heart crunches at the thought of Megan upset. I want to be there to comfort her. I want to hold her, to make her feel better.

Fuck. This is so screwed up.

Josh tilts his head to the side. "Why did you two break up?"

"I don't want to talk about it."

"Fine." Josh reaches for the book again. "Anyway, states of matter are basically just solid, liquid and gas. The changing between them is due to the arrangement of the particles at different temperatures. With water—"

"She broke up with *me,* anyway." I break into his lecture. "So why don't you give her the heavy-handed interrogation?"

Josh lifts an eyebrow. "You call this a heavy-handed interrogation?"

I throw my pen down on the coffee table, where it skitters and comes to rest against a coaster. "She said we were too different to be together."

"Did you disagree with her? Argue the point?"

"No. Because she's probably right."

Josh gives me a long look. "Okay. Indulge me. How are you and Megan too different to have a successful relationship?"

I glare at him. "You know how."

"I don't actually."

"Maybe because she's incredibly smart and I'm just a jock."

Josh's eyebrows now look like they're going to take off into orbit. "Seriously, Brandon? You're letting her walk away because you're insecure about the fact that she's smarter than you?"

I pick the coaster up off the coffee table and shuffle it in my hands. "No, I just think that ultimately she'll want more than me. She deserves more." I say the last part quietly, but from Josh's reaction you'd think I'd yelled the words.

His eyes widen and he shakes his head. "Oh, my God, I never thought I'd be sitting here having to boost your ego."

"Come on, Josh. You know what I'm talking about. Remember parent-teacher interviews in elementary school? When Mom and Dad walked out with information about the gifted program for you and remedial math homework for me? I overheard Dad saying to Mom, 'At least he's good at football.'"

"So what, Brandon? That was elementary school. You went to college. You're not dumb."

My shoulders slump. "When I told Mom about Megan I could tell she didn't think it'd work out."

"Did she say that?"

"Not in those exact words. She said how different we are. Which means she's talking about how smart Megan is compared to me." I'm still playing with the coaster, digging into the edges, my fingernails piercing the cork.

Josh just stares at me for a while before he finally speaks. "Yeah, well, our parents aren't always the most supportive, are they?"

I furrow my brow. "What do you mean?"

"I love Mom and Dad, but they can be intellectual snobs. Especially Mom. It's like she wanted a little clone of herself to parent, and she's disappointed that neither of us turned out how she wanted."

"Well, at least she came close with you," I say bitterly.

Josh screws up his face. "Are you kidding me?"

"Oh, come on, Josh. We both know I was the disappointment growing up."

"Yeah, that may be true, but now you're a professional football player and they're really proud of you. It's outside their knowledge base, though, so they just let you get on with doing your thing. I'm not that lucky. With me it's like 'Josh, why didn't you pick electrical engineering as your major? Coding is such an overcrowded field. Don't you want to come back and manage the business someday? And if you're going to do computer programming, why aren't you at least doing a doctorate so you'll stand out from everyone else?'"

I reel back. There's a sourness in his words that I've never heard from Josh before.

"And let's not even get started on the fact that Mom

isn't as okay with me being gay as she wants to be," Josh continues, his forehead scrunching.

"You don't think Mom's okay with you being gay?"

"You noticed it yourself. When I brought Megan home Mom was so excited at the prospect that I might be interested in a girl. As much as she waves the rainbow flag, deep down you know she'd prefer it if I was straight."

"I think now she'd just prefer not to potentially deal with Mason's father as an in-law," I say.

Josh huffs out a laugh.

"Shit," I say. "I never thought about it from your perspective. It always seemed like you had it easy." I finally finish my tormenting of the coaster and put it back on the coffee table.

"I don't think anyone really has it easy. Even if it looks like they do from the outside," Josh says.

We sit in silence for a minute.

Josh takes a deep breath before he continues, "I think in this case Mom is wrong. Different can be good. With you and Megan, the differences between you are your strengths. It just weirdly works, because she's never been wowed by the fact that you're a football star."

I snort. "That's for sure."

"She calls you on your shit, and it's healthy. You guys are good together. You make each other laugh. It doesn't matter if you're interested in different things."

I lean back on the couch, digesting Josh's words.

He's right. Megan challenges me, keeps me interested, and makes me laugh. God, just thinking about all the things I like about her gives me another sharp pang of missing her. "Ah, shit." I rub my hand over my face.

Josh studies me. "You really care about her, don't you?"

My stomach clenches but I meet Josh's gaze steadily. "Yeah, I do."

"Did you tell her that?"

I shift uncomfortably in my seat. "No."

"Why not?"

I shrug. "I don't think it would've made a difference. I don't think she feels the same way."

"She probably got freaked out by all that celebrity stuff. Because that's not her. You've been dealing with it for a while now so you're used to it. But I get how it can be intimidating for someone when they're exposed to it for the first time."

"I don't know if she'll change her mind about us being too different."

Josh is shaking his head again. "I can honestly say I've never thought of you as stupid. But I might change that opinion if you let Megan go without at least talking to her about some of this. Start with telling her how you feel about her."

I swallow.

There's a chance my little brother is right.

Now what am I going to do about it?

CHAPTER 40

MEGAN

SO, now I don't have a boyfriend, but the whole world thinks I do. Photos of Brandon and me have continued to be circulated widely on that lovely treasure trove of positivity called the internet.

WTF? Brandon Seaton could get any girl in the world, and he goes for her?

Now we know why Brandon Seaton fumbled that pass in the playoffs. Because he obviously needs his eyesight checked.

Some advanced human decided I resemble one of the trolls from *Frozen* and has made a meme about it, superimposing my face over the animated character. It's gone viral.

I just love people.

"What are you looking at?" Ashley asks as she comes and sits next to me in the lunchroom. I'm scrolling through my phone.

"Oh, just looking at what the internet is saying about me today."

"That's always a healthy pastime."

"Apparently I'm a troll." Using one hand, I take a bite of my sandwich. I pretend to look unconcerned as I chew.

"What? Did you attack someone online?"

"Not that kind of troll. I don't behave like one. I just look like one." I flash the meme on my phone at her.

She studies it for a moment, her face screwing up. "Someone who lives in their parent's basement with access to Photoshop and has got too much time on their hands," she says finally.

"Yep." I try to make my tone upbeat and positive, but the sympathetic look she gives me makes my throat swell.

"So, how are you doing anyway?" she asks.

"I'm fine."

"Don't lie to me." Ashley gives me a hard stare. Her skills are really wasted here at *The Science Journal*. She should be one of those hard-hitting TV journalists who expose human traffickers.

"I'm not lying," I say, putting my phone down on the table. "This stuff doesn't really bother me. They're just losers."

"I'm not talking about how you're coping with that stuff. I'm talking about what's going on with Brandon."

Just hearing his name is like being kicked. The past week has been awful. Actually, it's beyond awful—it's into the realm of horrific. I didn't quite realize how intertwined my life had become with Brandon until suddenly he's not there anymore, and now there's this giant, gaping sinkhole I have no idea how to fill.

I try to cover my reaction with a shaky smile. "What about Brandon?" I deliberately haven't told Ashley we've broken up. Mainly because I have tears that permanently seem to be on standby in my tear ducts right now, and I can't imagine getting through a conversation with her about this without them making an appearance.

"Well, you've lost that incredible glow you've had over

the last few weeks—you know, the glow of someone who's having amazing sex. Also, the amount of times your phone bings with messages has gone down by seven hundred and eighty-nine percent."

My stomach lurches but I concentrate on channeling a skeptical glance in her direction. "Are you making up random stats again?"

"No. Brett keeps track of it. He has a graph and everything."

Brett is the guy who sits in the cubicle next to mine. Oops.

"Anyway, are you going to tell me what's going on?" she asks.

I bite my lip. "We broke up." I say the words quickly, as if getting through them faster will cut down the pain they'll cause. No such luck.

Ashley's eyebrows bunch down. "Who did the breaking up?"

"Me."

"Why?"

I shrug, trying for a nonchalance that is so far from what I feel it might as well be in another galaxy. "It was never going to last. Why delay the inevitable?"

She narrows her eyes. "Are you listening to yourself?"

"At least now I have a head start on getting over him."

"Oh, that's amazing logic. Why bother going on dates at all with that kind of attitude? You might as well stay at home and begin getting over the relationship that never happened. While you're there, you can start knitting booties for all the cats that are going to keep you company in your old age."

"Knitting booties for cats?"

Ashley shakes her head. "Seriously, Megan, I've never

seen you as happy as you've been over the last few weeks. And you might want to pretend it has nothing to do with the incredibly gorgeous, nice man who treats you amazingly and worships the ground you walk on, but I think you know differently."

I don't need Ashley to tell me this. I know Brandon made me happy. And I hate how happy he made me, because it's got a direct inverse relationship to how unhappy I am right now without him.

"We're too different for it to work," I offer feebly.

"Do you know what I think you're doing? I think subconsciously you've broken up with him as a test to see how much he really cares."

Her words cause my heart to start hammering. I try not to let my unease show on my face. "Thank you, Dr. Phil. You know, you really need to stop reading all those pop psychology books."

Ashley throws her hands up in the air. "I give up. All I hope is that when you come to your senses, he's still waiting for you."

The idea of Brandon waiting for me is both happy and painful.

I'm about to ask Ashley what makes her think Brandon's waiting for me now—after all, he could have been out clubbing every night since we broke up—when we're interrupted by Brett opening the door.

"Um, Megan, there's someone here asking for you."

"Who is it?" I stand up, glad to have an excuse to exit this conversation.

He shrugs. "Some guy."

My stomach churns as I put the remains of my sandwich in the trash. I don't have any interviews lined up, so I'm not expecting anyone today.

Despite myself, hope surges in my heart. Has Brandon come?

Is that what I want? For Brandon to turn up and make some declaration of love and tell me that his feelings for me supersede any barriers the world can throw at us?

Ashley's comments play on my mind. Am I testing Brandon to see how he feels about me?

The fact that he didn't argue with me, the fact that he let me walk away and hasn't made any attempt to talk to me has cut at me. Maybe more than I realized.

Because the hope continues to swell inside me now as I walk back to my desk makes me recognize that I have been waiting for Brandon to make the next move. I do want Brandon to turn up and declare his underlying love to me. Tell me we belong together. That he can't live without me.

My breath is in my throat as my cubicle comes into view.

But it turns out it's not Brandon who's come to see me.

It's Tad Morton.

He's standing by my desk, his hands are in his pockets, and he shuffles uncomfortably from one foot to the other.

I stop abruptly. "What are you doing here?"

"I wanted to apologize to you. Properly this time."

I've lost the power of speech. I just stand, staring at him.

"Is there somewhere we can talk?" He flicks a glance at Brett, who's pretending to type on his laptop but appears to be hanging on every word. If he is typing anything, it's probably a transcript of this conversation to share with Ashley later.

I snap back to life. "I'll see if there's a conference room available."

The first room I try is free. Tad follows me in. I don't sit down though or offer him a seat. Instead, I lean up against the table, crossing my arms.

"How did you get in here?" I ask.

Tad fiddles with his phone. "I googled to find out where you worked. Then I told the security guard I was an old friend from high school. I showed him a picture of us together. He let me in."

It doesn't surprise me. Maurice, the security guard, is a softie. And I guess Tad doesn't look like an angry scientist about to extract revenge for the way his work has been misrepresented by journalists.

Not that we get many of those, but anyway.

"Let me guess. You showed him the photo of us from prom?"

Tad sticks his hands in his pockets, looking abashed. "Yeah. It was the only photo I had of us."

I don't want to think about that photo. About how wide my smile was. I was so happy that night. I had no idea it was all going to come crashing down a few hours later.

He shuffles from one foot to the other. "I try not to think about what I did because I know I was such a dickhead to you. I knew at the time it was an asshole thing to do, but I didn't realize quite how bad it was."

"It was an incredibly shitty thing that you did," I agree.

"Yeah." He rubs his face. "It wasn't until I had a girlfriend in college that I really understood how shitty it was. She told me about her first time, and I realized that I'd wrecked that for you."

"Yeah, you did. Then you humiliated me afterwards. Let's not forget that part."

He winces. "The stupid thing is, I really liked you."

I snort. "Whatever."

Tad's eyes slide past me to study the conference room

table. "I did. We had so much fun in chemistry, remember? You'd do that impression of Ms. Lindsey, and we'd talk about whether or not animals were smarter than humans and all that other random shit."

I'm stunned. I'm stunned that Tad Morton remembers what we talked about six years ago.

"If you liked me so much, why did you do it?" My voice is tight.

Tad bites his lip. "My friends started hassling me whenever they saw us talking." He rocks back on his feet, shoving a hand through his hair. There's a big pause before he continues. "I don't know. It's like in high school everyone is put in these groups, right? And you can't stray out of them."

"Yeah. I remember."

He finally looks me in my eyes. "For what it's worth, I'm really sorry about what I did. If I could go back in time and change it, I would."

What can I say? That I forgive him? Will I ever forgive him? He's right. He took something from me that I'll never get back.

"I appreciate you coming here and apologizing," I say finally.

"I'd better get going," he says.

"Yeah, okay." I don't make any move to see him out.

When he's got one hand on the door handle he turns back to me. "It's funny. It feels like the world has taught me that I'm not worth quite as much as I thought I was back in high school. But it looks like the opposite is true for you."

～

My conversation with Tad runs through my head the rest of the day. It's interspersed with reruns of what Ashley said. Basically, my head is just a conversation replay machine.

As I make my way home I'm still trying to process everything. I cling to a pole in the subway while people press in around me in a way that would be weird in any other context.

Secretly I've always loved the subway in New York. There's something just so...New York about it. In Tulsa, Oklahoma, you seldom get the chance to get up close and personal with a stranger's armpit.

My thoughts are pressing in on me even closer than the strangers.

It shouldn't take another guy standing up for me to make Tad suddenly realize that he needed to apologize for what he did. In an ideal world, if I'd confronted him back then, he'd have realized the implications of what he'd done and shut down his friends from hassling me.

But I'd never confronted him. I'd licked my wounds in private, trying desperately to pretend to the world that I didn't care.

But I did care. And I still care now.

The train pulls up at my stop, and I join the press of people leaving.

As I climb the stairs I walk past the poster of Karla, Conner's girlfriend. In the ad she's leaning back against a wall with one hand hooked in her jeans, a teasing smile on her face.

I stop and stare at it.

I've never taken my relationship with Brandon seriously. Because deep down I've never believed it would last. I've always assumed that Brandon should be with someone like Karla instead.

I'm making the same mistake I made in high school. I'm assuming I'm not good enough for Brandon. So I'm letting him walk away.

When I get inside my apartment, the first thing I notice is the Ken and Barbie dolls sitting on the counter.

Dropping my purse and keys, I pick up Ken and examine him. At first I thought Brandon was like this doll. Plastic. Clichéd. Defined by one characteristic: the fact that he's a football player.

But he's so much more than that. He's the guy who will verbally spar with me on any subject, take my mockery and give it right back, yet will always, always have my back. The guy whose biggest fear is looking stupid, but who agreed to go on a quiz show to raise money for vulnerable kids. The guy who understands that particular pain of not fitting in with your family but has bravely forged his own path instead. The guy who touches me so tenderly, kisses me so reverently, yet laughs at all my stupid jokes, even when they're at his expense.

The truth hits me so hard in the chest that I drop the doll.

I'm in love with Brandon.

I'm pushing him away because I'm scared that he's not going to love me back. I'm looking for excuses for why we can't be together so I can stop myself from getting hurt.

I scramble down to pick up Football Ken, dusting him off carefully. I place him next to Science Barbie, and I may or may not spend a minute trying to work out how to intertwine their hands. Because yes, I am that sappy.

The sound of the front door opening startles me and I turn, feeling my face flush guiltily.

"Hey, Megan." Josh takes off his coat and puts it on the hanger next to the door.

"Hey," I reply.

As Josh walks toward me, I think about how Brandon asked me once whether I would have picked Josh over him if Josh had been straight. I mangled my answer at the time. It seems so ridiculous now because there is a core truth I will never escape from. Despite how much Josh and I have in common, if I had to choose who was right for me I would always, always pick Brandon.

Because I love Brandon.

And being with him is worth the risk.

The fact strikes me like an asteroid, leaving me rocking and breathless. An incredible, aching urge takes over my body. I need to fix things with Brandon. And I need to fix them now.

I flick my gaze up to Josh, who's browsing through some junk mail on the counter. "Um...random question. Brandon's quiz show is tonight, isn't it? Do you know where it's taping?"

Josh tilts his head, studying me. "I'm about to go watch him in the studio. I just came home to get changed."

"Any chance I can come with you?"

Josh's eyebrows shoot up and a faint smile creases his face. "Sure."

An idea flicks through my mind. "First, there's something I need to make."

CHAPTER 41

BRANDON

FILMING a game show is like living in a surreal universe. A universe where everyone has thick makeup plastered on their skin, there are bright hot lights on you at all times, and every ten minutes or so all the action stops for a commercial break and makeup artists rush out to fluff your face with various brushes while other people scurry around adjusting lights and microphones.

Of course it's not just the hot lights that are making me break out in a sweat and keeping my makeup artist busy in the breaks. They're filming the show live, so there's no chance to fix things if you screw up, and I'm aware of the millions of people who are watching me every time I open my mouth.

The good thing about it being filmed live is you can see all the pledges people are making as the show progresses. Between the prize money I've won so far and what people are donating, we've already raised over $100,000 for the Active Coaches charity.

Given what a shit week this has been, it's nice to see the

gauge behind me rising and feel like I'm making some kind of positive difference.

And I'm doing okay with the questions, though I'm pretty sure they've dumbed them down to make it easier for us celebrities. After all, it'd be a bad look if we plunged into the water without raising any money.

Even though it's painful to think about her, I've been trying to remember Megan's technique for multiple choice —reminding myself that the right answer is on the screen and starting off by eliminating wrong answers.

It's my turn again. I take a deep breath as the question flashes on the screen.

What city hosted the 2000 summer Olympics?

a) Athens

b) Atlanta

c) Sydney

d) Beijing

The *Dunk the Dummies'* host, Jason, rubs his hands together. "Here's a sport one for you, Brandon. This should be easy."

Hmm. I decide not to point out I play in the NFL, which isn't an Olympic sport. And I was barely out of diapers in 2000.

Instead, I plaster on my best smile and focus on the question. It was a lot more relaxed answering Megan's questions on index cards rather than ones from a brightly lit screen when you're in a chair, overhanging a pool, and tipping closer toward the water with every wrong answer.

I remember watching the Beijing opening ceremony of the Olympics when I was about twelve, so it definitely isn't that one. One down, two to go.

Atlanta? I know Atlanta hosted it once, but I'm pretty

sure they would have made a big deal of it even in kinder-garten, if it had been in the States.

I vaguely remember doing a project about Greece when I was in elementary school. Well, I remember my mother having to reglue stuff in my diorama of the Parthenon after I'd made a complete mess of it. There's a good chance our teacher chose to study Greece because of the Olympics.

Which leaves Sydney.

"I think it's Sydney," I say.

Jason raises his eyebrows. "Why do you think that?"

I'm not going to talk through my warped logic on national TV so I shrug. "Gut instinct."

"And Sydney is correct! Congratulations, Brandon, you've won another ten thousand dollars for Active Coaches. How do you feel about that?"

"It feels... good," I say as the bright red gauge behind me climbs further.

The problem with celebrity quizzes is the game show host wants to interact with the celebrities. It appears that Jason believes I should have witty repartee hidden up my sleeve along with biceps that allow me to throw 70-yard passes.

Luckily one of my fellow contestants is Georgia Rye, a reality TV star who's famous for being ditzy, but somehow she's managing to use the craziest logic to talk herself into the right answers on most of the questions. It's much more entertaining than my struggle to justify my answers—or the other celebrity, Adam Francis, a daytime soap actor, who appears bored by the whole thing and is happily bombing out. At least it looks like I won't be the first person to get wet.

When it's my turn again, the question flashes up on the screen.

What color is Donald Duck's bowtie?
a) Blue
b) Red
c) Green
d) Yellow

I should know this. After all, I watched cartoons as a kid. But for the life of me I can't visualize his bowtie.

I guess green when the answer is red, and my chair does an ominous tilt toward the water.

Through the bright lights it's difficult to see the audience, but I've been scanning it relentlessly between questions, trying to find Josh, who promised he'd be here. I need to see one friendly face to calm me.

But when I finally spot Josh, it doesn't calm me at all.

Because I also recognize the person next to him.

Megan.

She's here.

My breath leaves me in a sharp gust.

I barely hear Jason laughing at something Georgia's saying about how she knew about endorphins because it was mentioned in the movie *Legally Blonde*. I'm too busy processing what Megan being here means.

It has to be a good thing, right?

At least it means she's changed her avoid-Brandon-at-all-costs policy, so I'll get a chance to talk to her. Unless she's come here just to see how dumb I really am, to reassure herself she made the right decision about our relationship.

But regardless, I need to take this chance. I need to tell her how I feel. To try to convince her to take a chance on us.

It's like my guts have been placed in a vice. Because the thought of confessing my feelings to Megan makes me want to throw up. If she doesn't feel the same way it will be beyond embarrassing.

Humiliating.

Devastating.

I vaguely register that Jason is talking to me again, and now there is another question for me to answer.

What battle is considered to be the turning point in the American Revolution?

a) Battle of Saratoga

b) Battle of Gettysburg

c) Battle of Fort Sumter

d) Battle of Trenton

I sneak a look at Megan in the audience. She has a grin playing on her lips, and I try to keep my face neutral, but seeing her smile causes a lightness in my chest.

"The answer is *A*, Saratoga," I say clearly.

Jason raises his eyebrows. "That was quick. I didn't realize football players had such an in-depth knowledge of American history."

"Yeah, it's a frequent topic of conversation in the locker room."

"And you're right! Well done, Brandon."

Awesome. More cash for Active Coaches.

My concern about what to say to Megan has swamped any nerves about this game show. Ten minutes ago I was desperately looking forward to the end of filming so the torture would be over. Now I actually want time to slow down. I want time to come up with the right thing to say to her.

You could tell her the truth, a little voice inside me suggests.

I want to interrogate the little voice about what the

truth is, but I get the feeling I already know the answer. The way I feel when I see Megan smile gives me the answer.

I'm in love with her.

Should I tell her that?

I've never been in love before, so I've never told anyone that I love them. The idea of saying it to Megan, when I have no idea if she feels remotely the same, is fucking terrifying.

A buzzing noise followed by a loud splashing jolts me back to the present.

I look down to see Adam swimming over to the side of the pool, his perfect hair plastered against his skull.

Jason turns to Georgia and me with a predatory smile.

"Now, Georgia and Brandon, you have a choice to make. You can walk away with the cash you've earned for your chosen charity and stay dry, or else you can go for an extra fifty thousand dollars. But be aware—if you get the question wrong you'll be getting wet."

He turns to me. "Brandon, would you like to see the question first before you make a choice?"

"Sure."

The question appears on the screen.

How many bones are there in the human body?

a) 104

b) 158

c) 192

d) 206

Fuck, this is something I should know. I'm pretty sure everyone watching at home will be screaming the right answer at the screen.

"So, Brandon, are you going to risk a dunking for the bonus question?"

"To be honest, I don't have a clue about the correct

answer, but I'm prepared to guess," I say. "I have a one in four chance of getting it right. And if I get it wrong, so what? I know how to swim."

Jason smiles. "Okay, Brandon, what are you going to choose?"

"A wise person once said to me, 'When in doubt, go for C.' So I'm choosing C," I say.

I know I'm taking a risk. But it's a no-brainer. Because the reward is so high, it's worth looking stupid for.

"Is C your final answer?" Jason asks.

"Yes, it's my final answer."

"Are you ready for what happens if you're wrong?"

I flick a glance at Megan. She's watching, her lips pursed.

"Yeah, I'm prepared for it."

A bright red light flashes and at the same time I hear Jason's voice.

"Sorry, that's the wrong answer. The correct answer is D."

And I tumble into the water.

Obviously on *Dunk the Dummies* they're prepared for people to get wet. The water is warm, and as soon as I'm out an assistant hands me a huge fluffy towel and ushers me back to the dressing room.

When I emerge, still toweling my hair, Jason is backstage with a beaming Georgia, who apparently managed to answer her question correctly and avoid being dunked.

The director and producer arrive and start gushing over us all. While I'm excited to hear about all the money raised, I'm also impatient to finish up, anticipation and uncertainty having a turf battle inside me.

As soon as we're free to go I'm on the phone to Josh. "Where are you?" I ask urgently.

"I'm on my way home, but I think Megan's waiting outside for you."

I release a breath. "Okay. Did she say anything to you about why she came tonight?"

Josh is silent for a moment. "You need to talk to her," he says finally.

"Yeah, you're right." I hang up and ask one of the production assistants which door the audience would have left by.

Following the directions, I jog out the main exit.

At first the street looks to be deserted, the streetlights shining down on an empty sidewalk.

Shit. Did she leave? The hope that's been swelling inside me abruptly deflates.

I'm fumbling with my phone when I realize a figure has detached itself from the side building.

"Hey," Megan says. She's wearing a cream sweater and jeans, her hair tied up in a messy ponytail, but she looks more beautiful to me than if she was a model on a catwalk.

"Hey," I reply cautiously.

"You did a great job." Her face is serious.

"Thanks."

We stand there, just staring at each other for a few moments.

What should I say? How do I lead in to telling her how I feel?

Megan bites her lip. "So, I...um...I know the show's over, but I came up with another flashcard for you."

Confusion runs through me. "Okay..."

She pulls a card out of her bag and gives it to me with shaking hands.

In marker pen she's written in block capitals another multiple choice question.

Megan loves Brandon because:

a) He makes her laugh

b) He makes her happier than she's ever been

c) He's the person she would choose to be stranded on a desert island with

d) Buried under his ego, he's the nicest person she's ever met

e) He's hot and great in bed

f) All of the above

I stare at the card, rereading it twice to make sure I fully get it, that it's saying what I think it's saying.

One look at Megan's face, and I know I've got the interpretation correct.

"I know you don't like multiple choice," she says, her voice cracking, "but I thought you might like this question."

"Yeah, I definitely like this question," I say softly.

Our eyes lock for a moment, and then suddenly she's in my arms, and I am holding her so tight, smushing my face into her hair, breathing her in. The best thing is, she's clinging to me just as tightly.

Eventually I pull back so I can see her properly. "It's the hot and great in bed one, right?"

"You seriously do suck at multiple choice," she says, a smile drifting up her face.

I look back down at the card still clutched in my hand then up at her again. "Do you have a pen?"

Her eyebrows tilt quizzically. "Of course." She rummages in her purse and hands one to me.

I let go of her. I turn the card over and scribble down something quickly. My heart is thumping wildly as I hand the card to her.

Brandon loves Megan because:

1. *She's the perfect girl for him and he can't*
   imagine being with anyone else.

"I decided to make it easy for you," I say. "I want you to get this one right."

Megan sucks in a breath and looks at me with shiny eyes. "I appreciate you making it easy for me."

She smiles at me, and I know I've got an ear-splitting grin on my face in return.

"We probably need to talk," she says, her grin fading, eyes sliding off to one side.

"I think we've just said the most important thing. Don't you?"

She rocks back on her feet. "Yeah. Definitely. But there're some things we need to discuss."

I feel a lurch of worry. "Okay. You feel like cheesecake?"

"I could definitely eat cheesecake," she says.

We arrive at Little Mama's and grab a booth down the back.

As soon as we've placed our orders, I reach across the table and lace my fingers through hers. "I'm really glad you came tonight."

"I'm sorry," she says, lowering her gaze and tracing a crack in the vinyl table. "I'm sorry I ran off like that the other night. I just heard some of your teammates talking about how your agent told you to settle down and get a girl-friend, and it freaked me out."

"Oh, my God, Megan. This is me, okay? You know I would never do something like that."

"I know. It's just, it cut me in the same place as what happened with Tad, you know? And I kind of freaked out because the celebrity thing was so full on and I was falling for you and I didn't think you felt the same way..." She pauses and takes a breath before continuing. "And I guess, deep down, I thought if you really felt about me the way I felt about you, you wouldn't have let me walk away without fighting for me."

I wince. "I'm sorry I didn't come after you. But I was the same. I thought you didn't feel about me the same way I felt about you. And I felt I wasn't smart enough for you. That eventually you'd want to be with someone smarter."

"What?" Megan's voice is incredulous. "You honestly felt you weren't smart enough for me?"

I shrug. "You know, with my family and all..."

Megan fixes me with a fierce look. "You're smart, Brandon. There are so many other types of intelligence besides academic. You're one of the best decision-makers on the field. You can read a situation and adapt to it in a split second. That takes smarts, you know."

"How do you know that?" I ask in amazement.

She rolls her eyes. "You don't think since he found out we're together my dad hasn't emailed me every news article about you he can find?"

"And you read them?"

"Well, I might have just scanned a few. They do get repetitive after a while. Brandon's good at throwing a ball a long way, blah blah blah." A smile has crept up her face.

I squeeze her hand. "So, are we doing this?" I ask. "Proper relationship, all in, hearts on sleeves, planning a future together—that type of relationship?"

Megan places her free hand on top of where ours are joined together. "We're definitely doing this," she says.

EPILOGUE

Megan
One Year Later

IT TURNS out it doesn't actually matter how large your budget is—apartment hunting is always hideous.

Although this time, instead of worrying about devil or feline-worshiping roommates, the stumbling block is whether any apartment has enough closet space for my boyfriend's abnormally large clothes and shoes collection.

"How do you seriously have a larger shoe collection than me?" I stand at the entrance of his wardrobe and stare. We've just been out apartment hunting, and Brandon's rejected a perfectly nice apartment on the basis that it didn't have enough storage. Which led us back here so I could personally inspect how much storage he needs. It turns out it's a lot.

"Hey, it takes effort to look this good," Brandon says.

"No, it just takes a large credit-card limit and question-able online shopping habits," I grumble.

Brandon snakes a hand around my body, pulling me closer to him. "But you love me anyway."

"Yeah, I'm pretty sure you brainwashed me into that."

"With my sexy body, charm, and sense of humor?"

"You can't forget your modesty," I say. "That was the trait that clinched it for me."

He kisses me, and finding an apartment soon falls down the agenda of the things we're doing that afternoon.

After a few more weeks of hunting, we finally find an apart-ment that suits all of our criteria. Close to the park, close to my work, separate office for each of us, and spare bedroom for my family—because there's been a definite increase over the last year in the frequency of them wanting to see me. And somehow the timing of my brothers' interest in visiting me always seems to coincide with the weekends that Brandon has a home game.

Our new place is also close to Josh's new apartment, which is great since it means we can still hang out. Josh has been through a lot in the last year after breaking up with Mason, and seeing how excited he is to be moving in with his new boyfriend makes it seem like all the stuff he's gone through has been worthwhile in the end.

The day after Brandon and I sign our new lease we're hanging out on the couch in my old apartment, watching our new reality TV addition, *Extreme Diving Expeditions*. It's even better than *Naked and Afraid*, although it seems sacrilegious to actually think that.

"I'll miss this place," Brandon says nostalgically, looking around the room.

"Technically, you've never actually lived here," I point out.

"Still, it doesn't mean I won't miss it. Do you think Barbie and Ken will like our new digs?"

I glance over at where Science Barbie and Football Ken have pride of place on the living room shelves.

I take a second look.

They've had an outfit change since I last saw them. My breath catches in my throat.

I stand up slowly and move closer to inspect them. Adjusting my proximity doesn't change what I'm seeing, though.

"Um...Brandon," I say, turning toward him.

"Yeah?" He's watching me closely, his eyes dark.

It takes me a moment to find my voice. "Is there a reason why Barbie and Ken are dressed in wedding attire?"

"I'm glad you've finally noticed. I thought it might be a nice lead-in to this."

Brandon reaches into his pocket and pulls out something small and suspiciously shaped. It looks like...a ring box.

And suddenly my mouth goes dry. My saliva glands have obviously decided to pick now as a good time to go on strike.

"Since we're moving in together, I kind of thought we should make it official," he says, swallowing hard.

My breath leaves me.

Oh, God. This is actually happening. He's actually proposing to me. I may have imagined this moment a few times.

I try to school my expression and keep the happiness that's bubbling inside me at bay. "That's it? That's your proposal?" I raise an eyebrow.

"Oh, yeah. You complete me, I love you with my entire heart, my life wouldn't be the same without you in it, I can't imagine anything making me happier than getting to spend the rest of my life with you, blah blah blah."

This time I can't fight the grin that swamps my face.

Brandon takes a few steps toward me and drops down to one knee, holding the ring box in the palm of his hand. "Megan, I'd like nothing more than a lifetime of mockery and laughter with you. Please say you'll marry me."

"Okay."

"Yes?"

The look of love and hope on his face causes me to swallow down a lump in my throat.

I shrug, feigning nonchalance. "I haven't exactly had any better offers, so I guess you'll do."

"I'm totally taking that," he says as he puts his arms around me and kisses me.

Thanks for reading!

Do you want more fun, romantic stories with a guaranteed happily ever after?

Sign up to my newsletter on my website www.jacquelineleeauthor.com and you'll receive my FREE short story collection 'It ended with a kiss', exclusive to my newsletter subscribers

Spoiler alert – all three stories end with a romantic kiss!

You'll also get emails every month giving you access to exclusive stories and special offers, plus you'll be the first to know when I have a new book out.

Three short stories that will leave you smiling...

Can you meet your soul mate while up a tree spying on your ex? Is his leaving party the best time to declare your love for your colleague? Is it possible that the kiss-cam at a basketball game is the right catalyst for moving from being friends to more than friends?

These funny, heart-warming short stories will make you swoon and then leave you smiling. Spoiler alert – all the stories end with some awesome lip-locking.

ABOUT THE AUTHOR

Jacqueline Lee promises you her stories will always contain funny conversations and deeply felt connections.

She's living her own version of happily-ever after on the East Coast of New Zealand, where she practices her banter with her husband and her sarcasm with her children.

You can keep in contact with her by signing up to her newsletter on her website www.jacquelineleeauthor.com or hanging out on social media.

https://www.facebook.com/Jacqueline-Lee-Author

https://www.instagram.com/jacquelineleeauthor/